Lure of the Tiger

Book 4

Aloha Shifters: Jewels of the Heart

by Anna Lowe

Twin Moon Press

Editing by Lisa A. Hollett

Covert art by Kim Killion

Contents

Contents i

Other books in this series iii

Free Books v

Chapter One 1

Chapter Two 9

Chapter Three 21

Chapter Four 33

Chapter Five 45

Chapter Six 53

Chapter Seven 61

Chapter Eight 73

Chapter Nine 81

Chapter Ten 89

Chapter Eleven 105

Chapter Twelve 119

Chapter Thirteen 131

Chapter Fourteen 139

Chapter Fifteen 149

Chapter Sixteen 159

Chapter Seventeen 173

Chapter Eighteen 185

Chapter Nineteen 201

Chapter Twenty 215

Epilogue 227

Books by Anna Lowe 233

About the Author 239

Other books in this series

Aloha Shifters - Jewels of the Heart

Lure of the Dragon (Book 1)

Lure of the Wolf (Book 2)

Lure of the Bear (Book 3)

Lure of the Tiger (Book 4)

Love of the Dragon (Book 5)

Lure of the Fox (Book 6)

visit www.annalowebooks.com

Free Books

Get your free e-books now!

Sign up for my newsletter at *annalowebooks.com* to get three free books!

- *Desert Wolf*: Friend or Foe (Book 1.1 in the Twin Moon Ranch series)
- *Off the Charts* (the prequel to the Serendipity Adventure series)
- *Perfection* (the prequel to the Blue Moon Saloon series)

Chapter One

Cruz steadied his breath and squinted across the moonlit landscape. The sea breeze teased his hair as he crouched, scanning for his target. The barrel of the rifle felt cool in his hands, much like the wind over the sweat on his back. The palm trees concealing him whispered an urgent warning as he focused on the task at hand. His target was somewhere over there — one person amidst the crowd gathered at the golf club a quarter of a mile away.

Something didn't feel right, but he fought the feeling away. When did a hit ever feel right?

The voice of his informant echoed through his mind for the thousandth time. *Northwest corner of the terrace. Look for a guest in black with black-rimmed glasses. The waiter will hand that guest a cocktail glass marked with a pink umbrella and an olive with a green toothpick. That guest is your target.*

Easy, he told himself.

But, hell. He must have lost his touch, because doubts crowded his mind. Not too long ago, in his active duty days, he'd been the top sniper in his elite Special Forces unit, and he'd never hesitated when it came to completing a job. He hadn't liked it, but he'd done what he had to do in wartime. This was different, though. This was…

This is war, too, his inner tiger insisted. *Finally, we get revenge on the monster who murdered our family.*

Cruz blinked hard and forced away the lump in his throat. *Get your shit together, soldier.*

Technically, he wasn't a soldier any more, just a civilian like the people partying in the exclusive clubhouse of the Kapa'akea resort. But his civilian status was just on paper. The soldier part would always be in his blood, just as his tiger side was in his blood. He was born to fight. To protect. To battle for just causes in a deeply troubled world. And revenge was as just a cause as any, especially when he considered the cruel manner in which his family had been wiped out. His parents. His younger sister. His brother. All of them murdered in cold blood.

A movement stirred on the side terrace, away from the crowd. He refocused through the sights. A woman in a sequined dress danced out of the French doors, giggling, followed by a man whose eyes were glued to her ass.

Cruz rolled his eyes. Definitely *not* his target.

A moment later, two businessmen stepped out onto the terrace, and the amorous couple scurried into the shadows of the garden. The businessmen didn't walk to the northwest corner of the terrace, but they stopped close enough to make Cruz's shoulders tense. When a waiter appeared, Cruz held his breath and adjusted the sights to get a better look at the drinks on the waiter's tray. Straight up bourbon, from the look of it. No miniature umbrellas. No toothpicks or olives.

He exhaled. Not his target. Still, he watched the men. Something about their tailored suits and self-important stances made him suspicious. Then again, humans always made him suspicious.

A cloud slid over the moon. When a shadow moved in the doorway, his blood rushed. His nose twitched, and every nerve in his body jolted with shocks of warning.

His tiger growled inside, lashing its tail from side to side. *Warning of what?*

Never in his life had he felt this strong a premonition. Not the day his family had been killed, nor the split second before his convoy had been trapped in an ambush, three years ago. Not even the day he'd met Silas, Kai, Boone, and Hunter, the shifters who were to become his brothers-in-arms. Destiny had forewarned him of each of those events, if only in a frustratingly vague way — and only seconds before the shit hit the fan.

But this premonition nearly knocked him to his knees. It was sharper, stronger, more intense than anything he'd experienced before. Something big was about to happen. Something that would change his life forever.

Cruz forced himself to breathe evenly. That feeling was to be expected the day he had the chance to avenge his family, right?

The curtains at the doors to the terrace stirred, and the two men turned to see who it was. Cruz pressed his finger against the trigger and held completely still.

"Come on, already," he whispered when the person hesitated in the doorway. His lips brushed against the barrel, and the acrid taste of metal filled his mouth.

Focus, damn it. Focus.

He turned his sights on the figure in the doorway. Was that his target?

The curtains flapped, and his pulse spiked. A young woman stepped into view. Proud. Graceful. But... sad, too. Conflicted, somehow.

The gears of his mind ticked over in agonizingly slow motion, and none of the messages firing through his nerves made sense. Why was she sad? What was her dilemma? And why did that seem so heart-wrenchingly important to him?

The thick-rimmed glasses propped back on her fair hair didn't match her youthful figure, just like her glum expression didn't fit her cheerily freckled face.

Another man pushed outside, passing the woman close enough to make her long black dress swish. Cruz swung the rifle toward him — a big guy whose combed-back hair didn't hide the bare patches on his scalp. The fancy suit didn't hide the gut hanging over his belt either. The two businessmen disappeared inside as the big man lit a cigarette and started talking to the woman. Make that, talking *at* her while her shoulders lifted in a sigh. When the man stepped closer — too close — and belched a plume of cigarette smoke, the woman flinched and stepped away.

"Slimeball," Cruz murmured.

Slimeball, his tiger agreed. The type it would be so, so easy to kill. Arrogant, manipulative, and self-assured. Cruz could see all that in the man's viper eyes.

Cruz pursed his lips. Was that his target?

Instinct tugged his attention to the woman, making it hard to focus on the man she obviously deplored. When Slimeball slithered closer to her lithe body, she rubbed her hands over her crossed arms.

Cruz was so mesmerized, he barely paid attention when someone else joined the pair. Then a white sleeve cut into his field of vision — a waiter, offering the young woman a drink.

Cruz's heart stopped.

A guest in black with black-rimmed glasses. The waiter will hand that guest a cocktail glass with a pink umbrella and an olive with a green toothpick. That's your target.

Cruz flicked his eyes to the drink. Pink umbrella. Green toothpick. Black dress.

Holy shit. That woman was responsible for the deaths of the people he loved?

The clouds slipped clear of the moon as commands thundered through his mind.

Shoot her!

Spare her!

Pull the trigger!

Don't! Don't!

He clenched his jaw. Maybe something had gone wrong. Maybe his informant had made a terrible mistake. But damn it, McGraugh had always been reliable, so how could that be possible?

If it had been Slimeball holding that cocktail, Cruz would have squeezed off a round and slipped away into the night without a second thought. But the woman…

The joints of his fingers seized up, refusing to pull the trigger.

Damn it. She could be a killer. Humans were tricky that way. And even if she wasn't the killer, what did he care? Humans were responsible for most of the problems of the world.

Then he caught himself. God, was he jaded. Was he really willing to kill a woman who might be innocent?

No. No, he wasn't.

He studied her from head to toe. She didn't have the look or stance of a killer. Cruz knew; he'd crossed paths with enough to be able to tell. Men and women both, and this woman didn't fit in. He sniffed the air. She didn't smell like a killer either. On the contrary, she smelled nice.

His tiger hummed, teasing her scent out of all those tangled in the sweet night air. *Like a sea breeze. Like wild roses that grow at the edge of the beach.*

Cruz frowned. Usually, he could settle his racing pulse with sheer mind control. But now, his heart revved just from looking at her. What the hell was wrong with him?

Destiny, a voice growled in the recesses of his mind.

He shivered in spite of himself. Destiny, what?

But that was it. One cryptic whisper from some dark corner of the universe and nothing more.

"Destiny." He cursed under his breath.

Some shifters revered a benign form of destiny they swore brought goodness, hope, and love. But Cruz knew the truth — destiny was a fickle and manipulative power that was more likely to fuck up a man's life than show him the path to bliss. Destiny rarely paid attention to mere mortals, but when it did, it was best to stay the hell away. Someplace like the house he had built for himself deep in the woods at Koa Point where no one could bother him. Not even Fate, who'd filled his life with so many regrets. All the times something had gotten in the way of visits home. All the times he should have called to say hello but didn't because a more urgent matter had come up. Big things, like the life-or-death missions assigned to his Special Forces team. Little things like canceled flights and crackling phone lines...

Don't add another regret, his tiger growled.

He slipped his finger off the trigger and watched the woman closely. She made a chopping motion and said something that made Slimeball shake a finger at her. Then she turned away with a firm set to her shoulders, prompting Slimeball to stalk back into the building and leave her alone.

Cruz's finger jumped back to the trigger. This was his chance, right? The silenced rifle wouldn't make much noise, and no one would notice her body thump to the ground. That would give him more time to cover his tracks. He could finish this mission, head home, and maybe even find a little peace in knowing he'd avenged his family at last.

She's not the killer. His tiger growled. *Don't shoot her. Don't!*

Wait a second. His tiger was usually the one desperate for revenge.

Killers don't look at the stars like they're looking for answers, his tiger said.

Cruz watched as the woman raised her glass and whispered a toast to the stars.

Not a toast. A promise, his tiger insisted. *And killers don't shift from foot to foot like they wish they were somewhere else. They focus, even when they're not on a job.*

That, Cruz had to agree with. If a person could teleport from one place to another, he'd bet that woman would be out of that pretentious club in a flash. Out of that silk dress, too. She looked more like the cutoff jeans and flip-flops type.

His tiger grinned. *I like her.*

No, he didn't. He hated all humans. Especially one who might be his mortal enemy.

She's not our mortal enemy. She's our destined—

The thought cut off as he jerked his head around to stare eastward where something caught his attention. Not so much a motion as the sense that someone was there. After a moment of searching, his keen eyes caught sight of a man. One moment, the figure was there, and the next, the man was hidden by the foliage. Then he was visible again and, holy shit — screwing together two long, metal shafts and aiming at the terrace. An M110 — a sniper's rifle much like the one Cruz held.

His first reaction was outrage. That woman on the terrace was his target. No one was going to have the satisfaction of eliminating that murderer but him. In a flash, he swung his rifle back to the woman on the terrace and took aim.

She's not a killer, a little voice insisted.

The woman gazed up at the stars, and the electric current that zapped through Cruz's body just wouldn't let up. He bared his teeth. Was he really going to let this chance go?

The woman turned, ready to head inside. It was now or never if he was going to get a shot off.

Now, the dark side of his soul called.

Never! his tiger growled.

He glanced to the right, where the second man was hurriedly taking aim at the woman.

No, his tiger roared. *No!*

A pop sounded, followed by an outbreak of laughter from the crowd on the main porch.

No! his tiger cried. *No!*

Cruz's heart pounded as he scanned the scene. Was that a silenced shot?

No — it was a bottle of champagne, bubbling all over someone on the main porch. Cruz ripped his gaze back to the side terrace, where the curtain flapped. The woman was gone.

She's inside! Safe! His tiger cheered.

He turned back toward the hit man, who'd also been distracted by the pop.

Destiny smiles on her, his tiger hummed.

Cruz wasn't so sure, because the second man kept squinting through his sights, intent on finding the woman for a second chance. Cruz sniffed for his scent, but the man was upwind.

Can't let him kill her, his tiger cried.

Cruz couldn't understand why it felt so important to keep that woman safe. But it did, and within the space of two heartbeats, the urge went from a vague feeling to a burning need.

Must keep her safe. Must get her away from this place! his tiger screamed.

Cruz cursed, disassembling the rifle in seconds flat, wondering what the woman had to do with the other shooter. Then he zipped the weapon into his bag and took off, racing through the woods with feline stealth. Within a matter of minutes, he'd concealed the rifle, plucked a stray leaf from his hair, and climbed the stairs to the clubhouse, straightening his jacket as he went. He hated suits — and crowds — but he'd worn his best tux tonight so he could fit in if necessary. A good soldier always had a Plan B, right?

He'd find the woman, get her someplace safe, and search for the truth in her eyes. Then he'd decide who to kill — the woman or the armed man in the woods. He could sense those preying eyes sweep the party like a searchlight in the night.

That woman is mine, he told himself, trying to mask his rage at the imposter.

That woman is mine, his tiger hummed in a totally different tone.

Chapter Two

Jody plastered a smile on her face as she headed back to the party. It might have been the world's fakest smile, but that seemed fitting, given the crowd she had to mix with. Everyone was dressed to the nines, posturing this way and that. Seeing and being seen, though she doubted anyone saw the real her.

The men saw the silk dress she'd been instructed to wear that evening — or rather, they did their best to see through it, undressing her with her eyes. The women eyed her overdone hair as if she'd sprouted Medusa's snakes instead of having submitted to two hours of styling prior to this black-tie event.

You're a model now, Richard had told her. *Act the part, honey.*

Richard, her new boss — a man she was ready to punch. She wasn't a model. She was just a woman who needed money for a good cause — and soon.

Her jaw hurt from the frozen-in-place smile, and her feet ached. She longed for her flip-flops — or better yet, to run barefoot through the grass. It was one of those beautiful Maui nights — too beautiful to spend cooped up at a cocktail party. The trees rustled, tempting her to escape. The birds seemed unusually still, as if something was lurking out there. Not a bad *something* so much as a mysterious, new *something* that pulled on her like a magnet. Which was funny, because it was usually the ocean that gave her that feeling. Like the breakers rolling into the shoreline not too far away, tempting her like a siren's call. That's where she belonged — carving the waves or running across the sand. That was her element. But there was something about the woods tonight that drew her in.

Then Richard had come along and reeled her back to the present with his cutting words.

Save the wild child look for the camera, baby. Now get your sweet ass back to the party and do as your contract says.

She scowled. Right — her contract. Everyone always warned her to read the fine print, but of course, Jody hadn't. She'd assumed the written version matched the verbal deal she'd made. There were all kinds of hidden clauses such as making appearances at events like this.

So once again, she'd shown a little too much faith in mankind. But, hell — if you didn't have faith, what did that make you?

Gullible? a voice dripping with sarcasm murmured in her mind.

"Thank you," she murmured, snagging a glass of water from a passing waiter and downing it in a gulp before heading back to work.

That's what this party was — work. A show. She was a product, and her employers wanted her on display. Jody Monroe, elite model in the new Elements fragrance line.

She scowled. Up until recently, she'd been Jody Monroe, surfer girl, up-and-comer on the pro scene. Back home, she was still Jody, daughter of Ross Monroe of Wild Side Surfboards. A girl who lived life to the fullest, the way her parents had urged her to. Not selling out to the mainstream. Marching to her own drum. Wiggling her toes in the sand.

With a grimace, she wiggled her toes in the too-tight shoes. God, what had she been thinking?

Then she straightened her shoulders and gave herself a pep-up nod. She'd been thinking of how much she owed her family and how this deal could solve all their problems in one fell swoop. She'd decided with her heart more than her mind. So, she'd do what she had to do, damn it. And when it was all over, she could go back to her old life with a sense of pride.

She paced through the hallway to the main porch where the bulk of the party guests gathered, glancing in a mirror as she went. Her blond hair was the right color, but it had been teased and sprayed into a swept-up hairdo to show off a pair of dangly earrings. Her blue eyes didn't sparkle the way they usually did — the way her dad said reminded him of her mom. Her shoulders were thrown back in their usual defiant pose, but that was it — a pose that hinted at the real Jody inside. But on the whole? She shook her head. Who that painted woman in the mirror was, she had no clue. It sure wasn't her.

"Darling, come tell us what it's like to work with Richard," a woman beckoned her onto the main porch.

Jody held back the retort on the tip of her tongue. *You mean Richard, the conniving, sexist pig?*

"Honey, I want to introduce you to one of our sponsors," a man said, snapping his fingers as if she were a circus animal at his beck and call.

"Sweetheart, how about a picture over here?"

She clenched her teeth. Did no one know her name? Still, she stepped toward the wide staircase where the others were gathered. Mingling was part of her contract, as Richard never failed to remind her. And if nothing else, she was outside where she could peek at the stars.

All for a good cause, she reminded herself, stepping outside. *All for a good cause.*

"Wait." A low, dark growl sounded from behind her, stopping her in her tracks.

It was the quietest voice in the crowd — a cross between a feline purr and an impatient snarl. Seductive yet scary at the same time. A firm hand closed over hers, tugging her back. She whirled, snatching her hand away and curling it into a fist.

"Watch it." Her contract didn't say anything about being touched, that was for sure.

Dark eyes blazed at her before darting over her shoulder to scrutinize the crowd.

Jody stared at the man. A new arrival at the party, no doubt. She would have noticed him earlier, for sure. His face was all hard angles and sharp curves where light danced with shadows. His eyebrows formed a dark, upswept line, much like his cheekbones. One second, his eyes were dark and mysterious, and the next, they shone yellowish-green.

"Get away from the stairs." He nodded her to his side. And damn it, his whisper was so urgent, so commanding, she complied.

"What's wrong with the stairs?"

Instead of answering, he boxed her in, shielding her with his body. The man wasn't much taller than her five foot eight — though all that muscle chipped into his frame made him seem twice her size — and he couldn't have been much older than her twenty-seven years, but there was a seasoned warrior quality about him. Raw, pulsing energy, too, like a powerful animal released from a cage.

Her defensive side wanted to demand what his problem was, but her soul wanted her to reach out, touch the man's arm, and help him talk through whatever it was that bothered him so much.

She settled for crossing her arms. Man, was he intense.

"What?" she demanded.

He stepped closer, and the edgy feeling she'd had all night intensified. The man was a one-man SWAT team, swooping in to protect her from whatever was about to go down — and something was going down, if she read his eyes right. That, or he was a lunatic of some kind.

He came so close, she shut her eyes and inhaled. He was the only man at the party who didn't smell like bottled chemicals. He smelled of the sea and of grass and of salt air. Even a little of sweat – fresh sweat that glistened on his brow as if he'd come hurrying over to her.

His nostrils flared, testing the breeze before he grunted a reply. "Come with me."

"I'd love to escape this party, but that isn't exactly what I had in mind," she shot back, keeping her voice low so no one could hear.

"You... What?"

The surprised flash of his eyes told her he was used to having his orders followed. Well, she was used to making her own decisions — for better or worse.

"Tell me why I ought to come with you, and I might consider," she said, staring him down.

The man stared back. Or rather, he glared, trapping her in the kind of standoff that ought to have ended in an angry huff with one of the two of them stomping away.

It won't be me backing down, she let her tipped-up chin say.

It sure as hell won't be me, his eyes blazed.

So they stood glaring, and a minute ticked by. But the longer she held his gaze, the more her body heated and the faster her heart thumped. The noise of the party receded, and the rise and fall of his chest mesmerized her. His chest, his scent, and the dark eyes that flashed like a wizard's...

Neither of them uttered a word. He seemed as tongue-tied as she was, though his stormy eyes never stopped dancing over hers.

Then he blinked, and his eyes narrowed on something behind her. "Shit."

A split second later, he lunged for her, and all hell broke loose.

Something whizzed by her arm, and a glass shattered. A woman screamed, and others followed suit.

"Gun! Gun!"

"Oh my God!"

"Get down!"

The deadly spit of a rifle chipped at the stone terrace, punctuating the cries. People rushed in all directions, knocking each other over. When a waiter with a tray went sprawling, glass splintered and champagne splashed.

"Quick. Follow me," the dark-eyed man said, grabbing her hand.

Another shot rang out, making the light overhead explode. Glass shards rained over Jody's back as she ran. Whoever this stranger was, he was right about getting away.

The man rushed her down the length of the porch, dodging panicked partygoers. He pulled her down a set of side steps and into the garden, away from the woods. Jody stumbled, but he hauled her to her feet and hurried her on like she was a football and not a grown woman. Then he rushed her around a corner of the building and crouched, pinning her against the stone foundation.

"What's going—"

"Shh," he hissed. His hand tightened around hers.

"Who's shooting?" She craned her neck for some avenue of escape, but she couldn't see a thing, not with his body sheltering hers.

"Take those shoes off," Dark Eyes said.

"What?"

"We have to run. Lose the shoes."

That suggestion, she was all in with. When she slipped off the heels, her bare toes squished into the moist earth, and her feet sighed with relief.

"What's going on?"

"You're in danger."

No shit, Sherlock, she nearly said. "You're in danger, too." When he shook his head, she scoffed. "Oh, and you're impervious to bullets? Do you have supernatural powers or something?"

He tilted his head at her, and his mouth opened then promptly slammed shut. "You're the one in danger. You need to come with me."

Whoa. Getting away was one thing. Taking off with a perfect stranger was another.

"Why should I trust you?"

His mouth twisted as he considered.

"I'm not sure you should," he finally said, so quietly she nearly missed it.

Jody gaped, trying to figure him out. But that, she decided, might just take a lifetime, given the hard-etched lines of his face.

He looked away then snapped his eyes back to her, going from not-at-all-certain to resolute warrior again.

"That way." He motioned. "Stay low. Go. Go."

He shoved her, and Jody had no choice but to comply. She sprinted across the lawn, away from the pandemonium in the club. Whatever was going on, she wasn't sticking around to find out.

Her feet hammered across the lawn, easily keeping ahead of Dark Eyes until—

A spitting sound whizzed by her ear, and she dove.

Dark Eyes dove, too, shielding her with his body. Jody hit the ground hard and came up wild-eyed, searching the woods. Shit. Someone really was shooting at her. Why?

A single red point glowed from far away, and her chest heated. She glanced down and yelped at a red dot that appeared on her shirt.

Death, she realized in a strangely removed way. Death had her in its sights.

She froze, incapable of twitching a muscle or drawing a breath. This was it. She was going to die.

Dark Eyes went wide-eyed. "Shit."

Shit was right. She didn't want to die. But she couldn't lift a finger, much less jump to her feet.

In the next instant, everything went from slow motion to superfast.

Dark Eyes's lips formed the word *No!* as he leapt for her — right into the line of fire. A moment later, he grunted and slammed into her — hard. They both jolted sideways before bashing to the ground.

Jody yelped. Dark Eyes groaned. And, *pfft!* Another nearly silent shot punctured the ground by her arm.

For one horrified moment, Jody lay still, waiting for the pain to register. But then Dark Eyes took a raspy breath, and she realized she hadn't been hit. *He* had.

And just like that, she charged into motion again.

"Get up. Get up!" she insisted, dragging him to cover behind the stone fountain that gurgled cheerily.

Outwardly, Jody was in control, but inside, a voice screamed. *Oh God. Oh God. He's hit. He took a bullet for you!*

The man kicked at the ground, pulling his legs into the small, sheltered space.

"Are you okay?" She crouched, snapping her head between her injured helper and the woods.

Please, please, let him be okay.

When she touched his back, her hand registered something hot and sticky. Blood.

A dozen garbled first aid instructions rushed through her mind, all jumbled together. *Call for help! Check airways! Monitor pulse!*

She ripped off the lower part of her dress, pressed it against his back, and started lying through her teeth. "You'll be all right. We'll get help. It will be okay."

She expected the man to groan or pass out, but instead, he rolled under her and worked his way up to his knees, swaying.

"We have to go," he rasped.

Jody blinked. "You've been shot. You're bleeding."

"I'll be fine." His face drew into ever sharper lines.

She'd felt the bullet propel his body against hers. How could he be all right?

"We have to get out of here," he said, grabbing her hand.

"We should wait for the police." And an ambulance, she wanted to add, but she didn't want him to panic. He was probably operating on some kind of extraordinary adrenaline rush. The second the pain set in, he was sure to collapse, right?

"My car's not far," he said, pulling her into cover behind a tree.

She dug in her heels. Flying bullets aside, she was nuts to follow a perfect stranger in a situation like this. But something about him was strangely believable, even if she couldn't put her finger on what that was. Instinct urged her to follow him and never look back.

Rationally, she knew it was crazy to even consider. But emotionally...

Go with your heart, her dad always said.

A second later, she was racing along with Dark Eyes, retreating into the night in another spontaneous decision she'd be sure to regret. But it felt like the right thing to do, even if a man that badly injured shouldn't be moved. He shouldn't even have been able to get to his feet.

"Are you sure you're okay?"

"It just grazed me," he said through clenched teeth.

The shot Jody remembered hadn't grazed anything. It had hit full on.

"But... but..."

"I've had a lot worse, believe me," he grunted as he ran.

She wondered what kind of man had suffered an injury — or injuries — worse than a gunshot. Although it must have just been a graze. Because he stood straighter with every jagged breath as he led her in a wide circle around the parking lot. He dipped, grabbing a bag of some kind, then strode along, pulling her through a hole in the fence and onto a gravel road outside the resort grounds.

"That way," he murmured while scanning the woods behind them. "My car is on the right." Then he eyed her bare feet and whispered in a gentler tone. "Can you make it?"

Jody's jaw hung open. The man had just been shot, and he was worried about her feet on the gravel?

Either he was crazy, or there'd been a miracle she'd somehow missed.

"Sure," she whispered as another little bit of her defenses crumbled. Maybe the tough guy thing was all an act. Maybe Dark Eyes wasn't quite as scary a character as she'd made him out to be.

A good thing she spent a lot of time barefoot in her usual daily life — her nice, quiet, safe life that had never seemed quite as precious as it did just then. Otherwise, she would have had a hell of a time picking her way across the gravelly path. It didn't bode well that Dark Eyes was leading her away from the resort, but with more shots spitting into the night, that seemed like her best option.

"There." He pointed into the shadows.

What started as a faint shape against the trees became a steel gray Lamborghini. Not at all what she'd been expecting, but she raced for the passenger side anyway. She couldn't guess what plan might have been racing through mystery man's head, but by now, she'd decided two things. Number one, he'd thrown himself in front of a bullet for her. If that wasn't proof she could trust him, what was?

Number two, she was all in.

He leaped into the convertible — really *leaped* in a single bound — while she clambered into the passenger side. And with a scream of wheels and scattering of gravel, they were off, skidding through a tight turn and zooming down the road. Jody rushed to buckle her seat belt then braced both hands against the dashboard. Dark Eyes didn't bother with a seat belt. His gaze jerked between the rearview mirror and the cone of light cast by the headlights. Seconds later, the chew of gravel under the tires turned to the smooth hum of asphalt as the car squealed onto the main road.

"Are you really okay?" Jody ventured.

He gave a curt nod and checked the rearview mirror, no longer hunching. No longer groaning either. It was uncanny.

"I'm fine."

She glanced at his back, but it was impossible to see any sign of his wound in the dark. For the next, long minute, there was no sound but the roar of the engine and the spin of tires over the road.

"I'm all for getting away, but do you have to drive at warp speed?" she asked.

"Yes. I do."

He pointed. The road ahead flashed with red and blue police lights, and a half-dozen squad cars rushed past, headed for the club. The wind lashed her hair as she swiveled to watch them race by, and when she twisted forward again, the wind whipped her hair all over her face.

Jody laughed out loud, and Dark Eyes shot her a sidelong glance. He seemed to do everything out of the corner of his eye. Sidelong glances, flashing glares that darted here and there.

"What's so funny?" he barked.

"Jeanette — the lady who did my hair — would have a fit if she saw me now."

He stared at her like *she* was the crazy one. He was the one who'd been shot, for goodness' sake! Although she must have been mistaken because, wow — he did seem all right. But how was that possible? She'd seen the red dot of the rifle's sights on her chest, and he'd jumped in the way.

Her heart beat a little faster. Why had he done that? Why had he risked his life to save hers?

"Are you *really* sure you're fine?"

He cast an annoyed look at the sky as if she'd been nagging him for days.

Jody squirmed in her seat. Okay, so he was all right. Slowly, she freed her hair from its tight bun and ran her fingers through the long strands. That simple action made her feel a little freer, a tiny bit more in control in a bizarre situation that had spiraled out of control. Enough that she even dared voicing the question that had been nagging at her ever since the first shots broke out.

"I don't understand. Why shoot at people at a publicity event?"

The man stared at her, and there it was again. The inner battle in his eyes — *that should I or shouldn't I* question that seemed so weigh so heavily on him. Why was he so wary of her?

He looked at the road, then the rearview mirror, and finally her face. "Not shooting at people. Shooting at you. He was shooting at you."

That *he* sounded much more specific than the vague *they* she had used. Had Dark Eyes caught a glimpse of the gunman?

"Me? How can you be sure?"

"I'm sure."

She shook her head. "Who would want to kill me?"

"There were two men out to kill you tonight. I saw one in the woods."

"Two?" she screeched. "Who was the other one?"

Dark Eyes looked away from the road long enough to pin her with a long, hard stare.

"Me. I'm the second man who wanted to kill you tonight."

Chapter Three

Jody sat perfectly still. If she didn't, she'd be shaking like a leaf. Two different people wanted to kill her — and one of them was the man driving the speeding car?

Why? What had she done?

"You want to kill me," she said, keeping a carefully neutral tone. Maybe Dark Eyes was a nutcase, after all. She gripped the armrest as he raced around another turn. "Um... by speeding?"

"I'm not going to kill you."

"But you just said..."

He tore his eyes off the road long enough to crook an eyebrow at her. "Are you trying to talk me back into it?"

The way he phrased his reply gave her the distinct impression he'd talked himself *out* of killing her. Which was good, but still. What was with this guy?

"No. I'm just... You saved me, but you wanted to kill me. Why? Did I do something to you? Because if I did, I'm really sorry, even though I have no clue what it might be."

His facial muscles twitched as if formulating words that refused to take shape. Shrubs at the roadside blurred past, and beyond them, the moon glittered over the Pacific, casting everything in black-and-white like a scene from a film noir. Which was fitting given the circumstances.

"You ever been to India?" he asked at last.

She did a double take. What did India have to do with murdering her on Maui?

"India? No. Not yet, at least."

"How about Detroit?"

She gave him a sidelong glance. Dark Eyes might be gorgeous in a swashbuckling, rakish sort of way, but he was definitely nuts.

"Nope. Are you from Detroit?" she tried. Maybe keeping him talking was the best course of action while she figured out what to do. Jumping from the speeding vehicle seemed fairly suicidal, and she'd dropped her tiny purse with her cell phone somewhere in her rush to get in. Still, in spite of everything, she felt remarkably calm, the way she did in the teeth of a forty-foot wave. Her mind told her to panic, but her heart told her to give him a chance.

When he didn't answer, she tried again. "Um, Mister..."

The road straightened long enough for the man to study her as he spoke words that made no sense. "Khala. Cruz Khala. My parents were Armin and Noelle Khala from Detroit. They, my sister, and brother were visiting my father's relatives in India when—"

Jody leaned as far away from him as she could when he trailed off. Whatever had happened to those people, it hadn't been good.

He watched her a second longer then gave a tiny nod. "She didn't do it," he whispered, more to himself than to her.

It was kind of spooky, the way he phrased it. Was the man a schizophrenic who held conversations with different personalities in his head?

The thing was, he didn't seem crazy. Bitter, world-weary, and pessimistic — yes. But crazy? Not entirely.

I didn't do what? she wanted to ask, but for once, she kept her mouth shut.

She studied him from the corner of her eye, trying to piece the tidbits of information together. India. Detroit. Maui. It was possible that his coppery skin wasn't all tan. But even if he had a splash of Indian heritage, what did that have to do with her?

"Listen, I don't know what's going on..."

"That's pretty clear," he said in perfectly dry tone.

"...but I've never harmed anyone, and no one has ever wanted to hurt me."

"Until now." He shook his head and muttered. "Fucking McGraugh was wrong."

She clasped her hands together, making sure the tremble inside her didn't sneak out. "Is he the one who was shooting?"

Dark Eyes scoffed. "He's my informant. He said you killed my family."

"Me?" she yelped, scuttling sideways in the seat. "Why would I do such a terrible thing? I don't even know you. And even if I knew you — even if I hated you — I would never do such a thing!"

The car thundered under a streetlight before plunging into darkness again, and shadows raced over his face. Another minute passed before he shook his head. "I know you didn't. I get that now."

She gulped, not quite reassured, as the car raced on. Where was he taking her? How long did she have to concoct an escape plan? She slipped the glasses off her head and folded them in her hands, wondering if she could use them as a weapon. They already were part of her defenses, in a way; she'd taken to wearing them lately just to piss Richard off. Because models, he never ceased to point out, didn't wear such clunky things.

"So, I'm staying at a condo in Honokowai," she said at last. "You can drop me off there and—"

He shook his head. "What happens when the gunman tracks you down?"

Jody stared. The man who'd planned to kill her was suddenly worried about her well-being? Then she caught herself. He'd jumped in front of a bullet for her sake, too. So maybe he really did care. But why?

"How about we just go to the police?"

"This is better," he muttered.

"What's better?" Her alarm grew when he pulled off on an unmarked road.

"Koa Point," he murmured as the car eased over a dirt road. His tone grew softer, gentler at the words. Sentimental, almost.

"Koa Point?"

He pulled up to a massive gate with a swirly pattern etched into it. A dragon shape? Jody stared into the darkness, but a cloud slid over the moon, hiding the details. Whatever the pattern was, that gate was the type to lock away an impressive private estate.

"Home," he said. Once again, his voice went soft — before he growled a few more words. "And no, I'm not going to kill you."

Either he'd read her mind, or her white knuckles had given her away.

"You promise?" she half joked.

"Would you believe me if I did?"

She crossed her arms. "No."

"Good." He tapped the steering wheel. "But for whatever it's worth, I promise." His voice dropped an octave, and his shoulders squared.

Well, damn. Maybe he did mean it.

Then she caught herself. She wasn't going to blindly trust anyone again. Not after learning her lesson the hard way.

She forced herself to take long, even breaths and whisper, "Great."

But it wasn't great. She was at this stranger's mercy, and she was all alone.

"I still think we should go to the police, though."

He pursed his lips. "Whoever was after you might be determined enough to track you to the next logical place. What if they have an inside man there?" He shook his head. "Like I said, this is better."

He tapped a code into a control panel set at the driver's side, and the massive gate slid open in an ominously silent motion. A moment later, Jody shrank in her seat as the gate ground to a close behind them, locking her in.

"You'll be safe here. I promise not to hurt you, okay?" The way he ran a hand through his hair indicated this wasn't all part of some premeditated plan. He was working on the fly, like she was. "We need to figure out what's going on, and this is the best place to do that."

Jody gulped and nodded. "Okay."

The driveway ended at a twelve-bay garage where he parked, exited the vehicle, and motioned her down a grassy path. Chest-high tiki torches flickered and danced in the darkness, making her wonder when they'd been lit. Was Dark Eyes some kind of reclusive tycoon? Did he have a staff who kept the home fires burning until he returned with women he'd decided to rescue — or women he'd decided not to kill?

God, he was confusing. And damn, it was a little spooky, too. Enough to make her recall her crazy aunt's warnings of all the supernatural creatures that haunted the world.

There are all kinds of evil spirits out there, Aunt Tilda would say. *Ghosts. Demons. Vampires...*

Then again, Tilda also told stories of more amiable creatures like mermaids and fairies, too.

Jody played it cool while she padded down the path in her bare feet. But inside, her emotions were all over the place. She told herself *weird* did not mean *terrifying* and that everything really would be all right. Her father had always told her to follow her heart, and somehow, her heart assured her she could trust this stranger. That, with him, everything would be all right. She nearly had herself convinced, too — until they stepped into a clearing that encircled a grass-roofed building where a taller, even more menacing man stood.

"This is our *akule hale,*" Dark Eyes murmured. "Our meeting house."

Our? Jody held her breath. Did that mean just Dark Eyes and Tall Guy, or did they share the place with a whole platoon of big, tough men? And yikes — a meeting? About what?

She eyed the foliage around the clearing, ready to sprint for her life. There only seemed to be that one other man there, but one was enough, considering the way he loomed at the edge of the open-sided building. Waiting, like he'd been expecting her all along. But Dark Eyes hadn't used his phone to call ahead, so how did Tall Guy know to expect them?

His eyes flicked up and down her body briefly before he extended a hand. "Silas Llewellyn. Pleased to meet you, Miss...?"

He didn't *sound* pleased, and he certainly didn't *look* pleased, but at least he wasn't downright hostile.

"Monroe. Call me Jody."

The man's look said, *I'll call you anything I want, and you call me Mr. Llewellyn.* There was something slightly formal, almost Old World and aristocratic about him. No accent, but he came off as someone older and wiser, even though he couldn't have been far over thirty or thirty-five.

"And you've brought Miss Monroe here because...?" Silas turned to Dark Eyes with a hard, icy look.

Jody made a hasty rearrangement of her hypothesis. Dark Eyes didn't own this estate; this guy Silas did.

When Jody's — Rescuer? Would-be assassin? — didn't reply with anything more than a flash of those midnight eyes, Silas prompted him. "Cruz?"

The two men stared at each other long and hard. Hard enough for Jody to grasp that on one level, the two were equals, at least when it came to pure male power. But Silas definitely stood higher than Dark Eyes — er, Cruz — on the totem pole of this estate.

Silas scowled. Obviously, he didn't approve of Cruz bringing her to their quiet hideaway.

Then Cruz shifted, and the light hit his back, revealing a huge, bloody stain, and she gasped.

"Oh my God. You really were hit."

"Grazed."

"But you must have lost a lot of blood..."

When she stepped closer, he stepped away, and she halted in her tracks. What was with this guy? He'd admitted to planning to kill her, not the other way around. So why was he so skittish around her? His eyes flashed, and she caught another glimpse of the striking, yellow-green tint that reminded her of a cat's eyes.

"I said, I'm fine," Cruz grumbled.

"What exactly is going on?" Silas barked.

Jody forced away a gulp and glanced toward the sound of waves rolling over a beach. Maybe she could run there, dive in, and swim the hell away.

Sometimes it's better not to think, she remembered her father saying as he'd taught her to surf, so long ago. *Just do. Listen to the elements and let yourself go.*

She took a deep breath. The sea breeze and whispering palms told her she could trust these men. The air hung heavy with promise, as if daring her to be brave enough to let things play out. So she shelved the idea of running away — for the moment, at least.

"I was shot at, and he, uh..." Jody said, struggling to finish the sentence. "He helped me get away."

"So I gathered," Silas said in a dry tone, staring down Cruz.

She watched as they faced off, perfectly silent, while their eyes blazed and their facial muscles twitched with nonverbal communication.

Communication that went something like, *What the hell were you thinking, bringing her here?* At least, that was how Jody interpreted the question coded into Silas's glare.

Cruz's weary look, on the other hand, said, *I have no clue.*

She'd never seen anything like it, except maybe with her grandparents, who'd been able to speak volumes in a few simple gestures and looks.

Jody noticed something else, too. The longer the eerily silent standoff dragged on, the more Cruz edged toward her, gradually shielding her from Silas's disapproving looks.

I won't hurt you, he'd said in the car. And more than his words, his actions convinced her. The man seemed determined to complete his 180 from would-be killer to protector. *Her* protector.

She took a deep breath and rubbed the goose bumps on her arms. Cruz had to be the strangest man she'd ever met — apart from some of the truly loony characters she'd spotted on the Santa Monica Pier — but the most fascinating, too.

Silas let out a deep sigh and motioned them inside the building. "Come in. Explain what this is all about."

The floor was covered with woven mats, and wooden beams arched high overhead. The sea breeze drifted in and out of the building, and the hum of waves told her the shoreline wasn't too far. Silas picked up a tablet that lay on a counter while

Cruz paced over to a living room area defined by couches set in a square. Jody stood beside one of the roof supports in between, not quite sure what to do. A clock on a side table said it was going on midnight. And, crap — it was going to be a long night, for sure.

Cruz paced back and forth, and Jody braced herself for an interrogation by two battle-hardened, soldier types. But then a calico kitten appeared out of nowhere and wound around Cruz's legs.

"Keiki," he murmured, scooping it up to his chest. Actually *cuddling* it like the kitten was family. And for one brief moment, a veil lifted, erasing the warrior and revealing a man capable of love, joy, and hope. If she'd blinked, she might have missed the brief relaxation of his shoulders, the softening of his jaw.

So Mr. Tough Guy had a soft side, after all.

The scent of coffee made her turn to watch Silas scoop rich brown powder into a machine that probably cost more than a month's rent in her tiny place back home. Then he tapped the spoon on the table. He might as well have slammed a gavel and said, *Let the interrogation begin.*

"Tell us what's going on. Why would someone want to kill you?"

Jody let her gaze slide over to Cruz. *He ought to know,* she nearly said.

But Cruz shot her a warning look, and she settled for a vaguer reply. "I have no idea. Someone just started shooting."

All three turned their heads as a flash of colored lights whirled through the night — police vehicles rushing by on the distant road, more sound than sight given how far the road lay from this tucked-away swath of private property.

"She's some kind of model," Cruz said, waving at her with a disapproving look.

She stood tall and shot him a withering look. "I'm not a model."

"Then what do you do?" he demanded.

"I surf."

"I mean, what's your job?" Cruz scowled. His yellow-green eyes shone. And gosh, they were beautiful. Fascinating. Haunted, too. She remembered the part about his family and swallowed away the lump in her throat. What might she be capable of if she'd suffered a loss that great?

"Like I said, I surf. I'm on the Women's Pro Tour. You can look me up."

Apparently, Silas already had, because he looked up from the tablet he'd been tapping on and arched an eyebrow. "Jody Monroe. Number eleven in the current standings?"

Jody shrugged. "Courtney Klein and I keep flip-flopping between eleventh and twelfth. Neither of us has ever broken into the top ten, though."

"Would she want to kill you?"

Jody snorted. "For eleventh place? Believe me, it's not like that. We're all competitive, but we're not *that* competitive."

Silas and Cruz exchanged glances that said, *You never know.*

"What other enemies do you have?" Silas went on as if poor Courtney was already headlining his list.

"Enemies?" No matter how hard she thought, she couldn't imagine anyone who'd want to kill her. She was a person who minded her own business. She helped her dad at his surf shop and did her best on the tour. "I don't have any enemies."

"You do now," Cruz growled.

Jody crossed her arms and shot him a look. *Like you, mister?*

The minute the thought flashed through her mind, she rejected the possibility. Cruz seemed to be the kind who was his own worst enemy, but instinct told her he wasn't *her* enemy.

"A jealous ex-lover?" Silas suggested.

She laughed out loud. She'd indulged in a fling or two with the athletes on the men's tour, but she would never mess around with another girl's man. "I wish my life was that exciting."

"It is now."

She made a face. "Not that kind of exciting, I mean."

"So what were you doing at the Kapa'akea club?" Silas asked.

She glanced at Cruz, boomeranging the question over to him. But his lips were firmly sealed, telling her she was the one testifying right now.

Jody took a deep breath and explained. "Ever since I made the pro tour three years ago, I've had sponsorship offers. It's all part of the scene. I've turned most down, but this year, a company came out of nowhere and made me an offer too good to resist." She trailed off, wondering whether she would have been better off turning it down. But, no. Her family needed the money, and that made it worthwhile.

"What kind of offer?" Silas asked.

"Modeling for a new fragrance line — 'Elements' by Wishful Desires." She made air quotes and scowled, making it clear that she hadn't signed on enthusiastically. "A total of three photo shoots, then I'm free. We did the first two in California, and we've come to Maui for the last one. After that, I cash my check, say goodbye to the cameras, and concentrate on the next competition in the tour."

She wiped her hands against each other, anticipating the day she could bid farewell to jerks like Richard. For a second, she stood taller, imagining the freedom she would regain. But then her shoulders slumped. Crap. The remaining photo shoot promised to be the worst yet.

"Who was that slimeball who talked to you on the terrace?" Cruz demanded.

Jody didn't have to stop and think who Cruz meant. "Richard? He's the product manager for the photo shoot."

"Would he want you dead?"

"He just hired me three weeks ago. I doubt he'd want me dead."

"Maybe someone wants to sabotage the campaign," Cruz said.

"That or get free publicity," Silas mused.

"You mean, by shooting the model?" A deep frown creased Cruz's face.

"Whoa." Jody put her hands up. "How is shooting me good publicity?"

"Any publicity is good publicity," Silas said. "That's how marketing goes."

A cold shiver went down her spine as she thought it over. "Richard did seem under pressure to get early buzz going. He said something about getting more press. But, killing me?" There'd been plenty of times she'd been creeped out by Richard and other members of the team, but she'd never considered she might become a target.

"Who knew you were going to be at the club tonight?" Silas asked.

Jody shrugged. "Who *didn't* know is more like it. It's all part of the publicity campaign. In the fine print." She sighed.

"You didn't read the fine print?" Cruz's sharp eyebrows jumped up.

She glared at him. No, she hadn't. Yes, it was stupid. But that was her business, not his.

Silas tapped his fingers on the counter. "What else does the job entail?"

"Nothing. Just the photo shoots. The last one is the day after tomorrow on a beach or under a waterfall or something. Well, it's supposed to be the day after tomorrow. Apparently, there's been some problem getting the props."

"What props?"

Jody shifted her weight from foot to foot. Being photographed in barely there bikinis was bad enough, but the props were the worst. The photographer had just about had her humping a surfboard in one shot and blowing suggestively into a conch shell in another. He'd also tried to get her to pose topless, insisting a lei was enough cover, but she'd drawn the line there. Each time, she'd contemplated quitting. It was that demeaning, that beneath what her father had taught her about pride. But each time, she'd convinced herself that the ends justified the means.

"The theme of the fragrance line — and the campaign — is 'Elements,'" she explained. "Earth, air, fire, water. They told me they were recruiting fresh faces for a huge campaign.

They've got a redhead off at a volcano somewhere doing the 'fire' photo shoot. The woman doing the 'earth' shots looks just like whatshername — that model from Eritrea. I don't know who they have doing 'air.' I'm the 'water' model."

"Earth, air, fire, water..." Silas's face went pale.

"I know, it's corny," she admitted. "Richard keeps coming up with things for me to be photographed with. He even wanted me to swim with dolphins, but the photographer said no way."

"So what's the prop?" Cruz churned the air with his hand to hurry her up.

She shrugged. "A jewel of some kind."

The men exchanged stunned glances. "What kind of jewel?" Cruz grunted.

"A sapphire." She paused in the sudden silence, wondering why Cruz took a step back. "Blue, like water. You get it?"

The clock ticked loudly, and an unbearably silent minute went by.

"Um, hello?" Jody said at last. "What's the big deal? It's just a piece of jewelry, right?"

Cruz looked at her like she'd just sprouted three heads. "Maybe," he muttered then looked at Silas. "Maybe not."

Chapter Four

Holy shit. Cruz looked at Silas, shooting the words straight into his mind the way strongly bonded shifters could. *Tell me this isn't happening.*

Silas didn't say a word.

Jody tilted her head. "Is something wrong?"

Normally, Silas was the quick-thinking one, but since he was uncharacteristically dumbstruck, Cruz did his best to cover up.

"Other than someone trying to kill an innocent woman, you mean?"

A second later, he cursed at himself. Where the hell did the *innocent* part come from?

Look at how clear those blue eyes are, his tiger said. *She's innocent, sure as we're guilty of too many sins.*

Which led him back to wondering who wanted her dead — and who had fed him false information — all over again.

Whoever it was, we'll find out and exact our revenge, his inner tiger growled. *Right after we get Jody settled in for the night.*

Whoa. Wait a minute. What the hell was the beast talking about?

"Listen, you've had a rough couple of hours," he found himself saying. "How about we call it a night?"

The woman crossed her arms, widened her stance, and tilted her chin up. "Call it a night?"

God, he wished she wouldn't do that perky-California-girl-meets-Amazon-warrior thing. Vulnerable yet feisty. Unsure yet tenaciously holding her ground. Every time she trained her sky-blue eyes on him, little bolts of lightning ran through his veins, and his tiger got all kinds of crazy ideas.

I like her. I want her, his tiger murmured. *She's my m—*

He cut off the impossible thought before it got any further and nodded to her. "You're safe here."

Her crossed arms tightened over her chest. "Safe from whom? You?"

Cruz couldn't decide how to respond other than *I hope you're safe from me, but I'm not really sure because my tiger is thinking all kinds of crazy things.*

Silas finally got his shit together and spoke. "Safe from everyone. Give us a day or two to investigate, and we'll get to the bottom of this."

She looked from one to the other. "What are you guys, detectives or something?"

"Something," Silas said.

Now her hands were on her hips. And dang, that was incredibly alluring, too. "We, who, are getting to the bottom of this?"

She'd make an awesome tiger, his inner beast hummed.

If he could have cuffed the animal upside the head, he would have. Jody wasn't a shifter. She was a human, which meant he had to stay on his toes. Humans were irrational. Unpredictable. In a word, dangerous. Humans had turned his world upside down by murdering his family in a bloody massacre. The trip of a lifetime his parents had been so excited about — visiting distant relatives in India and exploring remote jungles where Bengal tigers still roamed free — had turned into a deadly ambush that had never been fully explained. According to his sources, the villagers living near the scene of the crime had vehemently denied wrongdoing — of course. As rural, superstitious types, they'd tried pushing the blame to a whole muddled list of supernaturals. Vampires had done it, some villagers reported. Lion shifters, others said. Which was ridiculous — lion shifters didn't tangle with tigers and vice versa, and neither mixed with vampires. Those villagers were cowards who lied through their teeth. Typical humans, in other words.

Not all humans are liars, his tiger growled. *Like this one. She's scared shitless, but she's brave.*

Silas, meanwhile, had turned on a piercing look that could make the toughest opponent hem and haw.

"We — as in Cruz and I — will get to the bottom of this."

Jody didn't blink. Which only went to prove how crazy she was, even for a human.

"All three of us will get to the bottom of this." She jabbed her finger at each of them to make it clear she was insisting, not suggesting, and even Silas was taken aback.

Too bad Tessa — or Nina or Dawn — wasn't around. Any of the women of Koa Point could have helped ease this woman's fears. But Tessa and Kai, the dragon shifters, were over on the Big Island, using the cover of active volcanoes to practice spitting fire. Boone and Nina, the wolf pair, were in New Jersey, clearing out the modest house Nina had just sold. Bear shifters Dawn and Hunter, meanwhile, were enjoying their honeymoon in Alaska. Which meant it was just Cruz and Silas left at home, and hell. Neither one of them was the soft and fuzzy type.

I can be soft and fuzzy, his tiger insisted.

As if on cue, Keiki rubbed against his leg.

Cruz cleared his throat. "How about we figure out the details in the morning?" Going off a vague memory, he did his best to speak in a cheery voice. But, damn. He hadn't done cheery in years. Hadn't felt the need to bother, as a matter of fact.

Still, it worked, because Jody gave him and Silas one last *don't-fuck-with-me* look then nodded. "All right."

"Good," Silas said, though he didn't sound happy at all. "Cruz will set you up in the tree house."

If Jody's eyes grew wide, Cruz's just about popped out of his head.

"The tree house?" they both blurted at the same time.

The tree house was *his* place. His refuge. No one stayed there but him. No one!

Where else are we going to put her? Silas demanded.

Cruz cursed. The obvious choice — the guesthouse — still hadn't been repaired after damage sustained in a recent storm.

She can stay here in the akule hale, he tried.

Silas gave a curt shake of his head. *Seriously — you're going to make her bunk out in the meeting house?*

Well, Cruz sure as hell didn't want her bunking out at *his* place.

How about she stays at your *place?* he shot back at Silas.

The dragon shifter's eyes blazed. *I'm not the one who brought her here. Besides, you and I have to talk and make some calls. So get moving, already.*

"I'm sure you'll be very comfortable at the tree house, Miss Monroe," Silas said, dismissing them with a gesture toward the woods.

Silas rarely played his alpha-of-the-pack card, but when he did, no one dared question him. Not even Cruz, who had no choice but to lead Jody out of the meeting house and down the path toward his place.

You think she'll like it? his tiger asked all too eagerly.

God, he hoped not.

One night and she's out of here, Cruz told his tiger, walking faster.

Of course, he had been within a twitched muscle of killing her earlier that evening. The least he could do was put her up for one night.

"So, a tree house, huh?"

He shrugged. "You'll see."

It was hard to describe the rambling place tucked all the way back in the thickest woods at Koa Point. So he walked in silence, leaving the talking to her. And talk she did. Typical human.

"How big is this estate? It's got, what — ten fancy cars? And a helicopter?" She pointed to the rotors showing above the treetops, reflecting the moonlight. "Who owns this property? And wow — you get to live here?"

Cruz looked straight ahead. In truth, he had no idea who owned Koa Point. All he knew was that Silas had arranged the caretaking deal for their band of five shifters. The timing had been fortuitous; they'd all just earned honorable discharges and needed a place to settle down to transition to civilian life after years in the military. Only Silas knew the owner's identity, and he'd made it clear the owner wanted no questions asked. As long as the owner didn't visit — whoever it was had never come to Maui the entire time Cruz had lived at Koa Point — what did it matter? Cruz and his buddies took care of security on the sprawling estate and kept themselves busy with private investigative and bodyguarding work on the side.

"Who else lives here?" Jody asked.

Cruz wondered what she'd say if he told her the truth. *A whole troop of shifters. Two dragons, a wolf, a bear, and a tiger, to be exact.* Then he corrected himself, because it wasn't just the guys living there any more. With Kai, Boone, and Hunter mated, their numbers had swelled to eight.

A change for the better, his tiger nodded. *With Tessa, Nina, and Dawn around, things are... well...*

Cruz struggled for the word, too. *Nicer? More peaceful? Better balanced?* It was hard to explain, but the newcomers had all contributed to making the place feel more like a... a...

Home, his tiger filled in. *A community.*

Which was funny, because he'd never really thought Koa Point lacked anything before destiny had brought his friends' mates to their sides.

Destiny, his tiger hummed.

Jody stopped in her tracks at the first sight of a footbridge arching gracefully over the stream. "Wow. I mean... It's beautiful." She waved at the red and gold lanterns hanging overhead, lighting the way through the dark night.

Most evenings, Cruz didn't bother turning on the lights, preferring to stalk home in tiger form. But tonight, the light from the lanterns seemed softer, more welcoming than ever. A double-edged sword, he realized, because this wasn't about welcoming anyone into his private space.

Except part of him wanted Jody there. He wanted her to like it. Keeping people away meant he never got to share his most special place with anyone. Maybe it was time to change that.

"I love it," she gushed as a pair of myna birds fluttered overhead.

Jody's comment ought to have set off warning bells in his mind, but all he felt was a burst of pride. Tigers were hoarders at heart, and while he didn't collect junk, he had enjoyed bringing together little treasures to mark the place as his. Would Jody notice the details he'd put into the wooden handrails of the bridge? Would she spot the decorations on the Chinese lamps strung overhead?

"Wow, it's all carved," she murmured, running her hand over the rails. Her bracelets jangled, the only man-made sound in an otherwise peaceful night. "And, oh! Is that a tiger on that lamp?"

The swirling Chinese design was all claws and fangs. A subtle warning to potential trespassers — not that any dared explore Koa Point.

"Oh, there's a dragon, too. And a bear..." Jody oohed and aahed over each lantern.

In truth, the designs were Cruz's subtle homage to his shifter brothers — the men who'd become his second family after all they'd endured in their active duty days. They'd become family, and it felt fitting to acknowledge that in some way.

Crickets chirped from all around. Mynas chattered, and the stream gurgled under the bridge. On the whole, West Maui was relatively dry, but the mountains caught the trade wind clouds and kept the stream gushing, so his private corner of paradise was lush and green. His own private jungle. And, shit. It was being invaded by a human.

She's not invading, his tiger pointed out. *We invited her.*

Damn. Why the hell had he done that?

Because she has to be comfortable, and we have to keep her safe.

Which was a load of crap, Cruz knew, because what greater danger was there to her than him?

Jody's throat bobbed. "You swear you're not taking me somewhere to kill me?"

A shot of regret went through him. How could he even have considered killing someone as free of evil as her?

He shook his head. "I swear I'll never hurt you. Never." His voice grew raspy as he uttered the words, and inside, his tiger went one step further.

I swear I'll protect you to the end of my days.

Her eyes searched his, and she relaxed slightly. Most humans relied far too heavily on the spoken word, but Jody appeared to judge physical cues the way a shifter might.

She lifted her hand toward his, suddenly quiet. The space between them crackled, and he leaned closer. When Jody's eyes shone brighter, his pulse skipped. His palms grew sweaty, and his heart thumped. Inside, his tiger lashed his tail from side to side and hummed happily.

Christ, what was wrong with him?

"It's so peaceful," Jody said, breaking her gaze from his to look around while she continued down the path.

His tiger nodded with satisfaction at her hushed tone. *See? Not all humans are loud and bothersome.*

Cruz decided to withhold judgment for a little while.

You do that. Because she is our destined mate. Ours!

Someone could have hit Cruz over the head with a brick and he would have been less shocked. He didn't want or need a mate.

Want. Need, his tiger insisted with a low, throaty growl.

Jody stopped in her tracks, clapped, and choked out, "Oh my God."

"Nice, huh?" his tiger made him say.

"Nice? It's amazing," she said, looking up and around as his tree house took shape in the dim light.

Cruz did what he rarely did — namely, stop to admire his handiwork. Every member of their tight-knit unit had carved out a little corner of Koa Point for himself, and they rarely stepped foot on each other's private turf, choosing to gather on neutral ground at the meeting house instead. It was the perfect arrangement for a group of strong-willed shifters who'd stuck together through thick and thin. Now, each occupied his own custom home, and Cruz loved his.

It *was* pretty amazing. What had started as a single platform where a tiger could bask at midday had gradually expanded to a wide deck that encircled a four-story-tall monkeypod tree. A spiral staircase wound to the deck from the ground-level living area, and rope bridges extended from each side, leading to a number of side platforms — like bedrooms in a house, yet nothing like a regular house. The spartan living area held a hammock and a futon. One platform was suspended high up in the canopy of the forest, completely open to the elements — the perfect place for his tiger to swish its tail and stand guard. Another rope bridge led to the covered bedroom he used to stretch out in in human form. The double mattress had been hell to haul up, and the dresser was all dinged up, but it was home. A few little touches here and there and he'd have a real tiger palace all to himself.

Home, his tiger hummed in satisfaction.

He'd never had anyone out here except the other guys — and that was rare enough.

I like having her here, his tiger said.

Cruz made a face, but it was kind of nice, watching her react to it all.

"Who built this?"

His chest puffed out a bit. "I did."

"You?" She wasn't incredulous so much as impressed, and Cruz couldn't resist pointing out all the little features.

"There's a hot plate over there, a bathroom over there..."

Jody nodded and grinned. "My dad would love this place. He made us a tree house when we were kids, but it wasn't anything like this."

Cruz's tiger nodded in satisfaction. *Maybe some humans aren't crazy, after all.*

When she slid into the rainbow hammock and gave herself a push to start swinging, he had to fight the inexplicable urge to ease in beside her.

"Wow. This is way better than the condo at Honokowai."

He laughed out loud, then caught himself. What was he doing, joking around with a human he hadn't wanted anything to do with in the first place?

You're having a nice time, his tiger snipped. *Is that so bad?*

He cleared his throat and pointed around the living room. "The futon is pretty comfortable, and there are some extra towels in the bathroom." He pointed down the lantern-lit path.

"I've slept in some offbeat places, but this takes the cake. Oh — wait." She straightened in the hammock. "Where will you sleep?"

Usually, he slept in the bedroom area or on one of the other platforms suspended overhead. But he sure as hell wasn't going to sleep there tonight.

"I'll sleep in the meeting house. I do that all the time," he lied.

She hurried out of the hammock. "I can't oust you from your own home."

Exactly. She couldn't. He wouldn't let humans wreck his life ever again.

But damn it, his tiger had different ideas and made him communicate as much. "Of course you can. Here, you can borrow this." Without thinking, he took a clean T-shirt from a drawer and set it on the table so she'd have something to sleep in.

She sure can, his tiger hummed.

Even his human half swelled a little at the thought of Jody wrapped in his clothes. Her, covered with his scent.

He balled his fists and bumped his thighs a few times, trying to snap out of whatever had come over him.

"But..." she started.

He scuffed his boot against the ground. She didn't get it. If he stayed anywhere within sniffing, seeing, or hearing distance of her, who knew what his tiger might tempt him to do?

"It's fine, believe me," he said. A purr sounded, and little Keiki wound between his legs. He picked up the calico kitten and stroked her until her eyes closed with pleasure. He closed his eyes, too, soaking in the warmth and satisfaction radiating from the little fur ball. With Keiki, he could almost believe the world was full of goodness and hope.

Jody chuckled. "She purrs like a tiger."

Cruz's eyes snapped up. Did Jody suspect anything? But, no. The woman's eyes stayed on the kitten, and her smile was as innocent as Keiki's.

"Tigers don't purr," he pointed out.

"They're cats, aren't they?"

"Look it up. Tigers don't purr."

"Well, that little one sure can purr. Is she yours?"

"Mine? No. Cats don't like to be owned."

Cruz knew he could be a surly son of a bitch, and that usually succeeded in keeping people at arm's length. But Jody didn't seem bothered. In fact, she reached out to pet Keiki as if Cruz had invited her to. And the funny thing was, he didn't step away, as if he really *had* invited her to. As if he *wanted* this woman to come close.

Closer...

Closer...

Their hands brushed while they both petted Keiki, and Cruz found his eyelids drooping. Which was stupid, plain stupid, because there was a human invading his personal space. He couldn't help it, though. Petting Keiki always soothed his restless soul, and petting Keiki with Jody had the same effect times ten. So there they stood, like a couple of proud parents huddled over a newborn, marveling at the tiny ears, the button nose, and miracle of a tiny heartbeat under their hands.

Cruz inhaled the sweet night air, and Jody's scent snuck in like that of an exotic flower that had just bloomed amidst the familiar plants of home. That wild rose scent that tickled his nose. He closed his eyes and inhaled a little more.

"Sweet kitty," Jody murmured.

See? I knew she liked me, his tiger cooed.

Usually, it took him an hour of pacing and moving from one roost to another to settle down and relax. That's why he'd built so many different platforms radiating out from the tree house. But tonight... Tonight, he could have closed his eyes and drifted off to sleep there and then. A peaceful, dreamless sleep — the kind he hadn't had for years.

Then a bat whooshed overhead, too close for comfort, and his eyes snapped open again.

Shit. Silas was waiting.

"Gotta go," he said gruffly, pulling away. Not too far, though, because now that he'd caught sight of Jody's incredibly blue eyes, they mesmerized him.

"You sure this is okay?"

No, he wasn't sure. But he nodded anyway. "It's fine."

He transferred Keiki to her arms and drew reluctantly away. Then he fake-coughed a few times and forced himself to step toward the footbridge. His body ached, as if leaving her was wrong. But, shit. He couldn't keep Silas waiting any longer.

"Gotta go. Have a good night."

She nuzzled Keiki with her chin exactly the way he remembered his mom doing with his younger sister a long time ago. The way his mom had probably done with him back when he'd been too young to recall.

I remember, his tiger murmured. *In my heart, I remember.*

And for the next few seconds, warm feelings filled in the space usually occupied by anger and pain.

Jody went right on nuzzling Keiki, watching him go. "Goodnight. And thanks. For everything," she said before breaking into a wry grin. "I think."

Chapter Five

Cruz cursed himself all the way back to the meeting house.

First, for having brought Jody to his place. Second, for gazing into her eyes for far too long. If he hadn't been sure she was human, he'd have bet she was a witch, because she had cast a spell over him. He'd even handed Keiki over instead of hustling the kitten away. What was up with that?

Third, he cursed himself for dallying so long because he had a dragon to deal with, and dragons didn't like to be kept waiting.

"What took you so long?" Silas grunted the second Cruz came into sight. His breath held a little hint of ash as it always did when his patience was stretched thin. Spitting actual fire might not be far behind, Cruz guessed.

"I came as fast as I could," he lied. He'd stopped on the footbridge on the way back — twice — to turn toward his place and sniff the night air, teasing a little hint of Jody out of it.

Damn it, damn it, damn it. He could not — would not — fall for a human. He owed that much to the family members he'd lost.

Silas grumbled and ran a hand through his hair — a sign of the calm before the storm, Cruz knew. Any minute, the dragon shifter would unleash his ire. Silas had dealt well with all the crises they'd faced in the past months, but Cruz had rarely seen him this worked up. Silas's eyes glowed red, and a tic twitched at the corner of his mouth. What had Jody said that flipped that switch in him? Was it the hint of a jewel? Or was it something totally unrelated, like the rumor that had been going around about pressure to develop the estate into a luxury resort? The latter was unthinkable. Who would tear down the woods of Koa Point and crowd all that open space with bungalows and a golf course? Who could contemplate destroying the peace and magic of the place? And, shit — where would Cruz and his friends go?

The very thought infuriated him, so he pushed it out of his mind — for now. Right now, Silas was in a rare state, and Cruz wished Nina or Tessa were around. Each of them knew how to settle Silas down with a quiet comment or a steaming cup of tea. Cruz glanced at the coffee machine. Somehow, he doubted that would work tonight.

Sure enough, Silas whirled and showed the points of his teeth. "What the hell were you doing at the Kapa'akea club, anyway?"

Cruz shifted his weight from foot to foot. A good question. What exactly had led him there? He traced a crooked line through the memories that had seemed so logical at the time. But now, he wasn't sure. It all started with his informant. He scowled deeply. "Remember McGraugh?"

Silas nodded.

Cruz, Silas, and the other shifters of Koa Point had been in Special Forces together. McGraugh was an eagle shifter working for Navy Intelligence they'd collaborated with a few times. McGraugh had recently left the service, settled on the mainland, and went into private investigating, much like Cruz and his buddies.

"McGraugh tipped me off that the person who killed my family would be there."

Silas arched an eyebrow. "You said you'd made your peace with that."

Cruz glared at the ground. He would never make peace with the fact that he hadn't been with his family to offer protection or that he had never managed to pin down their killer.

"You said you weren't going to chase ghosts any more," Silas continued.

Cruz ground his teeth. He'd promised not to eliminate the entire human race, but given the opportunity to kill the actual murderer who had slipped away, he couldn't resist.

Jody isn't the killer, his tiger pointed out.

He snarled under his breath. "McGraugh's intel has always been good."

Not this time, it wasn't, his tiger insisted.

"So what happened?" Silas demanded.

Cruz took a deep breath and related the events of the evening. How he'd taken up position and waited for the cues he'd been told to look for. How Jody had appeared on the terrace, and how he'd seen the waiter hand her the drink. And then... He ended up trailing off at that point in the story, because he wasn't sure how to explain the instincts that had taken over at that point.

"What made you hold back?" Silas asked, studying him closely. Too closely.

Damned if Cruz knew. His tiger had just refused.

How could I let you kill our mate? the beast growled.

Cruz frowned at the floor. If destiny sent him a human as his fated mate, it was just fucking with him. He wouldn't fall for that.

He rushed ahead in the story — spotting the second shooter, watching Jody retreat indoors, and rushing over to drag her to safety before the sniper could get a clear shot.

Silas made a face when he finished. "I don't like it."

Cruz snorted. What was to like?

Silas went on before Cruz could get a word in. "I think we're right to keep her here, though. As long as it takes to get to the bottom of all this."

Something lurched in Cruz's chest — one section skipping for joy while another sank in despair. He needed to get Jody away — far away — before she wooed his tiger with crazy notions of love and destined mates.

"I thought you didn't want to get involved," he protested. "She is human, after all."

"We need Miss Monroe if we're going to find out more about that sapphire. If it's a Spirit Stone—"

Cruz bared his teeth. "You mean, use an innocent woman as bait? Come on, man. That could put her right back in the cross hairs."

"You're the one who was aiming the cross hairs at her, correct?"

A low blow, but Cruz deserved it. Thank goodness he hadn't pulled a trigger. But when he found the guy who did...

Silas made a sharp gesture, bringing Cruz's gaze back to his. "You need to stay focused. That sniper was probably a hired gun — and not a very professional one, at that. We need to uncover who set it all up. And in the meantime, Miss Monroe is safer with us than on her own."

Cruz had to give him that. He steeled his nerves, trying to reason things out. "The question is, who would want to kill her?"

"No, the question is who would want to frame you?"

"Me?"

"This whole situation smells like a setup."

His gut tightened. "Are you saying McGraugh turned on us?"

Silas pursed his lips. "I'd rather believe someone gave him false information."

"Who, then?"

They both went silent for a while.

"We need to find the waiter who served her the drink," Silas said at last. "Find out who set the bait."

Cruz felt his face heat. "Are you saying someone baited me with the prospect of revenge?"

"That wasn't the only bait," Silas added with a grim look.

Cruz tilted his head in a question.

"Her. Jody," Silas said. "She's bait, too."

"Whoa. What?" Cruz gulped away the fury that rose out of nowhere. "Why Jody? Who would be interested in her?"

Silas's eyebrows hit a deeper curve. "You. You like her."

Cruz's heart pounded away, breaking up his protest. "I... I..." Of course, he didn't like her. No way was he interested. Not in the least.

Silas arched one thin eyebrow that said, *Sure. Right.*

Inside, his tiger hummed. *I do like her. A lot.*

Cruz cast around for a better theory — one that didn't involve him and a human he couldn't possibly be attracted to.

"Bullshit. It's more likely someone is trying to sabotage the promotional campaign Jody mentioned. What did she call it? Elements?"

The color drained out of Silas's face as he gazed off into the distance.

Cruz tilted his head at the dragon shifter. "What? It's just an ad campaign."

Silas shook his head and murmured so low, Cruz could barely hear. "Moira."

Cruz froze. "Moira?" The she-dragon who had broken Silas's heart? "What does she have to do with this?"

Silas scowled. "I'm not sure. But that was one of the ideas she used to talk about trying someday — a fragrance line based on an 'Elements' theme."

Heavy lines marked Silas's face, and the tic at his cheek twitched away. Whatever had happened between Silas and the she-dragon had occurred before Cruz met Silas. All Cruz really knew was to steer away from the subject if he wanted to avoid sustaining third-degree burns. That, and he knew Moira had twisted Silas's heart before dumping him for another man in the most callous way. Kai had explained as much, though even he didn't know much more than that.

Moira is superficial, self-centered, and manipulative, Kai had once said. *The woman is poison. Silas is better off without her.*

Cruz thought about it. Most men were better off without the women they imagined to be their mates.

Not most men. Just some men. Look at Boone. Nina is perfect for him, his tiger pointed out. *The same way Dawn is perfect for Hunter and Tessa is perfect for Kai. They've never been so happy or balanced.*

Happy. Balanced. Cruz chewed the words over. Just because there were a few couples who really were made in heaven didn't mean destiny favored everyone. His friends were far and away the exceptions, damn it. He, for one, wasn't about to get goo-goo eyed about a woman.

So why did you have to blink so much when we left Jody? his tiger asked. The smartass.

"If Moira is involved in this..." Silas murmured, lost in his own thoughts.

"Elements is a pretty common theme," Cruz pointed out.

Silas stared into the night. "She used to talk about it exactly the way Jody described. Setting up photo shoots in different locations. Getting models with different looks to represent each element." He looked twenty years older as he shifted his weight from foot to foot. "And what Jody said about the campaign not getting enough press — Moira loves being the center of attention. She'd do anything for it. And on top of all that, this mention of a sapphire..."

"You think it could be a Spirit Stone?"

Silas's lips pinched into a thin line at the mention of the long-lost gems with magic powers. "Valuable jewels don't just happen to come along. It could well be that the other Spirit Stones are calling to it." He looked up at the hillside where his house stood. Somewhere in the rocky cliff behind the house was the location of his dragon hoard — or so Cruz guessed. Dragons loved treasures, and though most of Silas's inheritance had been stolen by a dragon lord named Drax, Cruz figured the shifter had to have a few treasure chests of glittering gems and gold around somewhere. That, and the three Spirit Stones — an emerald, a ruby, and an amethyst — he often locked away on behalf of the women of Koa Point. Tessa, Nina, and Dawn had each put their life on the line to obtain those stones.

"The Lifestone, Firestone, and Earthstone are all safe here," Silas continued. "That leaves two of five stones — the Windstone, and the Waterstone — a sapphire."

"Waterstone?" Cruz pictured a jewel that could conjure up monster waves or killer storms. "Do we really want to get mixed up with another Spirit Stone?"

"Do we have a choice?" Silas snapped.

Cruz held his tongue. He only knew his former commander as cool, collected, and calculating. But Silas's jaw worked left and right while his fingers tapped nervously on the tabletop. Was the weight of responsibility finally wearing him down? Cruz had never considered that before. Now that he did, he realized their little community at Koa Point was growing fast.

Hunter and Dawn were taking it slow, but everyone knew it was only a question of time before Boone and Nina — or Kai and Tessa — had kids. That threw a whole new layer of responsibility onto Silas's shoulders at a deeply troubling time. The world was already pretty messed up, but the question of the Spirit Stones complicated everything exponentially. Every ruthless, greedy shifter in the world would be after the next gem that turned up.

But there was more than worry in Silas's eyes. There was pain, too. Moira must have really pulled a fast one to agitate Silas to that extent.

Cruz tilted his head, seeing Silas in a new light. A mortal man, not a machine. A guy just as capable of losing his head — and heart — as Cruz was.

All the more reason for Cruz to be on guard against the foolish notion of a destined mate.

But... but... his inner tiger protested.

"First thing tomorrow, I'll track down the waiter," he said, composing a list in his mind. "Then I'll sniff around the woods where I saw the second gunman. Maybe I can pick up a trace of his scent."

Silas nodded. "We need to run a background check on Jody and dig into this Elements campaign, too." His voice grew rough and bitter.

"You really think Moira could be involved?"

Silas looked at the palms swaying gently in the night breeze. "I don't know. But this time, I'm not leaving anything to chance."

Chapter Six

Jody wasn't lying when she'd mentioned sleeping in some off-beat places. But a night in a tree house...

At first, she lay on the futon with her eyes wide open. The mosquito net draped gracefully around the bed kept the bugs out, but not the sounds or smells — and least of all, not the dancing shadows of the night.

Her nose twitched with the musky scent of virgin forest, and her ears tuned in to the multilayered chorus of insects and birds. Her eyes darted to every rustling leaf or swaying branch. But the atmosphere soothed more than it alarmed her, and before long, she was asleep. Asleep and witnessing the craziest hodgepodge of dreams she'd ever had.

There were scary dreams in which gunshots exploded everywhere, and no matter how she tried, she couldn't get her legs to move. Exhilarating dreams where a sports car raced down a highway so fast, the stars blurred. Confusing dreams in which an unfamiliar man seemed like the closest friend she'd ever had, while friends could not be trusted. Sensual dreams, too — of rolling in bed with a dark-haired man with greenish-yellow eyes whose gentle caress brought her to higher heights than anything she'd ever experienced.

She woke briefly then drifted right back to sleep, submerging herself in another round of dreams. In one, she surfed down the barrel of a perfect, aquamarine wave. In another, she swept the floor of her dad's shop with a steady swish, swish, swish. And in another...

Jody jerked awake, panting from the image of coming face-to-face with a huge striped cat. A tiger.

She blinked into the darkness. Holy shit. Where was she? And what was that purring sound that formed a bass to the orchestra of the night?

Something moved under her hand, startling her. But it was just a tiny kitten that yawned, blinked, and went right back to sleep.

"Keiki," she murmured, putting everything together. Keiki was the name of the kitten, and she was on Maui. But, whoa — was such a tiny creature truly capable of making such a loud sound? Or had she dreamed that persistent, growly sound the way she'd dreamed of the tiger's face?

Trees closed in above and around her, and something moved in the underbrush. A big something — or was her imagination at work again? One of the platforms suspended above her swayed as if recently vacated. She sat staring at it, clutching the sheet to her chest as her heart thumped away — partly from fear, but also from excitement. What would it be like to come that close to a wild animal in real life?

Like surfing, she supposed. That high that never grew old, no matter how many times she soared down the face of a wave.

She lay awake a while longer before her eyelids drooped, and the next time she raised them, the birds were singing at the top of their lungs, signaling morning. A good couple of hours into morning, in fact — much later than her usual wake-up time. Of course, it had been one hell of a night. Two men had tried to kill her, and one of them ended up taking her home.

She laughed out loud. How would she ever make that sound okay to her dad?

"Dad!" she yelped, suddenly anxious. Had he heard about the shooting? Was he worried? She stood quickly and looked around for a phone. But apart from a few light fixtures, the tree house seemed entirely off the grid.

A chair had been pulled up to the bed, holding a stack of clothes and a towel. So someone really had been there, if not a tiger. She shook the clothes out of their neat, military folds and brought a blue T-shirt to her nose, half hoping it smelled as good as the shirt she'd slept in. The shirt Cruz had given her carried a faint, alluring hint of the man, and she'd spent the night hugging it close. But this fabric had a flowery, detergent scent, as did the sporty shorts and the towel. A pity, really.

She took all three and walked around. The bathroom only offered a toilet and sink, but the quiet trickle of water lured her down a path into the forest. A path just wide and high enough for her to wander without swatting away leaves. Jody meandered this way and that, looking up and around. The place was like an aviary — lush, green, and alive with a cacophony of bird calls. Then the path opened upon a clearing and—

"Oh," she whispered in delight.

A row of lava stones held back a gurgling stream, creating a shallow pool wide enough to paddle a stroke or two across.

"You're kidding me," she murmured, spotting a bar of soap and bottle of shampoo beside the waterfall that nourished the pool. This was Cruz's shower?

She turned in a slow circle, looking back at the tree house with its spider web of interconnected platforms.

"Amazing."

The whole place had a Robinson Crusoe feel to it — Robinson Crusoe, luxury style, as if the castaway had had years to carve out the perfect home-away-from-home. And Cruz had constructed all of it. Who would have thought such a curt, grim man would create a Garden of Eden for himself?

Maybe there was a little bit of hope in the mysterious Mr. Khala, after all. Maybe even a dash of optimism in a man who wasn't entirely at home in his own skin. A man who'd held a kitten so tenderly and closed his eyes as if wishing upon an unseen star.

"Cruz Khala," she murmured to herself.

Assassin? Rescuer? Architect? A little of all three, she decided. She'd been scared of him at first, but everything he'd done since last night made her feel protected, not threatened. Yes, she'd been too quick to trust in the past, but her heart and soul insisted she could trust Cruz. That she *had* to trust him to survive.

She looked around. The place was secluded as could be. So she stripped and squealed at her first contact with the chilly water. Slowly, she lowered herself in and floated on her back, watching the one patch of blue sky visible through the dense canopy above. No matter how she tried to clear her mind, though, it kept mulling over the contradictory facets of Cruz.

She soaped up, washed her hair with the biodegradable soap — proving that Cruz had a heart for nature as well as furry felines — and dunked to rinse herself. The water felt crisp, clean, and softer than the salt water she spent so much time in. All in all, it was easy — too easy — to lounge in that pool and recall the best parts of her dreams. Especially the sensual parts. Jody ran her hands over her body, telling herself it was all about hygiene and not a hot fantasy. A fantasy of her host stepping quietly into the water behind her and soaping up her back. Sliding his hands over her skin... Touching his lips to her shoulder... Reaching lower...

She closed her eyes and imagined the low, growling sound from her dream. It formed the perfect background to the increasingly heated images running through her mind.

A bird fluttered overhead, chattering in surprise, and Jody splashed to a sitting position again. Whew. What was it about this place — and that man — that turned on the cavewoman in her? And why did she feel eyes burning into her skin?

"Morning," a deep voice sounded from the path.

Jody crossed her arms over her chest and whirled, not sure whether to greet the person or yell at him. It was Cruz, standing on the path. Shit. So much for trusting him.

But the man looked like he hadn't slept a wink all night, and he appeared genuinely surprised to find her in the pool — naked, no less.

"Good morning," she managed, determined not to get flustered. Not even with the man she'd just been fantasizing about. "I love your bathtub."

"Pool," he corrected with a little scowl.

"So peaceful. So private," she added, socking him with a look.

A tiny hint of a smile appeared at the corner of his mouth before he hid it away again. So the man really could smile. Could he laugh, too?

She stretched out an arm, making sure to keep the other over her chest. "You want to hand a lady a towel?" she asked, then immediately chastised herself. This wasn't some guy waiting for a good set of waves she could joke around with in a safe public place. He was a perfect stranger, and she was at his mercy.

A soft, growly answer sounded from his chest. "Trick question?"

She laughed out loud. "No."

His eyes flashed, and for a second, she wondered if he could read her mind.

She cleared her throat, getting herself back on track. "I'll get it myself."

"Sure," he said, opening his arms wide as if daring her to step out in full view, dripping and naked.

As if. She jabbed a finger in his direction then turned it in a circle. "And since you're such a gentleman and fabulous host..."

Cruz made a face that said, *Not.*

"...you'll turn around. Now." She made the last word a command and did her best to look like she could poke his eye out or crush his balls with her bare hands. In short, a woman not to be messed with, not even by a badass like him. So what if she was naked and essentially defenseless? It was all in the attitude.

Slowly, Cruz nodded and turned his back.

Whew.

"Such a gentleman," she murmured, as if she'd known it all along.

Cruz growled under his breath. "Such a lady."

Touché, she nearly chuckled. *Touché.*

It was kind of fun, provoking him. Way over on the dangerous end of fun, but somehow, she couldn't resist.

She rose, dripping. At a photo shoot a week earlier, she'd felt self-conscious no matter how much the photographer urged her to act sexy. Now, she felt feminine. Beautiful. Desirable, almost.

She caught herself there. Christ — any reasonable woman would heed the obvious alarm bells a man like Cruz set off. But instinct drew her toward him, like... like he was her destiny.

She pushed the thought away and made a mental note to save the sexy-as-sin heat for the next time she had to pose in front of a camera. Right now, she had to get dressed — fast.

She wrapped herself in the towel and called out. "I don't suppose room service at Chez Cruz includes a hairbrush?"

He turned, patting the messy hair that just reached his collar, and opened his mouth to answer. But no words emerged. He just stood there, soaking her in.

Jody took a deep breath and stared back. A hush fell over the forest — that, or her ears weren't working any more. Neither did her voice, because she couldn't manage a word. Her eyes zoomed in on his gaze and held it while everything else receded to a distant blur. A low, purring sound filled her ears again — so low, it was as if the earth were calling to her. Saying... what? She strained for the message.

He... is... your...

He is what? My what? she wanted to scream.

Cruz's eyes took on an otherworldly glow, and his chest rose and fell in deep, steadying breaths. Jody tightened her fingers on her towel. Had he heard the whisper, too?

What? She wanted to yell. *He is my what?*

Whatever it was teased at the corners of her mind, racing up to reveal itself before darting away like a wave rolling over the beach. Her heart beat faster, and her breath quickened. A buzzing sound filled the edges of her consciousness, growing into an angry hum until she tore her eyes off Cruz and looked up.

A helicopter zipped overhead. And, *poof!* The magic spell was gone.

Cruz cursed under his breath.

"Your helicopter?" she asked, wishing she could step back in time to figure out what had just transpired between them.

"Not ours. A sightseeing tour." He looked at her with mournful eyes as if he wanted another minute together, too. "You almost ready?"

She nodded, pulling the towel higher. “One minute and I’ll be dressed.”

He nodded and turned his back, all cold and hard again. But now that she’d caught glimpses of his secret, softer side, she wasn’t fooled.

She pulled the clothes on quickly, finger-combed her hair, and let her feet rustle through the leaves as a signal that she was done. When Cruz turned, his eyes played over her body. She’d purposely turned her right side to reveal the long, ugly burn mark that ran down her leg — a scar caused by a kitchen accident a long time ago. Her surfer friends never blinked an eye at it, while Richard and the Elements photographer frowned as if it were a fatal flaw and made sure it never showed in any shot. Was Cruz just another man who liked to chase outwardly perfect women instead of showing interest in the real her?

His eyes traveled up and down her body, barely slowing at the scar, and came to rest on her face. His lips moved, but then he dropped his gaze to the ground, mute.

A minute later, he kicked the ground. “Ready to get going?”

“Ready,” she murmured, though she wasn’t so sure.

Chapter Seven

When Cruz moved, Jody followed, straightening her shoulders as she paced over the footbridge. It was time to exit his little hideaway and face the real world. She snuck a glance at his face, but it was inscrutable.

Paths snaked this way and that around patches of lawn and clusters of trees. Most seemed to converge on a grass-roofed structure — the central point of the estate where she had met Silas the previous night. It all felt so surreal. Last night, she'd dodged gunfire. This morning, she was barefoot in the grass of a luxurious estate.

"So — Koa Point, huh? What does koa mean?"

His voice was a low bass, almost impossible to hear. "It's an elite class of warrior, named after the toughest kind of wood."

Her eyes flitted over his toned body. Yeah, *koa* fit, all right.

"Silas is at his place, checking into some records," Cruz murmured in answer to her unspoken question.

She stopped, slamming her hands onto her hips. "Whose records is he checking into? Mine?"

Cruz made a vague gesture then winced in pain, making her search his back for any sign of the wound he'd sustained. All she could make out were lumps of muscle that stretched out his shirt.

"Are you really okay?"

"Why wouldn't I be okay?"

"Well, you were shot."

He shrugged as if to prove his point. "Like I said. It barely grazed me."

"Right. Sure. Barely grazed," she muttered.

But Cruz just turned onto a different path — away from the meeting house and toward the garage — and segued straight into his next sentence. "So, we'll start at your condo..."

Her stomach growled, and she turned pink.

Cruz cocked his head. "Damn it. I didn't feed you, did I?"

She crossed her arms. "Hey, I'm not a zoo animal. But don't worry. I'll be fine."

His eyes darkened. "Don't joke about zoo animals." With a swipe of one big hand, he motioned her back toward the meeting house.

Jody didn't like the idea of caged animals either, but wow. Cruz really was touchy about that. Of course, the man seemed touchy about a lot of things. She followed him at a distance, just in case.

"Really, it's okay. I think I have a snack at the condo..." She didn't, but she didn't want to make a big deal of it.

Cruz stepped into the gleaming kitchen section of the meeting house. "Oatmeal all right with you?"

She nodded, expecting him to pop a sachet into the microwave. Then she stood, astonished, as he pulled out half a dozen fresh ingredients and started peeling a mango.

"Mango and coconut okay?" he asked.

"Sure," she said, trying not to stare. The man was a walking contradiction. She'd pictured him as more of a hasty, splash-some-milk-in-your-cereal kind of guy. In fact, everything in her field of vision was a contradiction — even the refrigerator. So far, she'd only seen Cruz and Silas on the estate — two big, tough guys who didn't exactly exude sentimental, social vibes. Yet the stainless-steel doors of the fridge were decorated with smiley face magnets, recipe cards, and photos. She leaned closer, looking at a snapshot of a happy couple sitting side by side on the beach. Another showed a man and woman giving a thumbs-up from the cockpit of a helicopter, and a third featured a striking beauty in a police uniform with a huge man at her side. Jody was sure the background was the arched garage Cruz had parked at the previous night. Were all those people visitors, or did they share the estate with Cruz and Silas? And if so, was one of them the property owner?

There was a clipped-out newspaper article, too, showing the charred remains of a helicopter. Someone had picked out two lines with a red pen — *Fiery Crash on Molokini. Pilot unable to regain control* — and next to it, had scribbled, *Great flying, Kai.*

Some kind of friendly gibe between friends, she guessed. She peeked back at Cruz. Something told her he would make a great friend — and a bitter enemy.

"If you want a smoothie, help yourself," Cruz murmured, nodding at the blender and a bowl of fruit.

It was uncanny, how the man seemed to know all her favorite breakfast foods.

Destiny, a faint voice whispered in her mind.

She shook her head and told herself not to read into the sound of palm fronds rustling in the wind. Cruz set a pot on the stovetop while she went about making a smoothie from grapefruit, blood oranges, and the strawberries Cruz pointed out in the fridge.

"What are the police saying about last night?" she asked, cutting the fruit into the blender. And, wow. It was all too easy to feel at home, as if she and Cruz made breakfast side by side every morning.

"They're keeping it hush-hush, at least for now. They have made an arrest, though."

She brightened. "Great! So I'm fine, right?"

Cruz jerked his head sideways in a curt *no* as he adjusted the flame. "I doubt it. They arrested one of the resort employees."

"And?"

His face soured. "It's one of the valets, Toby. The guy wouldn't hurt a fly."

She added juice and hit the *on* button, filling the space with the whirring sound of the blender. When the motor evened out again, she turned it off, opened the lid, and licked a splash of the concoction off her finger.

"I feel like a vampire," she joked, licking the bright red juice from her lips. "You want some?"

Cruz stared at her before jerking his gaze back to the pot.

What? she wanted to ask. *What did I say?*

But Cruz wasn't a man to be pushed, so she drank quickly and went back to the subject of the police investigation. "Why would they arrest the valet if he's innocent?"

Cruz shrugged. "Either they're idiots, or Toby is being framed."

"Framed?" she choked. "Who would do that?"

Cruz leveled a flat gate at her. "How about the same people who wanted you dead? The same people who made sure I was given false information. Who knows how far they're willing to go?"

That made her lose her appetite, although a sniff of the oatmeal made her hungry all over again. She remained silent, sipping the smoothie while Cruz finished the oatmeal and surprised her — again — by spooning it all into a plastic bowl.

"Can you eat on the go? We need to check your condo before anyone else does."

"Sure," she said, worried all over again.

The man was truly a mystery — gruff one second, considerate the next. She hurried to follow him to the garage, tasting a spoonful of oatmeal on the way. It was warm, sweet, and solid. Just the thing to get her started on what was sure to be a difficult day.

Cruz led her to the leftmost bay of the long, arched garage and motioned for her to get in the car — a red Ferrari convertible this time. The Lamborghini occupied the next spot in the garage, and a vintage Jaguar filled the next bay. How many cars did the man own? Or did they belong to Silas — or whoever the property owner was?

"I do this too," she joked.

Cruz shot her a quizzical look.

"Drive a different car every day. But Tuesdays are my Rolls-Royce days. I save my pink Ferrari for Fridays."

In truth, she'd barely paid off half of a decade-old Chevy, but it was nice to pretend.

Cruz looked at her for a second. "Wednesdays are Rolls-Royce days."

She stared then cracked up. "You're kidding."

He broke into a tiny grin. "Yeah. But seriously — we need a different car in case anyone spotted the Lamborghini last night."

"Oh." Maybe he really was a detective or a PI or something.

She stepped to the passenger side, trying to play it cool. When she sat, she mashed her knees together. If she dropped a bit of oatmeal, it was going to land on her, not the leather seat.

"Why would the police keep things quiet?" she asked when Cruz slid into the low-slung vehicle with a practiced motion.

He handed her something — the purse she'd dropped in the other car the previous night, and she couldn't help but blush for some reason.

"I don't think it's them so much as the Kapa'akea club," he said. "They seem to be doing their best to keep everything hushed up."

"They hushed up attempted murder? Wouldn't the guests post pictures to social media and tell all their friends?"

Cruz fired up the engine and backed out of the garage with a squeal of tires. Jody hung on to her oatmeal while he accelerated up the driveway toward the gate.

"Those club members aren't the type to spread the news around, believe me. With a pro golf event scheduled to take place there next month, they're probably worried about scaring people away." He shook his head in disgust. "They love locking people out of their club, but they love showing it off at the same time."

"Seriously?"

"Seriously."

The estate gate slammed shut behind them, and a second later, Cruz was racing down the road.

"Oh!" she yelped between spoonfuls of oatmeal. "My dad. I should call him in case he's worried."

"I doubt he heard anything, but you can call."

She yanked her phone out as Cruz shifted through one gear after another, speeding down the main road. Ignoring the list of missed calls, she dialed and waited, squinting into the bright sunlight reflecting off the ocean.

"Wild Side Surf Shop. Hello?"

Jody couldn't hold back a grin. "Hi, Dad. Just checking in."

She waited for him to break out in worried father tones, but apparently, Cruz was right. The shooting really had been hushed up.

"Hey, sweetie. How are you? You surviving that modeling gig?"

Jody took a deep breath. She'd only told her father about the modeling contract because she couldn't bear to keep secrets from him, and he'd done a fairly good job hiding his disappointment. He'd always lectured her against selling out to the highest bidder, and she'd always agreed. But when she pictured the look on his face on the day she'd get to share her paycheck with him, her mood brightened again.

"Almost done now."

"Have you gotten a chance to surf?"

Not nearly enough. Jody turned her face seaward, sniffing the ocean. She could practically feel the swell building. "I hope to get out today."

"Well, get us some good pictures while you're at it. The shop needs some exciting new shots in the front windows."

Wild Side Surf Shop, she knew, needed a lot more than some exciting new photos to keep the business alive. Customers were loyal and business was brisk, but its prime location on a what had become a trendy section of beach made the shop vulnerable to take-over by bigger businesses.

"I promise," she said, making several extra silent promises on the side. With the money she earned...

"Decent shots," her dad joked. "None of those shots that are all — what do they call them these days? — assets. No assets, you hear me? I want shots that show off how my baby can surf."

Jody laughed. "I'll make sure to keep my assets covered."

Cruz glanced over with one eyebrow arched high. She pointed forward and muttered, "Watch the road."

"Yes, ma'am," he said with the dawn of a grin.

"Someone there?" her dad asked.

Jody winced. How the hell was she going to explain? *Actually, I'm in a Ferrari with a perfect stranger. In fact, I slept at his tree house last night. Not that he laid a hand on me. He just made me fantasize about sex all night. He cooked me oatmeal for breakfast, too, and it's as good as what Mom used to make...*

She pursed her lips and changed the subject. "A friend. How's Eileen?"

Her dad's tone became somber. "Your sister's doing okay, considering."

Considering her latest fertility treatment failed, Jody added. *Another couple of thousand dollars she couldn't afford in the first place down the drain.*

"But you know her. She's a Monroe, and she never gives up. They're looking at other options."

Options Eileen and her husband couldn't afford. Jody nodded and flexed her fingers. Well, she was a Monroe, too, and she wouldn't give up either. But she wasn't about to go into the details, not with Cruz able to hear every word.

"Hey, I'd better go. I just wanted to say hi," she said as Cruz raced around another bend of the highway. "Talk to you soon?"

"Talk to you soon, sweetie. Have a great day. Oh, and don't forget to look up Teddy."

Oops — she had forgotten. The second she had some free time — and was sure no one was trying to kill her — she would look up the living legend of surfboard shaping as she'd promised.

"Will do. Love you. Bye."

A pang hit her as soon as she ended the call. God, it would be so easy to hop on a plane, fly home, and do what she loved best — helping her dad in the shop and surfing in her free time. No photo shoots, no madmen trying to kill her, no competitions. She loved surfing, but after three years on the pro tour, she'd just about had her fill of the hectic schedule and long flights. Maybe it was time to settle down and live a quieter life designing surfboards of her own.

Of course, Seal Beach wasn't the place it used to be, and part of her yearned for a quieter place. A slower pace.

She tilted her head back to face the sun. Someplace like Maui would be nice. Maybe even with a man at her side. Maybe she could get a job with Teddy Akoa, design boards, and see more of Cruz. California was okay, but Maui seemed like paradise.

She stopped the runaway thoughts there. No one had ever shot at her in California, so there was that.

"Do you know Teddy Akoa?" she asked, taking another bite of oatmeal.

"You mean Akoa's Surf Factory?" Cruz nodded. "Funny old coot, him."

She smiled, because her father had used almost the same words. The *factory* part had to be an overstatement — Teddy Akoa only produced a board or two a month — but his work was known to insiders around the world.

"I've been to Maui four times, but I've never been able to track him down. Does he really shape custom boards in a shack by the beach?"

Cruz shrugged. "Wouldn't surprise me. He keeps to himself. The place is farther down the coast."

Jody wished Cruz could make a U-turn and take her there to meet the great man himself. She heaved a quiet sigh and looked forward, resigning herself to her reality. She didn't have time for frivolous side trips, not as long as she had a target painted on her back.

"When should we go to the resort?" she asked.

Cruz shook his head. "I already did."

"You what?" Jody glanced at the clock on the dashboard. When had he found the time?

Cruz went on without batting an eye. "They're not talking. And the waiter who handed you the drink — the signal that singled you out as a target — says he got the message from another guy. And that other guy said he was given the order by another person, who doesn't remember who ordered the drink for you in the first place."

Jody stared at him. "What time did you get up this morning?"

Judging by the dark lines under his eyes, the question really ought to have been how late he'd been out the previous night. Cruz didn't say a word, though.

"Hey," she whispered. "Thanks. For everything." Obviously, the man wasn't used to looking out for anyone but himself. But he was trying — genuinely trying — to help her. He'd saved her from a gunman, offered her his place for the night, fixed her breakfast...

Without thinking, she touched his arm. Within the space of two heartbeats, the creases on his brow eased away. He stopped gnashing his teeth, and as for Jody — well, whew. She felt it, too. A warm sense of connection and comfort she couldn't explain. She closed her eyes and breathed deeply, the way she did to welcome the peace of a quiet morning on an out-of-the-way beach.

Wow. Cruz really did have an effect on her. And she did on him, too.

Your mom and I... We just knew, she remembered her dad saying with misty eyes.

Jody took a deep breath. Her dad believed in soul mates, and her great-aunt Tilda went a step further and chattered on about destiny. Then again, Tilda believed in lots of things, including vampires, ghosts, and mermaids, which just went to prove how crazy she was.

So Jody hadn't really believed the destiny part, but damn. She sure was tempted to now.

A horn beeped, and she opened her eyes in time to catch Cruz jerking the car back into its lane. Had he also drifted out of focus for a moment or two?

Or three...or four... Because when he glanced over and their eyes met, the world slowed down all over again.

Beep! Beep!

Cruz swept his focus back to the road and glared through the next few miles of winding coastal road until the condos of

Honokowai came into view.

"This one?" he pointed to the fourth building, speaking in gruff, choppy syllables.

Jody nodded and got out of the car. She ran her hands over her arms and looked around before stepping to the entrance with Cruz. The words he'd uttered the previous night raced through her mind. *What happens when the gunman tracks you down?*

Cruz craned his neck, scrutinizing balconies and windows with narrowed, professional eyes.

He's a sniper. A hit man, a little voice screamed in the back of her mind.

He saved you. You can trust him, a second voice chipped in.

"Damn it." She punched in the key code for a second time and hurried into the cool, carpeted lobby. She strode toward the elevator and hit the button several times, tapping her foot the whole time.

"Just grab what you need, and we'll head back to Koa Point," Cruz murmured as the elevator doors slid open.

When she reached her unit on the sixth floor, Cruz motioned for her to step aside. He kept his body up against the wall by the door, and the moment she tapped the code into the keypad, he shoved the door open with a sharp kick.

"Whoa. Are you a cop or something?"

"Special Forces," he grunted, peering in carefully.

Special Forces? That explained the eagle eyes and coiled muscles, but not the Ferrari, the Lamborghini, or what he was doing on Maui.

"Bad news," he said, making her freeze. "The place has been ransacked."

Her blood ran cold as she looked over his shoulder. "Where?"

"Look at the place. It's a mess."

She pursed her lips and nudged him aside. "It's not that bad."

He stared as she walked in and picked a pair of shorts and a towel off the floor. She'd been in a hurry to leave for the party. So what?

"You mean, this is normal?" He sounded horrified.

She glared at him, and he glared back. Normally, she could hold her own with any guy. But wow, this man was about as easy to stare down as a cat. A very big, potentially lethal cat.

A full minute later, she broke the impasse by making a face. "You sound like my father."

He didn't laugh as her dad would, though. He just stalked around the tiny unit, thrusting open doors and checking closets while she gathered up her clothes. She was just pulling her wet suit off a chair on the balcony when the front door rattled, and they both froze.

Cruz looked at her with a look that asked, *Were you expecting someone?*

She backed away from the front door. No, she wasn't.

Cruz stalked forward, looking dangerous as ever.

"Mr. Special Forces," she whispered. "Don't kill housekeeping, okay?"

He scowled but didn't relax the slightest bit. And neither did Jody when the door handle rattled a second time.

Housekeeping, she realized, would knock and announce themselves. Whoever it was out there was sneaking in.

Cruz motioned for her to take cover while he prepared to throw open the door. Jody hurried to one wall, clutching her duffel bag. God, she'd already been shot at and voluntarily abducted. Now what?

Chapter Eight

Cruz steeled every muscle and prepared to pounce. Blood coursed through his veins — blood and rage — and his heart drummed. Who was trying to break in to Jody's place?

It was exhilarating — as exhilarating as anything since his Special Forces days. Which was strange because he wasn't fighting for his country right now. He was just protecting a woman he barely knew.

Just? his inner tiger growled. *What do you mean, just?*

That feeling of rage was unusual, too. He usually operated in a calm, professional way. The last time he'd gotten anywhere near as worked up was—

He gulped. That was back when his family had been killed.

Out of nowhere, a memory flashed through his mind — Jody licking the blood-red smoothie off her lips. *God, I feel like a vampire.*

She'd been joking, but it had brought back all kinds of doubts. Like the fact that the villagers near the scene of the crime had blamed vampires and shifters for the heinous crime. Of course, they would have said anything to absolve themselves, but...

Cruz flexed his fingers while watching the door handle jiggle. If he didn't watch out, his nails would turn into claws. Jody was definitely getting under his skin. The instinct to protect her was as strong as the instinct to avenge his family.

She's getting under our skin in a good way, his tiger murmured.

Every move she made, every word she uttered sent tingles through his weary bones and shooed back the darkness framing his soul. Just the way she tossed her hair and looked at the sky made him want to look up and check for shapes in the clouds.

Look, it's a rocket, he remembered his dad saying one quiet summer day a long time ago when they'd stretched out side by side.

I see an elephant, he'd replied.

His sister had called it a snake, while all his brother had found were sheep. But it didn't seem to matter because it was just for fun. Fun, like Jody.

She was definitely getting under his skin, bringing back good memories to dilute the bad. Making him smile from time to time. He'd already taken to listening for the quiet jangle of her bracelets and the soft sound of her step.

Give us a couple of days, Silas had said to Jody.

Cruz took a deep breath. In a couple of days, he would be in way over his head with this woman. Even now, her wild rose scent teased and taunted him, and the soft timbre of her voice did all kinds of titillating things to his soul.

Why is that a bad thing? his tiger demanded.

Because it could never work. Because he hated humans. Because he lived in a world of darkness while she inhabited a sunny universe of hope and light.

He worked his jaw. First, he'd kill whoever it was behind the door — unless, of course, it was housekeeping, though he really doubted it — and then he'd figure out how to keep himself immune to Jody's charms.

With hate? With fear? His tiger growled.

Cruz scoffed. He wasn't afraid of anything.

Not even of falling in love?

Someone whispered behind the door, dragging his focus back to the intruder. Little clicks sounded as a code was tapped in, and a man pushed the door open. In a flash, Cruz grabbed the man's wrist and sent him sprawling. By the time Jody yelped and the guy on the floor groaned, Cruz had the second, bigger man thrust face first against the wall.

"Whoa," the big guy protested, though his words were slurred, given that his lips were mashed against the wall.

"Richard?" Jody squeaked at the man on the floor.

Cruz did a double take. Who the hell was Richard? He glanced over to where the first man lay. A tubby guy with a polyester Hawaiian shirt who smelled of stale cigarette smoke. A guy he recognized from somewhere.

His tiger growled. *It's Slimeball.*

"You know this guy?" he grunted.

Well, of course Jody knew Slimeball. He'd seen them talking at the Kapa'akea resort.

Jody made a face aimed more at Slimeball than him. "He's the product manager for the photo shoot."

"Call the police, Jody. Quick," Slimeball urged, rolling away from Cruz.

Jody stuck her hands on her hips. "Sure. I'll call the cops and tell them you and some hoodlum broke in to my unit."

"We weren't breaking in. We had the code."

"And how exactly do you have that?"

The woman was even more beautiful when she was angry. Cruz grinned in spite of himself.

"We were checking on you," Richard protested. He stood slowly, keeping his hands up.

"You and who are checking on me?" Jody glared at the second guy, not the least intimidated by his bulk.

The man's muscles twitched, and Cruz tightened his grip, giving the guy a clear message he'd better not budge.

"Me and my bodyguard," Richard said.

Cruz nearly laughed. The guy he had against the wall might have muscle, but he lacked reflexes and the most basic training.

"Your *what*?" Jody screeched.

"My bodyguard. I nearly got shot last night."

"Wait a minute. I was the one who nearly got shot last night." Her words cut off before she could tack *asshole* on to the end.

Slimeball wiped his sweaty brow. "I'm not taking any chances."

Cruz's blood boiled. "What about Jody?"

Slimeball looked around, confused. "What about her?"

If Jody hadn't given Cruz a look of warning, he would have punched the man there and then.

"What about Jody's safety?" he repeated, grinding the words out.

A burning sensation registered in his eyes — the first signs of a telltale shapeshifter glow — and he blinked hard, trying to wrestle the rage back. That was a losing battle until Jody touched his arm, making his broiling emotions settle down again. Cruz blinked as a new image popped into his mind. Instead of picturing the carnage he'd like to wreak, he saw beams of sunlight breaking through the trees on one of those perfect afternoons in his patch of jungle on the estate. The wild pumping of his heart slowed down slightly, and his fists unclenched.

He took two more breaths then opened his eyes — on Jody.

Wow. Her eyes are so blue, his tiger cooed. *Like the sky in summer.*

Cruz almost forgot where he was until Slimeball spoke, breaking the magic spell.

"I swear I was going to get Jody a bodyguard, too," Richard said.

I bet, Cruz thought.

"Don't need one," Jody barked.

Richard scowled and jerked his thumb at Cruz. "Oh no? Who is this guy?"

A sly grin flitted over Jody's face and she crossed her arms. "Maybe he's *my* bodyguard."

The way she emphasized *my* made Cruz warm, totally distracting him. It wasn't until a second later that he processed her words and went wide-eyed. Her *what?*

"No, seriously," Richard protested. "Who is he?"

Now Jody really looked pissed, and Cruz was, too. Their eyes met, and his mind spun. She was serious. She wanted him to be her bodyguard.

Say yes. Yes! his tiger cried.

But that meant sticking with her, night and day, for as long as it took to find the gunman and close this case. That meant sniffing her intoxicating scent. Watching her graceful moves. Listening to her cheery voice. That meant feeling things he wasn't prepared to deal with.

It meant betraying his family, too. Letting a human into his heart.

No, it doesn't. It means living. Maybe even loving, his tiger whispered.

"When did you have time to find a bodyguard?" Richard demanded.

Jody glanced at Cruz with an expression that said, *He found me.*

His heart skipped, and his tiger whispered inside. *I didn't find you. Destiny led me.*

Cruz swallowed hard and answered Jody's unspoken question with a tiny nod. *Yes, I will be your bodyguard. Even if it kills me.*

He shoved the big guy against the wall in warning then let go and stepped forward. He bristled, forcing Richard to step back — way back. "Like she said. Her bodyguard." And just like Jody, he left off the *asshole* at the end.

Jody stared as if she hadn't expected him to take her up on the challenge, and in a way, that hurt. She hadn't expected him to do the decent thing. Hell, he hadn't expected it either.

So, damn. Just how much of a shithead had he become in the past couple of years?

Jody stuck an accusing finger at Richard. "What exactly are you doing here?"

"Like I said — checking on you. Making sure you'll be ready for the photo shoot."

Jody's jaw fell open. "You're kidding. I got shot at yesterday, and you want to go ahead with the next session?"

Richard shrugged. "The show must go on, baby."

Not your baby. Cruz could see the retort flash over Jody's face.

Richard shuffled closer, and Jody's nose wrinkled. "In fact, we're ready to go ahead this afternoon. Unless, of course, you want me to sign the contract over to someone else, along with the paycheck. How would you like that?"

Jody's face became a tight, angry mask.

"How would you like the paycheck to go to someone else, huh?" Richard goaded. "Someone who could help their sister or mother or whoever—"

"My mother is dead," Jody said in a totally flat tone.

Cruz whipped his head around. He knew the pain concealed in Jody's even voice. He knew the feeling of a hole in his heart and the regret of so many important things left unsaid. Words like *I love you* and *Thank you* and *Sorry for everything I put you through as a kid.*

See? his tiger said. *Humans mourn, too.*

Richard flapped his hand. "Whatever. The point is—"

Cruz's vision went red. Whatever? He stalked forward. "Now you listen to me—"

"I got this, Cruz," Jody hissed, clenching her fists.

He glowered at them both. "No photographs today. Period."

Richard was too terrified to protest, but Cruz could see the gears move in the man's mind. He would come up with some sneaky way to force Jody to pose — that, or he'd fire her.

"Tomorrow," Jody said, stepping between them. "I think a day is reasonable, don't you?"

Richard made a face. "The big boss wants results, and she wants them soon."

Cruz leaned forward. *She?* Was that Moira?

"We need to make a splash ASAP and get this campaign in the news. Especially since these two-bit island cops refuse to let me hold a press conference. We can't even get any mileage out of last night."

Between *two-bit island cops* and *mileage*, Cruz was ready to snap. Dawn, his buddy Hunter's mate, was an island cop, and she was a damn good one. And as for getting mileage out of an attempt on Jody's life...

She touched his arm, and he took a deep breath.

"Two days," Cruz snarled at Richard. "Minimum." Then he locked eyes with Jody. "As your *bodyguard*, I insist."

Just saying the word made his tiger want to roar loud enough for folks over on the Big Island to hear.

Her bodyguard. Hers. Finally, you're catching on.

Jody's expression started out steely and grim, but the longer they stood there, the softer it became, and all kinds of emotions Cruz didn't know he possessed stirred and rumbled inside.

"Two days," Richard grunted. Keeping the wall at his back, he slunk toward his hired thug and the door. "Tuesday at noon. If nothing else, it gives me more time to arrange for that damned jewel."

Cruz's ears perked. Maybe that was a good sign. If there'd been some complications obtaining the jewel, that might mean it wasn't a Spirit Stone being drawn out by the others.

"Be ready at noon — or else," Richard snapped. "I'll call you with the location. And you, idiot," he snapped at his bodyguard, "are fired."

Cruz wanted to shove them both out the door, but he refrained, if only barely. He settled for closing the door with a thump and faced it for a moment, getting his shit together again. Then he turned and—

Jody's shoulders were slumped. She stared at the too-busy pattern of the rug, and her hands knotted tightly. Even right after being shot at, she hadn't looked so unhappy. Like a bird with clipped wings staring out from a cage. His heart ached just seeing her like that. He reached for Jody's hand the way she'd reached for his when he needed it.

A moment later, she tossed her hair, back to her usual self.

"Asshole," she muttered, glaring at the door. She stuck her hands up quickly. "Him, I mean. Not you."

In spite of himself, Cruz grinned.

Chapter Nine

Jody was glad to have a bodyguard. She really was — especially one with dark, flashing eyes, slabs of muscle, and the kind of rugged looks that helped distract her from the fact that someone wanted her dead. But a bodyguard who insisted on stalking around every corner like a predator did seem a bit over the top.

Of course, the man had started out as her potential killer, and part of her still struggled with that. But a far greater part of her trusted him, as crazy as that seemed. Bone deep, she knew he meant her no harm. She slung her bag over her shoulder and followed Cruz closely.

"Do you really think this is necessary?"

"You wanted a bodyguard? You got one," he said without glancing back.

When she'd first announced the idea, she'd surprised herself as much as him. Once again, she hadn't exactly thought things out. Should they discuss terms? Payment? God, could she even afford his fee, whatever it was? She doubted it. And damn, she really ought to ask, because she'd learned the hard way about verbal agreements.

Or maybe not, because she didn't want to talk business with Cruz. She didn't want to be his client. She wanted to be his... his...

She got stuck there. What did she want to be? His friend? His future one-night stand? More?

She caught herself staring at the stacks of muscle on his shoulders and gulped. Maybe she ought to stick to *client*, after all.

"Do we really have to snoop around like this?" she asked as he peered into the condo's foyer, holding up his fist in some kind of sign. Mr. Military on high alert.

She placed her hand on his shoulder. Big mistake, because she nearly started kneading the muscle and purring to herself.

"Do you want to be shot at again? Let's go."

He hurried her across the parking lot and into the car. Before she even had her seat belt buckled, he gunned the engine and took off.

"Whoa, Nelly," she murmured, hanging on to the door. Maybe the previous night wasn't an exception. Maybe Cruz always drove like a maniac.

She crossed her arms and watched scrubby bushes and a row of condos blur past. A minute later, she opened her mouth in spite of herself. "How exactly did you get into bodyguarding?"

He turned and shot her a look that matched his tone. "It all started at this party at a fancy club. . . "

She swatted his arm. "I mean, how did you start in the business?"

He sighed. "Do you really want to know?"

Yes, she did. She wanted to learn everything about this fascinating man. This assassin-protector. This contradiction on two feet.

"I do. Really," she whispered.

For a moment, his eyes softened, and the electrons zipping back and forth between their bodies strained even harder, trying to draw them closer. Then Cruz blinked, leaned back, and grunted one of his not-quite-replies.

"How did you get into surfing?"

The question was meant to shut her up, she figured, but heck, she'd be happy to talk about that all day.

"My dad got us started — my sisters and me. He was a pro surfer for a while. His parents surfed, too. Did you ever see those old movies where women balance on men's shoulders while they surf?" She laughed out loud. "My grandparents did that. So I pretty much grew up with surfing." She waved toward the ocean as they raced along. "I've always loved it, and I thought it would make a great job. Making your own hours. Being out in the sun, in the water, riding the waves. And when you catch the perfect ride..." She closed her eyes, imagining herself inside the barrel of a breaking wave. The roar of the water, the drop in temperature in that gravity-defying pocket of air. The feeling of harnessing one of nature's greatest powers. She took a deep breath, opened her eyes, and finished the thought. "It's a job, but it's not a job."

She braced herself for the lecture that was sure to follow. *How much of a job is number eleven on the women's tour? When are you going to earn real money?* Her father never said that, but just about everyone else did.

Cruz remained silent, digesting her words for the next half mile before he finally replied.

"I don't get it."

"What don't you get?

He motioned back the way they'd come. "That asshole — Richard, I mean."

Oh, she knew who he meant, all right.

"Why do you work for him?" Cruz finished.

Jody frowned. *Because I didn't listen to my father?*

She tried the kind of answer most people could understand. "There's a thing called money, Cruz. Maybe you don't have to worry about it on that fancy estate of yours—"

"It's not my estate," he cut in. "And believe me, I know about money. I know about hard work. What I don't get is selling yourself out."

She choked on her next words, then jabbed a finger at the steering wheel. "Pull over. Stop. Stop the car right now."

He threw a hand up in a placating gesture, but she wasn't having any of that.

"Stop the car," she ordered.

For an agonizingly long second, she wondered if he would ignore her, but to his credit, he turned into the next pullout.

"Whoa. Hang on," he protested.

She was that close to jumping out of the car and slamming the door, but she didn't. Not yet, anyway.

"I am not selling out," she hissed, staring at her reflection in the vanity mirror of the visor. "I am not selling out."

"No? Then why agree to modeling if you dislike it so much?"

She crossed her arms. He would never understand. "Maybe I want to get rich."

He looked at her — really looked at her, like no one at the party had bothered to do — then snorted. "Liar."

She nearly smiled at the conviction in his voice. It felt good to have someone believe in her, even if that was a man she barely knew.

"Maybe I want to be famous," she said, testing him.

He cut the engine and turned to her. "If you wanted to be famous, you already would be."

"What's that supposed to mean?"

He flapped a hand. "I've seen how some women market themselves with their own YouTube channels and stuff. You could sell those 'assets' of yours."

"Assets?" she protested, shrill as an angry cat.

Cruz threw his hands up. "Your word, not mine."

She made a face. Damn. She'd have to be more careful what she said around him.

"I bet you get lots of offers," he went on.

She rubbed her hands over the scar on her leg. Actually, she did. Ever since she was fifteen — regardless of the scars. But her dad had protected her from preying agents and made sure she kept her head screwed on right.

You don't need them, her dad had warned her. *They take all the pureness out of the sport. The fun.*

How right he was. Representing products she didn't believe in wasn't any fun. The Elements fragrance line had engaged a prominent photographer for this gig — a man who'd shot several *Sports Illustrated* swimsuit issues. But, damn. She'd always had a different image of how she might make it into the pages of that magazine.

"I know how it goes." Cruz's voice grew chilly. "If you have the looks, you can get rich and famous for nothing more than notoriety. But you don't strike me as the kind of person who wants that."

She stared at the sunlight sparkling off the waves. Some of her closest friends didn't know her as well as Cruz.

"So why do you do it?" he asked, more softly this time.

She ran her fists over her thighs, deliberating whether to tell him. She hadn't even explained to her father, for goodness' sake. Which might have been why she ended up telling Cruz, just to get it all off her chest.

"My family needs the money."

He didn't look convinced.

"My dad..." she started then trailed off. This wasn't just her secret. It was her father's, too. Should she really share that with Cruz?

If Cruz had pushed and prodded and insisted, she might have clammed up. But he just sat there, letting her tell as much — or as little — of her story as she was comfortable with.

"My dad is my main sponsor — well, the surf shop is. That way, I can compete on the tour without being trapped in too many contracts. Even back in his day, my dad hated how commercial the pro tour was becoming, and now it's even worse. Especially the women's tour, where some of the sponsors don't see us as athletes — more like so much tits and ass. I've even heard a couple admit as much — off-camera, of course." She scowled, remembering the first time she'd discovered how right her father was. "Having my dad's business sponsor me is a win-win, because it really has brought attention to his shop."

So what's the problem? Cruz's furrowed brow implied.

"The problem is, he's gained enough attention for bigger operations to want to buy him out. They have the money to buy the place out from under him, too. He's been holding out, and I thought everything was okay, but I just found out he mortgaged the business."

"Your dad has a problem he never told you about?"

She made a face. No, her dad didn't have an addiction or owe money to a loan shark or anything like that. "Problem? Yeah, he has a problem. He loves us too much."

Now Cruz really looked confused.

"He sponsored me so I could surf on my terms and make the most of my chance, in part because he couldn't make the most of his chance, back in the day."

"Why couldn't he?"

She couldn't resist a smile, because the story always lit her up inside. "He quit the pro tour after he met my mom and my sister and me. When I was little, I mean. My mom was a single mother with two young kids. But one day, my mother and Ross met on a bridge. So technically, he's my stepdad, but he's always been just Dad to me." Now she was beaming, because she loved imagining the scene, though she only had the vaguest memories of that day. "My mom's car broke down in the middle of the bridge, and no one stopped to help her. No one. She was stuck with the two of us crying in the back, but then my dad came along." She chuckled. "He always says it was destiny."

"Destiny..." Cruz's face grew serious. Deadly serious.

Jody nodded. "And my mom always said it was love at first sight."

Most men rolled their eyes at that, but Cruz just studied her with his lips drawn in a tight line.

"His pickup wasn't much better than our car, but he towed us home — my mom couldn't even afford tow insurance — and, well... The rest was history. They fell in love, got married, and he adopted my sister and me. He quit the pro tour and opened his shop to help make ends meet. And it worked. We went from barely getting by to doing okay." Jody took a deep breath. Before long, she'd be telling poor Cruz about every bedtime story her dad had ever told her. How he'd wiped her tears when her mother died of leukemia, and how he'd quietly shed his own before picking up the pieces and managing to keep them going through all that.

"These were my mom's," she whispered, showing him her bracelets. Each was a flat, quarter-inch titanium bangle etched with a geometric design — a family heirloom her father's aunt Tilda had given to her mom on her wedding day. "She had six, and we each got two. I never take them off."

Cruz sat motionless, looking at her.

She cleared her throat. "Anyway, my sisters and I grew up working in the shop."

"Sister or sisters?"

"Sisters. I have an older sister and a younger sister — my mom and dad had her two years after they got married. My older sister still works in the shop."

So what's the problem? Cruz didn't quite ask, though it was written all over his face.

"My older sister and her husband have been trying to have kids for years, and they're running out of options. Mike is a welder, but he just started out, and the treatment they're trying is expensive. So my dad mortgaged the shop to loan them money. Not that he told us about the mortgage part, of course." She'd tried to be annoyed at her father for that, but she'd never really succeeded. "Like I said, my dad loves us too much. He's put his business on the line for both of us. Now, the property tax on the shop is going up, and he's left himself without any leeway to meet the difference. So I figured I would accept this one contract just this one time and take care of it all."

"Why you?"

She stared at him. "Why not me? All my life, my dad has made sacrifices for us. It's about time I make a sacrifice for him and help my sister at the same time. Maybe you see that as selling out, but I don't."

A truck rushed by on the road, buffeting the sports car with its drag, but Cruz didn't blink. He just watched her like a new species he'd never encountered before.

"That's not selling out," he whispered.

Jody exhaled. Funny, how good it felt to have someone else say that. She tipped her head back to the perfect blue sky. A java finch fluttered past in a blue and gray blur, and she smiled.

"Beautiful," she murmured. "Look — that bird is beautiful. Maui is beautiful. Life can be beautiful if you just concentrate on the right things." Her parents had taught her that.

Cruz, though, was looking in the side mirror, watching clouds gather over the jagged mountain peaks. "Sometimes life is beautiful. Sometimes it sucks."

She was tempted to smack his arm for ruining the moment, but his eyes were focused somewhere far, far away, and the corners of his mouth turned down. Then all she wanted was to cup his cheek and ask him what he had done or seen — or lost — to feel that way.

"Sometimes it sucks," she agreed. "But mostly, it's beautiful. I picture my sister holding a baby, and I know how precious it would be to her. And even better — I picture her handing her baby to my dad, and how over the moon he would be. And *that* is beautiful."

Cruz looked over, his eyes shining with pinpoints of — hope? Denial?

"Seriously?" he asked. "Bringing a baby into a world as messed up as this is beautiful?

She nodded firmly. "Beautiful. Now repeat after me, Mr. Cruz Khala. Life is beautiful. Love is beautiful. You just have to believe."

One side of his mouth went up while the other went down. "Believe, huh?"

The word sounded foreign, as if he was just learning it. Or trying to, anyway.

"Yep. You ever try that before?" She meant it as a tease, but the longer she looked into his eyes, the more serious the moment felt. The more time slowed down. And the more she wondered if this was how her mother had felt the day she'd met Ross Monroe on that bridge.

Cruz shook his head slowly. "No. Not for a while, at least."

"Maybe you should," she whispered so as not to jar herself out of the magical, mystical feeling of the moment.

Cruz's chest rose and fell with each deep breath, and his voice was a low rumble. "Maybe I should."

Chapter Ten

"Hey. What's gotten into you?" Silas prodded Cruz.

Cruz snapped to attention, trying to remember where he was. Right — in the *akule hale*, the meeting house on Koa Point. His feet were propped on the lower edge of the stool he'd pulled up to the breakfast counter, and Tuesday's newspaper lay before him. A mug of coffee steamed at his elbow, and the rich scent woke a dozen memories, like his father and mother standing in the kitchen of the house Cruz had grown up in. A place far away in place and memory.

Always crooked, his mom would fuss over his dad's tie and jacket in that mix of adoration and exasperation she'd perfected over the years. A tone she had used on Cruz, too.

Good thing I have you, his dad would say, giving her a parting kiss. *And you and you and you,* he'd say, kissing each of the kids in turn.

Cruz closed his eyes. So many good memories, but so much pain, too. And, damn. The more time passed, the more he had let himself get mired in dark memories instead of good ones.

Life is beautiful. Love is beautiful. You just have to believe.

He took a sip of coffee — carefully, because it was hot. But, oops. The steaming coffee was lukewarm. Apparently, he'd drifted off again. He'd done a lot of that in the past few days, sometimes reliving the pain of losing his family, other times marveling over the sunshine that Jody seemed to carry wherever she went.

Jody. Let's think about Jody, his tiger said, preferring more recent memories. Good ones.

So, yeah — he'd spent far too much time thinking about her. The two of them had spent Sunday confronting her slimeball manager then retracing her steps at the club. Despite his best efforts, he hadn't been able to pick up any clues to the gunman. Then they'd hunkered down at Koa Point for most of another day, with Cruz making investigative calls while Jody worked out on the shore and in the water, carving stunning moves into the waves at Koa Point's private surf break. Not that Cruz had been watching or anything.

Well, okay — maybe he had watched for a little while. How could he resist? It was so damn effortless, the way she harnessed those waves. Even the way she paddled out fascinated him. Left arm, right arm, left arm, all the way through the incoming surf. And just when he thought the next wave would push Jody back, she would duck and shove her board under the oncoming wave. Then she'd pop up on the other side, not even sputtering.

And that was just paddling out. Watching her lie on her board waiting for the perfect wave was just as fascinating. Quietly, patiently, she bided her time exactly the way a tiger lay in wait for his prey. Watching. Waiting. Coiling her muscles and coming out of nowhere to jump on the perfect wave. She would take off ahead of a ripple of water that looked like it wouldn't amount to anything. But that ripple would lift and climb higher, chasing Jody in an all-out race to shore. A split second after the crest lifted and broke, Jody would rise, too, jumping to her feet and zooming down the face of the wave.

Of course, he'd seen plenty of surfers in his time. But he'd never really stopped and studied one — especially one as good as Jody.

It was breathtaking. Thrilling. Exhilarating — and hell, he was just observing from shore. What would it be like to fly down a rushing wall of water moving with that force and speed?

He had no idea, but, damn. It looked amazing.

The biggest waves, Jody rode diagonally, running away from the curling, foaming tip, crouching lower and lower in the tunnel of water underneath the breaking wave. Cruz crouched, too, listening to the roar of the waves, practically tasting the salt water on his sun-dried lips. He couldn't even imagine how loud it must be for Jody inside. A thunderous roar? A continuous hiss? She wore a look of total glee all the way down the ever-closing barrel until Mother Nature gave up and let her go. Jody would surf out the waning wave, give her surfboard a barely visible pump, and turn around over the tail end. Then she'd drop down to her board to paddle out and do it all over again.

Of course, she switched it up every couple of waves. Sometimes, she rode out a wave in one long, effortless glide. Other times, she'd spin her hips and twist the board around, carving a white line across an aquamarine wall of water like an artist signing a masterpiece. And sometimes, she'd launch off the lip of a wave and rocket into the air. Like gravity didn't apply to her. Like a bird. Her feet stayed rooted to her board even though she was nearly upside down, and she'd yank her head around to judge her landing the way a cat came out of a fall. When she landed, she bent her knees, adjusted her balance, and sliced right into her next turn.

Every once in a while, she'd goof, and the foamy crest of a wave would consume both woman and board. The wave would thunder as if to proclaim victory, but Jody would pop up laughing a minute later, still having a ball.

Life is beautiful. You just have to believe.

Cruz had to shake his head, impressed. Jody didn't just say the words. She lived them.

You just have to believe, his tiger had echoed as she turned and paddled out again.

Cruz blinked a couple of times and cleared his throat. Okay, okay. So he had spent a little time watching Jody surf. So what?

"You have to stop obsessing about the past," Silas said, pacing back and forth, pulling his focus back to the business at hand that Tuesday morning on Koa Point.

Cruz kept his eyes fixed on the coffee. Actually, he was obsessing about the lithe, lanky human who was getting closer and closer to his heart. A human he absolutely, positively, was not attracted to. Not in the least.

Not when she smiled that special way of hers — straight from the heart. Not when she brushed against him the couple of times they'd drifted close, sending shots of electricity through his body. Not even when she lay spread out on his futon at night, staring at the sky. Because yes, he'd prowled by once or twice in tiger form and peeked. Bodyguards had to keep an eye on their clients, right?

"Right," he muttered.

Silas gave a satisfied nod as if Cruz was affirming his comment — whatever it had been.

"So, let's go over this again," Silas said, stalking around and around. His pacing was driving Cruz crazy.

"Yes, let's," Kai, Silas's cousin, said. "I'm still not following you."

Kai and his mate Tessa had returned late the previous night from their trip to the Big Island — too late for Cruz or Silas to fill him in on the details, which they'd agreed to catch up on now.

Cruz frowned. He might be obsessed with Jody, but Silas was fixated on Moira, his ex-fiancée. In the past two days, the dragon shifter had grown sullen, haggard, and shifty-eyed. He'd been taking marathon flights in dragon form that lasted half the night. The beat of mighty wings had reached Cruz at his perch in the jungle, and he'd caught glimpses of Silas's shadow sweeping over the trees. Years ago, Moira had betrayed Silas, and those wounds ran deep. Open wounds, apparently, not the healed scars Cruz had assumed them to be.

"How does Moira fit into all this?" Kai asked.

"Moira owns and runs the Elements fragrance line," Silas said. "It took me a while to dig through all the middlemen she's set it up through, but I was able to track the final connection yesterday. It's her, all right."

Kai scratched his brow. "So Moira owns Elements, and Jody is one of the models. And someone tried to kill Jody..."

Cruz scowled. He'd snuck over to the Kapa'akea resort a second time and still hadn't been able to find a trace of the gunman. Not a whiff of a trail, not a footprint except for those of the police. It was uncanny. What kind of hit man didn't leave a scent?

"And Jesus — what's this about McGraugh?" Kai went on.

Cruz shook his head, because he still hadn't digested the latest news from their friend Ella, a desert fox.

Silas heaved a weary sigh. "Ella has been assisting our investigation on the mainland. McGraugh was found murdered in his office twelve hours ago. Ella said the police were calling it a botched burglary, but she doubts that."

"Moira... hitmen... modeling... And we fit into this... how?" Kai asked.

"I wish I knew," Silas said. "Moira must know we're based here on Maui. She could be trying to provoke us — or frame us. Cruz was close to killing Jody himself. And if he had—"

Cruz looked at his shoes. God, he'd been so damn close.

"—he might have been caught. Imagine the trouble we'd have with half the Maui police force investigating everyone at Koa Point." Silas set his mug down with an aggravated thump. "That's the last thing we need."

Cruz scowled. Other than the occasional speeding ticket, everyone at Koa Point abided by the law. They were shifters, a secret that could never be revealed.

"Does Moira know about the gem?"

Cruz wanted to groan. Yet another complication he didn't need. "Moira has to know about the three Spirit Stones we have. But from what Jody says, I doubt Moira knows about the jewel the product manager is trying to bring in. It's all his idea, and he wants to pop the secret on his bosses to make a big bang."

Silas stood wearily and checked his watch. "I'm going to go call Ella and see what else she might have discovered. That, and I'll try to find out which jewel this Richard person is planning to bring in."

Kai and Cruz watched him go, exchanging silent glances. Then Kai leaned closer. "Okay, now you fill me in on what's going on."

Cruz furrowed his brow. "We just did."

Kai lifted one eyebrow. "Did you? Because I still don't understand why you're the one sitting here, clean-shaven like it's date night, while Silas is the one pacing around like a caged tiger. Pardon the cliché."

Cruz was about to protest when Kai caught sight of something behind him and murmured, "Let me guess. She's the reason."

Cruz whirled far too eagerly. Yep, it was Jody, who'd been teaching Tessa to surf in the calmest patch of water off their private beach. Jody broke off from saying something to Tessa and focused on him. Their eyes met and—

His breath caught, and his blood rushed.

Mate, his tiger rumbled.

Jody's step hitched, but she covered up quickly, strolling up as casual as can be.

Cruz struggled to do the same. Every time he saw her, he lost his breath. And not from her clothes or her makeup or the way she did her hair, because he rarely noticed any of that. It was the sparkle in her eyes, the bounce in her step, the grin on her face. Yes, she was beautiful. But she could inhabit an entirely different body and still take his breath away. It was all in her personality, her breezy way of dealing with — even celebrating — life.

"That was great," Tessa said as they ducked under the shade of the meeting house. "I could surf all day."

"Me, too," Jody sighed. "But I have to go to the photo shoot. Are you ready to go?" she asked Cruz.

"Ready," he said, standing quickly.

Rea-dy, his tiger growled, licking his lips.

Cruz scolded him. *Stupid beast. You know you can't have her.*

He'd been trying to compartmentalize his feelings for Jody into clear halves. Not always succeeding, but trying. His tiger side could covet Jody all he wanted, but his human side was smarter than that.

A rumble of protest built in his chest.

"Hmm?" Jody asked, looking around.

He covered up with a cough and a last sip of his coffee. "Nothing. I'm ready." He ducked under the lowest edge of the thatched roof and cast a glance at the sky. "I'm not sure the weather will cooperate with the photo shoot, though."

Jody's mouth twisted in a wry grin. "Fingers crossed."

"See you later," Tessa called.

Cruz watched Jody from the corner of his eye as they walked to the garage. Her bracelets jangled as she walked, and the breeze played with her hair. She must have rinsed in the outdoor shower, because her scent was more wild rose than salty, and that drove his tiger wild.

"Which car today?" she quipped, waving at the low, arched bays of the garage.

Cruz hesitated. The Land Rover had tinted windows so no one could spot the passengers. The Ferrari was usually Boone's ride. Cruz preferred the Lamborghini for raw speed.

"Lady's choice," he said.

"Lady's choice?" She faked a bored sigh. "Well, I suppose the Lamborghini will do."

He grinned in spite of himself and motioned her in. A minute later, they were humming down the road with the coast blurring past on the *makai* side and cane fields on the other. They got stuck behind a slow-moving rental car, though, and he couldn't help muttering under his breath.

"You don't like people much, do you?" Jody asked.

Visions of his loved ones, lying lifelessly with wide, shocked eyes flashed through his head. Or so he'd taken to picturing the scene of the crime. Having been stationed in a war zone when it happened, he hadn't been able to see for himself.

So, of course, he hated people. They'd murdered his entire family in cold blood.

His hackles rose, but when he took a deep breath, Jody's soft scent calmed his pulse. Without thinking, he brushed a hand against hers, and that helped, too.

He shrugged, struggling to make sense of the conflicting emotions welling up inside. "People are irrational."

"Says the guy who lives in a tree house." She laughed.

His lips moved, but his brain just wouldn't supply an answer, so he gave up. Maybe he needed to stop thinking everything through so much. And okay, maybe humans weren't the only irrational beings on earth. But he liked his tree house, damn it.

Jody does, too, his tiger said in a satisfied undertone.

"Are you okay?" she asked a moment later, all gentle and concerned. "Whatever's got you so worked up—"

You, he wanted to say. *You have me all worked up.*

"—you're better off putting it behind you." She made a tossing motion over her shoulder.

As if it was as easy as that.

Maybe it is, his tiger whispered. *Maybe you should give it a try.*

"You need to lighten up a little. Laugh more."

He made a face, but she just grinned and launched into a joke. "So, you know how to get a surfer to school on time?"

Cruz looked over. It was kind of cute, the way the corners of her mouth twitched, ready to laugh at her own joke.

"Tell her the waves are no good." She grinned at the punch line and went right into the next joke. "What's the difference between a surfer and a large pizza?"

Cruz tapped his fingers on the steering wheel.

"A large pizza can feed a family of five." She giggled. "Oh. Oh. I have a good one."

"Finally," he murmured, trying not to smile.

"Why is surfing like sex?"

He looked at her expectantly. That, he had to hear.

"When it's good, it's really, really good. And when it's bad, it's still pretty good."

She joked all the way down the Honopi'ilani Highway and through the high-end resorts of Makena. Her eyes shone like a little girl's, and Cruz couldn't help smiling either.

But the joy faded out of both of them the closer they got to the turnoff to the secluded beach where Richard and the photographer would be.

Make that, Richard, the photographer, and several other people Cruz wished he never had to meet.

"Finally, you made it," Richard snipped, flicking his cigarette butt into the sand of the pristine beach.

A rumble sounded in the distance — a storm cloud moving in.

"Finally?" Jody muttered under her breath.

A woman hustled over with a happy wave of her hands. "Just wait till you see the outfit I've picked out for you!"

Jody looked like she really could wait, but she trooped dutifully over to the trailer parked at the side of the road. Well, she started to before turning back to Cruz. Her eyes were mournful. and her shoulders drooped like they were parting forever. Cruz's gut churned. They hadn't spent much time apart in the past seventy-two hours, and even when they had, they had both been at Koa Point. Time had a way of stretching there, while distance felt compressed, so even when she'd been out surfing, she hadn't felt far away. But now...

Her lips moved, but no sound came out.

"So where's that jewel?" the photographer, Guy, asked.

Richard grumbled. "We couldn't get it, after all. That son of a bitch said he'd have it for us, but he didn't come through."

Cruz was so focused on Jody, he barely registered the words. When he did, he was strangely relieved. Obviously, Silas had been wrong about another Spirit Stone being called to by the three they already had at Koa Point. And a good thing, too. Spirit Stones brought trouble, and Jody had enough of that as it was.

"You coming?" the wardrobe lady called.

"Coming," Jody said, turning away slowly.

Cruz watched her for a long minute before pinning Richard, the photographer, and the other men present with a *Don't even think about it* glare.

She's mine, his tiger added, lashing its tail.

Five pairs of eyes hit the ground in submission, and Cruz grunted in satisfaction.

"Get moving," Richard barked at the others. "We need to get this shoot finished before the rain sets in."

Cruz set off to secure the area, hoping the storm would sweep in as fast as possible and cut the photo shoot short. He sniffed the air, inspected every path, and eyed the hills that boxed in the bay. Richard had an assistant stationed at the head of the dirt road to turn casual visitors away — something Cruz was sure Richard didn't have a permit for, though it suited him. The fewer people who wandered through the area, the better.

He kicked at the dirt and sniffed the air for the tenth time. No sign of interlopers, but then again, neither had there been that night at the resort. Then he set off to comb through the area a second time. He said he'd guard Jody, and he meant it.

He was just coming back from his third pass when the trailer door slammed open and a woman called out in glee.

"We're ready."

It was the wardrobe lady — or maybe the hair lady — Cruz wasn't sure. He didn't care either, not when he saw Jody step out.

"Gorgeous, honey," Guy, the photographer, called. "Let's get started."

Cruz's mouth hung open. The woman in front of him was gorgeous — undeniably, amazingly, mouthwateringly gorgeous. But she wasn't Jody. Not the Jody he knew.

Her hair had been twisted and teased, sort of like she would look when she came back from surfing, but nothing like that at all, because it had all been arranged to look that way. Her lips were a shade too red, her eyelashes a tick too dark. And her bikini — two little purple triangles and a high-cut thong — well, that was about four sizes too small. Jody never would have picked it out herself. He knew; he'd seen the loose-fitting, comfortable clothes she brought over from the condo.

"Gorgeous. Jeanette, get a little more shadow on her. We want those tits to stand out," the photographer said, snapping his gum.

Jody winced.

Cruz growled. Was the man serious?

Apparently, he was, and Cruz was powerless to stop the transformation of the spunky woman who so fascinated him into little more than a hunk of flesh. Guy led her over to the water's edge and turned her by the shoulder — actually *turned* her like a potted plant — dispensing orders the whole time.

"George, move the light over there. And put some of that seaweed around that rock. Jeanette, what can we do about her ears?"

Cruz narrowed his eyes. What was wrong with Jody's ears?

The makeup lady scurried over and sprayed something then attacked them with a little brush.

"All set. On your knees, baby," the photographer said.

"Was that thunder?" The makeup lady squinted into the sky.

No, it was him, barely swallowing a growl. What right did that asshole have to tell Jody to drop to her knees? It was all so coarse. So overtly sexual. So, so... wrong.

Jody didn't like it one bit either. Her eyes blazed.

"Um, boss?" George, the assistant, ventured. "How about we start with the boulder shots? The light is perfect for that."

Cruz decided George was okay. Richard and the photographer, he could kill.

Guy stuck out his hands like a frame. "Not a bad idea. Hop up on that rock, honey."

George offered Jody a hand up, but she ignored it, hopping up to the four-foot boulder in one easy bound. Cruz would bet she could scale a cliff if she had to.

"Okay, good. Turn a little," Guy said, still chewing his gum. "A little more... Right leg back... More. Perfect."

Then Richard cut in. "Wait — what's with the bracelets? Jeanette?" His voice dropped to a threat.

"Not my idea," Jeanette rushed to her own defense.

Jody made a face. "I always wear them. I told you last time."

Cruz's eyes froze on the bracelets as a memory flitted through his mind — Jody, fingering the bracelets as she talked about her mom.

These were my mom's. I never take them off.

"They'll ruin this shot. Lose them," Richard barked. "George, get us a light reading, damn it."

For a moment, Jody looked defiant, but she managed to hold on to whatever words she was about to launch off the tip of her tongue. Then she pulled her teeth over her lower lip and slowly pulled the bracelets off.

"I'll take them." Jeanette reached up.

Jody looked down, and he could practically read her thoughts. *But they were my mom's.* Then she looked past Jeanette and right at Cruz. "Will you hold them for me?"

He stepped forward without thinking, and when he reached out, their fingers brushed, sending a tingle all the way up his arm.

Damn it, it was just a couple of bracelets. Why did he feel like she'd just entrusted him with a royal heirloom?

He slipped them into one of the deep pockets of his cargo pants, snapped the button over the top, and patted them to let her know they were safe.

Jody smiled, and for a moment, his whole world lit up. But then Richard opened his big mouth and ruined everything again.

"All right, already. We don't have time to lose."

A roll of thunder sounded over the mountains, underscoring his point. The light was spectacular, with a perfect blue sky to seaward and the leading edge of ominous clouds to the east.

"Chin up. Eyes to me. Shift your weight to the back leg." Guy motioned with one hand. "Don't slouch, baby."

Don't call me baby, Jody's eyes blazed.

"Right hand on the hip. Give me negative space."

Cruz formed and reformed a fist. He'd love to give the man some negative space — whatever that was.

"Trace your hands over your hair and twirl the end," the photographer went on. "Perfect. Everything but that expression. Don't give me ax murderer. Give me sex. Hunger. Desire."

Jody's jawline went even stiffer. She looked more like an ice queen than a sex kitten, but who could blame her?

"Come on, already," Richard called over the photographer's shoulder. "You're acting the story, remember?"

Jody rolled her eyes, and Cruz wondered what the story was supposed to be. A woman swallowing her pride to work for a sexist, asshole boss?

"Okay, let's back it up a little. Hop down and walk out into the water to about knee-deep."

Jody did as she was told, and for a second, Cruz thought she might bolt and swim out to sea.

"Perfect. Now turn around and walk toward me."

Jody walked while the photographer backed up, shadowed by George who held an oversized white umbrella that had something to do with the light.

"Come on. I need to *feel* you come up this beach," Guy said. "We need to see how much you want this in your eyes."

All Cruz saw in Jody's eyes was grim resignation.

"Do it again. And remember the story. You're a mermaid, washed up on the beach."

Cruz covered his face with one hand and shook his head. He could come up with a better story than that.

"Swing your hips more. Give me attitude."

Cruz hid a grin. She was giving him attitude, all right.

"Back up. Do it again. But dunk this time. I need mermaid vibes," the photographer insisted, popping his gum.

Jody dunked, keeping her head back when she stood. Salt water washed over her body in a thousand little rivers and waterfalls.

Cruz's mouth opened a crack, and time slowed down then suddenly rushed ahead. The dunk had washed away a little of the model and brought more of the real Jody to the surface. Her hair was slightly less than perfect, her makeup more subdued. And wow, she really was beautiful.

"Gorgeous, sweetheart. Now walk toward me." The photographer motioned. "Slower this time. Remember the story. Something drew you here, though you're not sure what."

That part wasn't so outlandish, Cruz had to admit. Shifter lore was full of stories of heroes or heroines following instincts to fulfill their destiny. There were even stories of mermaids, though like many shifter species, those had gone extinct.

"You've been having the same dream over and over," Guy narrated as the camera clicked away. "But when you wake up, you can barely remember what it was. Only that it took place on this beach."

Cruz grimaced. He had lots of recurring dreams, and he remembered every one in detail. The nightmares about his family, and more recently, hot dreams of him and Jody, wrapped around each other in his bed...

...beside his bed...

...in the shallows of the rock pool...

Jody's eyes drifted to his and warmed, making him wonder if she, too, wished for a different ending to their encounter by the rock pool that first morning on Koa Point.

"That's the look we want!" Richard cheered. "That exact look. Are you getting this, Guy?"

"Bet your ass, I am. Now one more time. Give me heat, baby. Heat."

Jody splashed back into the water, dunked, then turned and strode up the beach with a little more sass in her step.

Cruz stood perfectly still. Now he was the one feeling the heat.

"There we go. Work it. Work it. Be the mermaid. Look for your destiny."

Jody's eyes drifted over the beach as the camera shutter clicked madly away.

Cruz watched her. Humans used the word *destiny* so lightly. Did they even know what power it possessed?

"Okay, let's do it again."

Jody repeated the coming-out-of-the-water shot a dozen more times, warming up to the camera on each pass. The stiffness faded from her limbs, and her expression grew ever more wistful, like she really had bought into the story. Cruz had to admit he was getting sucked into it, too. Between the repetition and the singsong quality of the photographer's voice, the scene took shape before his eyes — with one addition. He was the guy that mermaid was drawn to. He was her destiny.

"One more time. You're the mermaid, and you're following an invisible force that brought you here."

Jody sauntered slowly up the beach as droplets of water accented her perfect curves.

"You're hungry. Give me hungry, baby. Give me desire."

Jody faltered for a moment, and her eyes wandered listlessly over the beach. But then her gaze landed on Cruz, and the heat in her expression shot up a hundred degrees.

"That's it! Perfect," the photographer called, crouching between Jody and Cruz. "Now you know what's drawn you here."

In a tiny, almost imperceptible movement, Jody licked her lips.

"Yes! Yes! That's what we want," Guy said. "That need. That desire."

That desire was about to make Cruz's army pants much too tight, but he couldn't drag his eyes away. Jody's chest rose and fell with every breath, and her nipples pebbled under the fabric of the bikini.

"You're hot. You're hungry..." the man droned on.

Cruz stared at Jody, imagining everyone else right out of existence. Imagining Jody coming to him just as wet and hungry, but back at his place where they would have some privacy. Like she'd come straight from her silent fantasies in the rock pool and over to him in the bed.

She dipped her chin the slightest bit, and his tiger growled inside, forming a picture in his mind. Jody would be assertive but submissive enough to let him take the lead. He'd lay her out on the mattress, pin her arms over her head, and give her all the loving a hot-blooded woman ever desired.

The photographer clapped once and lowered his camera. "I could not ask for a better take. Let's move on to the next shot while this light lasts."

Jody jolted the way a person did when yanked out of a dream. Cruz did, too. The air tingled, and he couldn't tell whether the electricity stemmed from the impending storm or the sheer chemistry between them.

Jeanette handed Jody a bottle of water, and she gulped it down. Cruz gave himself a little shake and turned away to scan the surrounding hills. He was supposed to be guarding Jody's life, not lusting after her. And damn it, she was human. There was no way he could be thinking — dreaming — desiring all those fantasies in his mind.

"Okay, now get on your knees." The photographer snapped his fingers, and Cruz whipped around.

Jody looked at him, not Guy. Slowly, she dropped to her knees. A puff of wind swept through the enclosed bay, teasing her hair.

Cruz's mouth went dry. Sweet Jesus, how was he supposed to look at Jody and not imagine her as his? He looked up, praying the gathering storm would put him out of his misery — his sweet, sweet misery — before it was too late.

Too late, a voice chuckled in the back of his mind.

Chapter Eleven

Sand scratched at Jody's knees, and salt water pinched her skin. The heat of the sun on the beach burned her shins, but that was nothing compared to the heat sweeping through the rest of her body. She gulped again but the feeling didn't go away, and neither did the raging fantasies.

"Put your hands under your breasts and push up a little," the photographer said.

On any other day, she would have walked out on the spot. That or she would have grabbed the camera out of Guy's hands and swung it at Richard, who was leering again. Nothing was worth posing for shots like that. But with Cruz there, looking at her with glowing eyes and slightly swollen lips, her hands fell into position right away.

There, Cruz, she imagined herself having the nerve to say. *For you. Do you like what you see?*

A bead of sweat rolled slowly down his temple, and the corner of his mouth twitched. Yeah, he liked it, all right.

Of course, it was crazy to lust after a man who'd admitted to having her in his gun sights at one point. But all she'd ever witnessed was Cruz's fierce, protective behavior. He'd shielded her from a bullet and let her stay in his home. He'd proven a dozen times that for all his gruffness and hostility toward the world, he cared. Deep down, he cared. About her. About Keiki. About his friends.

So, yes — she'd let herself lust after a man like that.

The camera clicked away, but she barely heard it. The photographer murmured instructions. She obeyed while the rest of her brain outlined a dozen ways she and Cruz could consummate the desire that had been building inside her over the past few days.

"Tilt your head," Guy said.

Her eyelids drooped as she pictured touching — tasting — licking Cruz.

"Push back your hair..."

She imagined Cruz's hands doing that for her then holding her in place as his hips moved.

"Push the left strap of your bikini off your shoulder..."

Thunder rolled over the upper slopes of the mountains. Were the mountain gods angry, or did they approve?

She pictured Cruz slipping the bikini strap aside then touching her bare skin — and stopped just short of giving the photographer more than he'd asked for. God, what was coming over her?

She rocked back on her heels. Yes, she'd fantasized about guys before. And yes, she'd acted on those fantasies, too. But those were all fun, flirty flings. No man had ever made her feel like she'd die if he didn't touch her. No one had ever made her forget where she was and what she was doing except loving him.

No one but Cruz. He stood directly over the photographer's shoulder, staring back at her. His hands were clenched into fists, his body angled to hide the erection his cargo pants barely concealed.

God, she wanted him. And he wanted her, too.

Thunder rumbled, closer this time — a long, low grumble that unrolled over the slopes of Haleakala. Just enough of a warning to make her check her sanity. Cruz had admitted to wanting to kill her at one point. Why on earth should she trust him?

The temperature cooled, and goose bumps rose on her skin as the heat in her body raged on.

"Shit. We're losing the light," Richard said.

Jody glanced at Cruz. The sky might be growing dim, but his eyes flashed at her in a mix of promise and desire.

Guy flapped his hand. "Just a couple of more shots. Tilt your head back, honey. Way back."

Jody arched, and the photographer clucked in delight.

"Perfect. Tilt your head this way. George, give me all the light you can. Jesus, Elements is going to love these shots. Keep it up, honey."

Purplish-black clouds swirled above, chasing away the blue part of the sky. Any second now, those clouds would burst and soak her to the bone. Energy crackled and swirled around her like a prowling beast. Cruz was just like that — hard and edgy. Always on the brink.

"Now, look up. Right at the camera. Keep that expression," the photographer called.

She looked past the camera to Cruz with his smoldering eyes. A one-man storm cloud focusing all its energy on her.

I want you, she whispered in her mind. *I need you.*

It didn't matter whether he heard the words or not. He would understand her body language, all right.

Cruz's body stiffened. *Watch what you wish for,* his eyes flashed.

Oh, she'd watch it, all right. She'd watch him peel his clothes off, followed by hers — if only he'd give her the chance.

"Shit. It's starting to rain," George said.

"Last few shots," Guy insisted, clicking away.

Jody was amazed the droplets that hit her bare skin didn't sizzle and evaporate.

I can handle you, mister, she let her shoulders tell Cruz.

His lips formed a tight line. Most likely, he had one of those dark knight complexes that made him think he'd seen and done too many terrible things to deserve a fair maiden like her.

She nearly chuckled out loud. Some maiden she was.

"Hang on to that vixen look. Hang on," the photographer begged, shifting around for a different angle.

She ignored him completely and arched an eyebrow at Cruz. Her, a vixen? Ha.

Cruz's nostrils flared. Okay, so maybe the vixen thing worked. And hell, it was working for her, too. Another few minutes of this and she'd come to a screaming orgasm just from the look in the man's eyes.

But she wanted more. She wanted the real thing.

"Guy," George murmured as the droplets turned to rain.

Guy jogged around her. "Just a few more shots with the clear part of the sky..."

The sky was about as clear as her thoughts were, but Jody didn't care.

"Richard?" the hair lady called. "That call you were waiting for has just come through. I have them on the line."

Richard hurried away, and good riddance, too.

"Can you stretch up and spread your arms?" the photographer asked. "Yes, like that. Just like that."

Jody threw back her head as rain tapped over her chest. Boy, did it feel good. Cleansing, as if the sins she'd committed by thinking dirty thoughts were forgiven. Like those weren't sins so much as perfectly natural desires.

A clap of thunder shook the sky, and the drops intensified to a deluge. Guy covered his camera with his shirt. "Okay, it's a wrap. Run for it, everyone. Run for it."

The sky exploded, pouring buckets of water down. Jody found herself running and laughing with the sheer joy of it. All that power in the sky. All that desire in her body.

A hand closed around hers, and though she knew without looking it was Cruz, she peeked anyway. His hair was matted down with rain, his shirt stuck to his chest, and he looked at her like... like...

"What?" she shouted over the drumming of rain.

He opened his mouth then closed it again, and she wanted to shake the words right out of him. But then Cruz did something totally, utterly surprising. Something much, much better than telling her what was on his mind.

He smiled.

A huge, open smile like that of a kid on a roller coaster out on the greatest adventure of his life. A real smile, from the heart. From his most hidden, secret territory, in other words. A pity she wasn't a photographer, because that would have been the shot of the day.

But, hell. She could do better than a photo. She could kiss him.

So she did.

She pulled up short and kissed him full on the lips while the thunder rolled and waves crashed over the beach. Her arms wrapped around his shoulders. Visions of snaking her legs around his waist danced through her mind, and it was all she could do to pull back and give a very surprised Cruz her best vixen look.

"Just a sec," she yelled, ducking into the trailer for her things.

She nearly ran into Richard, who stood with a hand stuck up in a stop sign, holding a phone to his ear. "Great news. We can get the gem for tomorrow."

Paying no attention, she darted back out, grabbed Cruz's hand again, and ran. Every hurried step splattered her bare legs with mud, but she'd never had so much fun. The dirt track leading to the beach was already awash with brown torrents rushing downhill.

"Wait, Jody. We can get that jewel, after all," Richard yelled from the trailer door.

"No way," she called over her shoulder. "I'm done."

Actually, she was just starting — starting on every dirty act she wanted to share with Cruz. But as far as modeling was concerned, she was through.

"We could do a bonus session," Richard yelled. "I'll pay you extra. Just think..."

She squeezed Cruz's hand tighter and splashed onward. There was only one thing she could think about and that was getting intimate with him. But, hell. How was she going to hold out until they got back to his place? Even the quarter mile to where the Lamborghini was parked seemed too long to wait.

"You going to let me drive in peace this time?" Cruz yelled over the sound of the rain.

Jody laughed. She was going to let him do a whole lot more than that.

They split at the last possible second, each diving into opposite sides of the car and out of the rain. For one frozen moment after the doors slammed shut, neither of them moved or spoke. But the second their eyes met...

Jody leaned over — make that, practically leaped over the gearshift — and covered Cruz's mouth with hers. A heartbeat later, the rest of her body caught up, and she straddled him. Rain hammered on the roof, not quite covering her greedy whimpers or Cruz's heavy breaths. Her hips gyrated over his, and she moaned out loud.

Cruz tasted so good. He smelled good. He felt good. Overwhelmingly good. His hands on her hips communicated how badly he wanted her. The heat radiating from the broad chest that heaved under hers did, too, not to mention the unmistakable prod of his erection between her legs.

Rivers of rainwater trailed from her body to his, and she became aware of the mess they would make in the car. She broke off the kiss and reached for the towel she'd grabbed — a towel not much drier than her body after that sprint through the rain — but Cruz growled and pulled her back, slamming his mouth over hers.

I want you here, the gesture told her. *I need you here.*

"The car..." she murmured between desperate kisses. If it were the decade-old Chevy she drove at home, she wouldn't have hesitated.

Cruz didn't slow one bit. His tongue swept over hers in bold, possessive strokes, and his eyes flashed with barely controlled desire. The windows fogged up within a minute, sealing them away from the world.

"God, Cruz..."

There was so much she wanted to say, and no way she could get it out right. Her body was doing a pretty good job getting the message across, though, what with the way she stroked her lower body against his and surged against him with her chest. She was a one-woman storm, a lot like the one raging outside, unleashing all its pent-up energy at once.

Then Cruz nudged her back and looked at her. Just looked at her.

Jody held her breath, wondering what he'd do next. Push her away? Insist on finding a better place? Tell her he had come to his senses and changed his mind?

His eyes flashed as he slid a finger under her bikini strap and pushed it slowly down her shoulder.

Mine, his eyes seemed to announce. *You are all mine.*

Yes, she wanted to cry out. *Yes, yes, yes.*

The wet fabric of her bikini clung stubbornly to her skin until Cruz got the strap all the way past her elbow, when it finally rolled to the side. And just like before, he waited — a brief hesitation like the pause before a clap of thunder. An inhale. A ready. . . set. . .

One second, her eyes were locked on Cruz's yellow-green orbs. The next, she tipped her head back and cried out as his mouth closed over her nipple.

"Yes. . . " she moaned.

The man moved fast as a cat, and she danced in place as he consumed her. He sucked the nipple into his mouth and nibbled it with his lips — a hard, insistent nip that had her seeing stars. One big hand closed over her breast, working her willing flesh, while he slid his other hand around her hips and pressed her against his erection.

She moaned unintelligibly, because he had her everywhere at once. Or nearly almost, because her body cried out for one more point of contact.

"Inside. I need you inside."

She wiggled over his cock, wishing he were wearing as little as she was. Wishing she could work down his fly and let their bodies connect.

"Soon," he murmured in a rough, uneven voice that made her toes curl. Then he went right back to her breast, circling and kneading with his fingers and tongue.

It was so good — and damn, they were moving fast, like a train barreling down the tracks. A different kind of *fast* than the giggly, groping fun she might have engaged in with any other man. And it wasn't *fun* so much as *intense.* Her heart was beating halfway out of her chest. Her body was melting down, her nerves firing a dozen messages at the same time.

More. Need more.

Good. So good.

Right there. Harder. Closer. . .

She really ought to think this over before she went too far, but she didn't want to.

Sometimes it's better not to think, her dad had said in those first surfing lessons he'd given her, so long ago. *Just do.*

She stifled a naughty giggle. She was pretty sure her dad hadn't been encouraging something like *this.*

Cruz moved to her left breast, not bothering to move the scrap of fabric aside.

"Oh, yes..."

The more he suckled and bit, the more control she lost. The friction of the bikini only heightened the pleasure, and she leaned so far back, her head bumped the roof.

"Mmm," he murmured. "Salty."

"Salty comes with the package," she managed, arching to give him better access.

"Taste test," he said, finally pushing the fabric aside. "Without..."

His lips closed over her nipple and squeezed. Hard, as if he put as much time training that set of muscles as the rest. Then he let go long enough to drag the fabric back and forth over her sensitive flesh, driving her wild.

"Now with," he whispered, in a deep, hungry voice, covering her with the bikini and tasting her again.

Jody closed her eyes and pulsed against his body. His free hand pulled and released her in a slight pumping motion, setting the pace.

I am in charge here, the motion proclaimed. *I control your pleasure.*

Jody whimpered, ceding all control. Instinctively recognizing that with Cruz, there was no other way. And given what a master he was... no hardship there.

"What do you like better?" he asked in a hoarse whisper.

Her muddled brain tried to make sense of that. Did he mean the bikini — with or without?

She stroked her hands over his chest and took hold of his shirt, rolling it upward before he could protest. "Without. Definitely without."

He grinned — an honest-to-God, *you're funny and I love this* grin — and helped. A damn good thing, because the soaked cloth was a bitch to get off, and the vee of his chest didn't make it any easier. Jody laughed as she finally plucked the shirt off and tossed it aside.

"What a mess you are."

His eyebrow arched. "What a mess I am?"

"Yes. You're all wet and sticky."

His eyes flashed with renewed desire. "Wet and sticky, huh?"

"You have a dirty mind," she scolded, hunkering to lower her breast toward his mouth.

"Right. I'm the one with a dirty mind." He lapped at her nipple, flicking his tongue like a kid with a melting ice cream.

The clever comeback she'd had poised on the tip of her tongue evaporated the second he touched her breast. She was going to explode from ecstasy. Christ, the car was going to be a mess. She was already a mess, and Cruz hadn't even—

She moaned as his left hand advanced between her legs. She shuddered, and every muscle in her body melted, clenched, and melted all over again.

"I think you like my dirty mind," she whispered.

"I like more than your dirty mind."

Rain pounded on the roof like a set of Polynesian drums, driving her crazy with desire.

"So good..."

He traced her folds then dragged a knuckle over her clit, making her cry out.

"Yes..."

The hem of her thong moved with his hand, and her body ached all over.

"Please... more..."

"More here?" he teased, circling her clit. "Or here?" He slid farther back toward her entrance.

"Trick question?"

He chuckled and rocked his hand beneath her, giving her a little of both before finally sliding a finger inside.

Jody let her head flop back. God, that felt good. So good...

Cruz circled then slipped a second finger in, muttering to himself. "You're so beautiful. So tight..."

She didn't feel tight. She felt absolutely ready for the monster erection pushing against her thigh. He could swell to twice that considerable size, and she'd still have space for more. Then she gulped, because something told her, in reality, accommodating him might be a stretch, indeed. Just imagining the sweet burn made her moan out loud.

"Good?" he whispered.

"Real good."

"Gonna make it better."

"Be my guest," she muttered, gyrating over his hand. Driving his fingers deeper. Deeper...

He curved his fingers inside her, making her cry out. She leaned forward, and his mouth closed over the skin of her neck.

"I am going to make you come so hard," he murmured into her skin.

She wanted to come up with a smart aleck retort. Something like *Not as hard as I'll make you come,* maybe, or *Wanna bet?* But damn, he was right, and she knew it. And though her lips moved, the only sounds she could produce were desperate moans.

The aching need built higher and higher, driving her in an upward spiral. Every muscle in her body coiled while she fought her release. The downpour outside was a roar in her ears. Cruz's sure motions drove her further and further past her limits until she cried out once more.

"Just like that..." Cruz whispered, pushing deep, deep inside her as she shuddered and came.

Ecstasy swept over her like a wave — a huge, winter wave that tumbled her off her surfboard and laughed in her face. Like nature, reminding her who was boss — or rather, Cruz, reminding her he was a man of his word.

I am going to make you come so hard...

The man hadn't been kidding — she really was putty in his hands. Just as her muscles slowly gave in to the heat wave melting her from the inside, an aftershock hit her, and she arched, crying out. Cruz pumped twice more before letting her glide gently back to earth.

She slumped over his body, panting into his neck.

"Good?" The word rumbled from his chest, and the sound wave vibrated through her body.

She kissed his neck. "Pretty good."

"Pretty good?"

She laughed out loud. "How much do you want me to stoke your ego?"

Cruz's breath tickled her ear. "Maybe just a little bit."

His tone was light, but his arms tightened around her. She thought of his tree house, hidden way in the woods. The dark, warning looks he flashed to anyone who dared approach his personal space. The way he'd cuddled Keiki.

Maybe her bodyguard had spent a little too much time alone. Maybe he really did need a few bolstering words. Or even more than words. Maybe he needed love.

She pulled her head back and looked deep into his eyes. Her hair was a cascading mess but it curtained the outside world away, and that was good. She cupped his face with both hands and let her lips play over his.

"That was more than good. That was great."

His yellow-green eyes seemed to glow, and his hands tightened over her waist.

"So good, I might just be purring," she added.

He grinned then pressed his ear to her chest. "I don't hear anything."

She snorted because he had to hear her heart hammering away. "Okay, maybe not *purring* purring, but purring inside. Like a cat."

He pushed closer until she couldn't see his face, then murmured, "Like a tiger."

She laughed. "You said tigers don't purr."

He looked up at her again, dead serious. "They do inside."

She nodded slowly, trying to figure out how to tell him just how good he made her feel. How secure. How at home.

But words were only one way to communicate all the emotions welling up inside — and not always the best way. So she dropped tiny kisses across his lips, his nose, and the sharp line of his cheekbones. All the places that had been off-limits until now.

Cruz held her silently, seriously, and closed his eyes.

She pressed closer and snuggled her nose against his, hoping the gesture wasn't too intimate for him. A different kind of intimate than his hand against her skin or his mouth over her breast. More intimate, in some ways. That was flesh, parts of a body. This snuggle, though, was more.

She moved her nose slowly, tipping her head this way and that. Cruz mirrored her movements, pushing harder then backing off and snuggling at a whole new angle. Her cheeks stretched into a smile so broad, it hurt. Maybe Dark Eyes didn't want to keep himself shuttered off from the world. Maybe he just needed the right woman to open the door to his unlocked cell.

"Hey," she whispered. Not a question or a demand. Just a placeholder for other words she was tempted to try out sometime. Words like, *I love you.* She wondered how long it had taken her mom and dad to get those words out in the open. Not too long, from what she'd heard, because there really was such a thing as love at first sight.

How long would it be until she dared utter those words to Cruz?

"Hey," he murmured, tipping his head against hers.

Outside, the rain slowed to a cheery tap over the roof of the car as the worst of the storm swept out to sea.

She and Cruz held each other in silence. It was a tipping point, she realized. A time to transition to whatever came next. Like a lot more sex, hopefully.

"Oh," he murmured, stirring at last. He popped the button on his pants pocket and pulled out her bracelets. "These are yours."

As if her heart weren't already close to bursting.

"Thanks," she said, slipping them back on. He watched her, and she gulped away the lump that filled her throat. "I won't be as easy on you next time," she added, going for a lighter mood.

Cruz smiled. "Next time, huh?"

"The sooner, the better," she admitted, snaking her hand down his chest. All that time, he'd been taking care of her. Now it was time to take care of him.

But Cruz closed his fingers over hers — gently, yet firmly — and shook his head. "Not here. Not until I get you to a bed."

She made a sad puppy face. "Soon?"

"Soon." He laughed and brushed a kiss across her knuckles.

She heaved a theatrical sigh and retreated slowly from his lap, making sure to bump and grind a few more times. She left him with a long, sloppy kiss.

"You're torturing me," he growled.

"Gotta keep your eyes on the prize." She yanked on her bundled up T-shirt and pointed to the ignition. "Warp speed, Captain."

Cruz arched his eyebrow. "Warp speed?"

She tapped his thigh, enjoying the rare, lighthearted feeling of the moment. "Come on, already. Vroom, vroom."

He started the engine with a roar and wiped a narrow path across the condensation on the windshield. He was chuckling, though, and looking like he hadn't had this much fun in years.

"Vroom, vroom," he murmured, hiding a grin. Then he sped off, making the tires squeal.

Chapter Twelve

Wolves howled their emotions. Dragons spat fire. Bears chuffed.

Cruz's inner tiger roared and pranced in delight.

All right, already, he muttered, tightening his knuckles around the steering wheel.

It was hard enough to keep the car on the road with the rain, a raging hard-on, and the soft play of Jody's hands over his thigh. To have a tiger roaring in his head at the same time — really roaring, wanting to announce his joy to every living beast across hundreds of miles and remind them who was boss — well, that just made it harder to steer a straight line.

The rain had settled into a steady shower, and the slice of blue in the sky was down to a narrow band far out on the horizon, over past Lanai. That wouldn't last long, though — not with the storm chasing the sunshine away.

"Gonna last a while," he murmured, worried that an awkward silence might settle between them.

Of course, he was with Jody, and there was nothing awkward or silent about her.

"The good thing about ridiculously expensive sports cars," she said as casually as if discussing the weather, "is that they can rush you from one side of a tropical island paradise to the other — fast."

"Not fast enough."

Jody nodded in agreement and tapped her foot impatiently. She slid her hand over his on the gearshift, and that felt nice. Really nice.

"Not too cold?" he asked. They had the air conditioning on to counter the condensation on the windshield, but even sitting there shirtless, he was still plenty warm inside.

Jody fanned herself with her hand. "Hot. Way too hot."

Which only ratcheted up his core temperature another few degrees.

He clenched his left hand around the steering wheel and subtly adjusted his pants. Every car on the road had slowed to a snail's pace in the rain, and he wanted to cuss out each and every one. If he didn't get home soon, he'd end up stopping at a motel just to avoid dying from lust.

But he didn't want a motel. He didn't want to screw Jody in the car. He wanted to lay her out on his bed and make slow, sweet love to her there. Or maybe hot, hard sex. Whichever. And as for her being human — well, he couldn't bring himself to care anymore. She was an exception, a one of a kind.

Jody sat with her eyes closed and a wicked look on her face that said she was imagining all the things he'd do to her — or what she'd do to him — the second they got home.

Home, his tiger murmured. *Home is wherever she is.*

Yeah, well, the bed was at Koa Point. He sped up, overtaking another car, then slowed behind a truck. This drive was going to kill him.

I wonder what she's thinking, his tiger said.

Slowly, tentatively, he reached out with his mind. Closely bonded shifters could read each other's thoughts, and destined mates could, too. Not that Cruz wanted to examine that possibility too closely — not in the state he was in. But he was dying to know what she was thinking — even a tiny little hint.

Her free hand slid over her thigh. Her lips moved. And gradually, an image formed in his mind. A feeling. The feeling that Jody might tiptoe her fingers up his thigh then creep in along the crotch of his pants.

He sucked in a deep breath. If she did that, he'd be tempted to unzip his pants to let her touch.

He concentrated a little harder, and the image grew clearer. How she'd slide a hand in and fist his cock. Stroke it. Tickle it. Explore from the thick base to the slit at the tip. Then she'd stroke just hard enough to—

"Stop," he grunted, as much to himself as to her.

Her eyes flew open. "What?"

He looked over and found her eyes hazy with lust. Wow. She really had been thinking along those lines.

"Stop thinking that." He shifted in the seat before the pressure in his dick killed him.

"Thinking what?" Her voice was all innocence, but her sidelong glance at his crotch gave her away.

He snorted. "Stop thinking about sex."

Like you haven't been thinking about it? his tiger pointed out.

She frowned. "You didn't like what we did?"

"I did, and you know it. I can't wait to... to..."

Her breath caught as he struggled for words.

"To what?" she asked.

He stared past the swishing wipers. Would Jody prefer him talking dirty or should he pretend to be a gentleman and find some polite euphemism for screwing her senseless?

Be direct, his tiger said. *She likes direct.*

So, bam — without a further second's deliberation, the words flew out of his mouth. "I can't wait to fuck you in my bed until we both come undone."

Her mouth fell open. Her nipples pebbled under the shirt that clung to her chest. Her hands trembled in her lap.

"Oh," she mumbled.

"Oh?"

She wiggled in her seat. "If there is such a thing as a verbally induced orgasm, I think I just had one."

A low, rumbly, satisfied sound came from his chest. It was incredible how Jody managed to push every one of his buttons. And they were still miles away from home.

She drew her knees up to her chest and watched the road quietly before whispering, "Say that again."

He couldn't hold back a choke of surprise and plucked at his pants. "You really are going to kill me, you know that?"

"Just once. Say it just once, and I promise to be a good girl."

"You're a minx, and you know it." He couldn't keep a smile off his face, though. "You're a minx, and I can't wait to fuck you in my bed until we both come undone."

She pursed her lips, not giving away anything. But the sugary scent of lust filled the car, so strong he nearly swerved.

A few minutes later, she was at it again. Thinking. Fantasizing. Filling his mind with all kinds of sensual plans. Like how he would lay her out on his big bed and thrust into her in one smooth stroke. Or how she would fall to her knees and give him the blow job he'd fantasized about. Or—

He growled, looking over. "Minx. Minx, minx, minx."

"Are you reading my mind or something?"

Something, he wanted to say. "It's pretty obvious," he said, hoping she didn't press him on it.

She didn't. Another minute of silence passed, and she started taking deep breaths. Really deep, loud, rattly breaths.

"Now what are you doing?" he demanded once they inched through the intersection at Ma'alaea.

"Ujjayi breathing."

"Ujjayi what?"

"Like in yoga. I'm trying to center myself."

He shifted up a gear as traffic thinned again. "Center yourself?"

"You know, to transport my mind to a different plane. Like those monks who levitate."

"I don't know much about monks."

She laughed. "Would never have guessed."

Cruz grinned. Yes, he couldn't wait to get home, but this was kind of fun, too. Jody made everything fun. Even nearly perishing from desire.

"Is it working?" he asked, going with the flow for a change.

"Nope. You ever try it?"

"Levitating? No. Though my feet might have left the ground for a minute or two while you were posing. What the hell were you thinking about?"

She gulped water from her bottle and offered it to him before answering casually. "I was thinking about giving you the blow job of your life."

Cruz choked back the water that caught halfway down his throat, nearly spitting all over the dashboard.

Jody put up her hands and grinned. "Sorry. I promise to shut up for the rest of the drive."

"That, I have to see," he said, not quite concealing the chuckle in his voice.

"Watch me." Jody crossed her arms and shut her mouth tight.

He wondered how long she would last, and the funny thing was, that was kind of fun, too.

She opened her mouth at least three more times throughout the interminable drive but snapped it shut each time. He leaned closer, anticipating her words, but she just crossed her arms more tightly and looked away.

"You know you want to say something," he teased.

Her lips folded inward in a totally sexy way. Of course, anything she did at that point made him think of sex, so now he was the guilty one.

He sped down the road, weaving in and out of slower traffic — in other words, every other car on the road — until finally, finally! — he could take his foot off the pedal and let the car coast down the driveway to Koa Point. Cruz grabbed his shirt but didn't put it on. Jody, meanwhile, straightened her shirt and bundled up the rest of her things before stepping out of the car. They both slammed the doors behind them and stood peering out from under the roof of the garage.

"Gonna have to run for it," he murmured, watching the pelting rain.

She laughed. "I'm getting good at that. You, too."

He had to work hard to hide his smile, but when she sidled up beside him and ran a hand up his chest, his mood became serious again. Where was all this leading? He was falling for her, hard and fast. Breaking every cardinal rule of a warrior who didn't mess around, especially not with his heart.

She took both his hands, telling him she wasn't messing around either, and whispered, "Hey."

He took a deep breath and rested his forehead against hers. "Hey."

Her chest rose and fell in time with his breaths, and the chill that had started to creep into him in the air-conditioned car gave way to her body's warmth.

"Am I allowed to think dirty thoughts now?" she whispered.

He nodded slowly, making both their heads bob. "Now is good. But first, are you ready to run?"

"Ready."

He didn't count down and shout, *Go!* but Jody took off across the lawn the second he did. She sprinted along, laughing like it was the most fun she'd had all week. And it was fun, he had to admit. That build of anticipation. The sloppy, splashy run through the grass and mud. They raced down the winding path and over the footbridge to his place. The forest canopy closed overhead without blocking the rain — it just made the downpour jump from leaf to oversize leaf on the way down. They both rushed into the shelter of the living room and stood panting, looking out at the rain.

"Almost there," Cruz said, gesturing up to his bedroom.

Jody gripped his hand and stared at him. "You weren't kidding, huh?"

He shook his head. No, he hadn't been kidding about wanting her in his bed. And yes, he wanted to lead her across the rope bridge to the platform that held his big, solitary bed. His private bedroom — though private was relative, since it had a roof and no walls, like the living room Jody had slept in for the past few nights.

"You sure?" she whispered.

See? His tiger hummed inside. *She gets it. She gets* us *and how important this place is.*

He looked around. "Well, since this room looks like it got hit by a tornado. . . "

She play-slapped his arm. "It's not that messy."

It was, but he didn't care. Not about the towel she'd left hanging over the chair, nor about yesterday's clothes in a heap on the floor, and not even about the magazine turned upside down halfway under the couch. All he cared about was her.

She bit her lip, growing serious again. Was she getting second thoughts about all this or giving him a last chance to opt out? "So, you ready to show a girl a good time?"

An instant later, he towed her along, rushing up the connecting platform to the shelter of his bedroom above. Then he hit the brakes and gave her a moment to take it all in.

"This is amazing," Jody breathed.

It *was* amazing. The roof stood out a good three feet wider than the floor. And with water free-falling from all four edges to the ground far below, he had the feeling of being out in the tropical rainstorm while staying perfectly dry — at least, apart from the water they'd carried in with them, now dripping slowly down their bodies in the most sensual way.

"You're amazing," he whispered, letting his shirt drop from his hand as he prowled toward her.

No more waiting. No more wishing, his tiger growled.

The scent of lust spiked as Jody backed away with that vixen grin.

"You're shivering," he murmured.

"Not inside, I'm not." She backed up another step. Not escaping so much as teasing, and he knew it. She peeked behind her, stopping near the edge of the platform. Out of space.

A moment of truth. They were finished playing games. It was now or never, and he waited for her fear to show.

But Jody just let her chin jut a little, showing him — and maybe herself — she wasn't about to back down now.

"Cruz," she whispered, holding out her hand.

He held his out, too, but they were still a foot apart. "Be sure you want this, Jody. Be sure."

He needed to hear it from her. They were moving awfully fast, and while sleeping together had the potential to complicate his wonderfully uncomplicated life, it was even more momentous for her. He was a shifter. A recluse who lived in a tree house. A man with far too many ghosts in his closet. Did she really want to tangle with a guy like him?

His outstretched fingers trembled a tiny bit.

"I want this, Cruz. God, do I want this." As if to cement the point, she yanked her shirt off and let it drop to the floor.

Cruz stared, exploring every inch of her body with his eyes. His gaze swept over her breasts and belly before stopping at the barely there thong that was the only thing she still wore.

Heaven, his tiger murmured. *I'm in heaven.*

Jody slid her hands to her hips until she found the sides of the thong and waited. "Do you want me to take this off, or do you want to do it yourself?"

Cruz didn't answer. Instead, he pounced. Really pounced. One second he was a foot away, and the next, he had her on the bed. He came over her, covering her mouth with his, claiming everything he touched.

Jody's eyes were wide and startled, but they were delighted, too.

"I'm all wet," she squeaked.

"I like you wet," he said between kisses.

Those idiots from Elements had one thing right. Jody and water went perfectly together. Water became her, somehow. It brought out her inner shine, her one-of-a-kind spunk.

Opening her mouth, she welcomed him in. She wrapped her arms around him and whimpered, driving him wild.

Mine. She is mine. My mate forever, his tiger growled.

Cruz had never felt as powerful — or as powerless. He plundered her mouth with his tongue and touched her like... like... well, like a pirate. But Jody egged him on, assuring him she wanted to be plundered, at least by this privateer. She already had her legs wrapped around him, her shoulders thrust back, her hands threaded through his hair.

When he'd touched her in the car, he'd managed to keep cool — mostly. But now, he was a fumbling teenager, unable to decide where to begin. So he tried to touch her everywhere, which didn't really work. He couldn't even get his pants off — and maybe a good thing, too, because he wasn't that much of a brute. He'd told Jody he'd fuck her until they both came undone, and that meant pleasuring her first.

She wants to be taken. She wants to be ours, his tiger yowled.

The irresistible image of sinking his teeth into her neck to deliver the mating bite flashed through his mind.

He shook his head hard. Humans didn't know about mates. *We are not taking it that far. This is just our first time. So don't ruin things by trying. Got it?*

Got it, got it, the beast huffed.

That gave him just enough mind space to get his shit together and love Jody the way she deserved. The way he and only he could deliver, unlike any other man, anywhere, anytime.

Hey! Why did you stop kissing? his tiger complained.

Jody's tight grip on his hair asked the same thing.

Not stopping. Just redirecting, he assured the tiger.

Ah, the beast sighed as Cruz started moving down her body. *Now I see your plan.*

Jody moaned, moving beneath him as he reached her collarbone. Her hands played with his hair, giving him free rein.

He trailed a line of kisses down her chest, getting high on her sweet, wild rose scent. Loving the way her body surged under his, leading him to her breasts. On a sharp inhale, her nipple came up to his mouth in open invitation. He took it as gently as he could then worked it harder, plucking and sucking until her moans were louder than the sound of the rain.

Just for you, buddy, he told his tiger, running his tongue over the bumps of her areola.

Just for you, my ass, the beast chuckled back.

He chuckled, making Jody mumble, "What's so funny, mister?"

That was his Jody, always a minx, even when she was at his mercy. Did nothing daunt this woman?

"Funny is me barely able to keep my head screwed on straight."

She liked that one; he could tell by the chuckle in her chest. A chuckle that made her breasts wiggle, prompting him to turn his attention there once more. He gathered the soft flesh together and dragged his tongue over her nipple again and again. Then he switched to the other side, circling and pinching until her nipples peaked so high, they popped right into his mouth.

"Oh..." she panted, arching her body. "Cruz..."

It had been a long time since he'd heard anyone say his name that way. Not a barked order or a frustrated sigh. Not a cold dismissal or an intimidated whisper. Just needy. Happy. Eager.

A twinge of fear went through him, but he chased it away. He could hurt this woman, and she could hurt him. In the heart, not the body.

We can trust her. We need to trust her, his tiger said.

He shifted his weight and crept lower, tracing the ridges of her centerline. Her belly button tempted him to linger, but the scent of her core called, and he dropped lower.

"Yes..." she moaned, spreading her legs.

Jody. He wanted to sing her name the way she sang his. *Jody, Jody, Jody.*

He ran a hand down her folds and breathed deeply, savoring her scent.

"More," she cried, wiggling under him.

He spread a hand on her belly, stilling her, letting himself savor the moment. "Been dreaming of this every night."

"Me, too. Believe me, me too."

Another moment to preserve in his mental album, but Cruz figured he shouldn't push his luck. Not with his woman offering herself up this way. And since she was...

He pulled back, lifted her hips off the mattress, and hooked her legs over his shoulders. *Go big or go home.*

The second his tongue touched her softest, most hidden flesh, Jody made a choked sound and thrust her hips up. He licked more boldly, letting her get used to the feel of his mouth on her. And judging by the sounds she made and the tightening of her thighs, she was all on board.

"Oh... Yes... Oh..."

He licked in one long line, closing his eyes. Up and down the length of her in one long, delicious swipe. Then he stopped at her clit and circled the tight bud.

Jody thrust against him in an unmistakable rhythm, making him lick lower. Deeper. Tasting her until she was wild with pleasure, and he was, too. When her muscles coiled all around him, he pressed a thumb to her clit, circling there while his fingers pushed deep inside.

"Yes… So close…"

He was close to exploding, too, and his cock hadn't even seen any action yet.

He flicked his fingers and sucked at the same time, making her shatter in ecstasy.

"Don't stop…"

He wouldn't dream of stopping. Not before he'd milked every last drop of her orgasm. And when he was done…

He grinned. When he was done, he'd bring her to her next orgasm. And the next and the next until her mind was blank of anything but him.

Jody bucked, gyrated, then slowly settled on the mattress again. He rested his head on her belly as it heaved with wild, panting breaths.

"God, Cruz…" She patted him on the back.

He grinned and soaked it all in. The heat of her body. The shell-shocked satisfaction in her voice. The scent of his own desire intertwined with hers. The peace in his soul. Human or not, it didn't matter any more. Jody was Jody, and she was his.

My destined mate, his tiger hummed.

Slowly, he kissed his way up her body again until he was at her mouth. A second after Jody cupped his face and kissed him deep, her eyes flew open. He tilted his head as she gave a tentative swipe of her tongue.

Holy shit, her expression said. "Is that… Is that me?"

He broke into a huge grin. Man, he loved how she showed her feelings like so many signal flags. He smothered her in another kiss then let go with a little pop. "Yes, that is you on my tongue."

His tiger preened and pranced in delight, knowing he possessed even that tiny, fleeting part of her. Her taste. Her heavenly taste.

"You look so proud of yourself, you big lug. Just wait until I get payback." She licked her lips.

His dick hardened in his pants.

"Speaking of which," Jody murmured, reaching for his zipper.

He dropped down over her and rocked his head back and forth against her chest. "You are amazing, you know that?"

She laughed. "No, I'm not. It's just that my brain stopped working. The fucking me senseless thing is working, in case you didn't notice. But there's one more thing..."

Her hand crept inside his pants — the sodden, soaked-from-the-rain pants he wanted off, pronto — and fisted his cock.

"Yeah," she murmured, shifting for better access. "One more thing..."

Chapter Thirteen

Jody held her breath and reached deeper, determined not to lose her momentum. The *senseless* part was true because part of her brain really had turned off. Her filters had shut down a while ago, and whatever she felt, she said.

Like, *I was thinking about giving you the blow job of your life.* Or saying, *just wait until I get payback* while licking her lips.

But, heck. She wasn't exaggerating. She was just feeling a little, er... bold. Not just bold as in, assertive around a guy, because that had never been a problem. Rather, bold as in assertive around *this* guy, who could probably kill a tiger with his bare hands.

The pouring rain might have contributed to her mood — seeing, hearing, *feeling* a tropical storm had a way of doing that to a girl. That, and she had come twice already — another excuse for why her tongue had loosened so much. But the second she closed her hands around his cock, she clammed up for a few seconds because, wow. Maybe he wouldn't fit inside her. Not that she wasn't going to give it her best shot.

Cruz's eyelids drifted shut as she slid her fist up and down. His breath hitched, and he shifted his hips to get closer.

"Um, help?" she murmured, struggling to remove his rain-soaked pants.

His eyes snapped open as if he'd popped out of a dream. "Here I was thinking you could do anything."

"Almost anything. But these pants..."

Together, they worked them down, and Cruz kicked them to the floor.

"Now you're the sloppy one," she pointed out.

"Don't care." He shifted into position above her in a way that didn't broker any doubts. His face was a mask of seriousness, as if making love to her was something he had to get exactly, precisely right.

Slowly, she dragged her hand down his length — a long, mouthwatering ride. When she pulled back up, the return trip seemed twice as long, his cock twice as hard. She circled her fingers down for a little variety and tugged on the foreskin just enough to make Cruz groan.

"Minx."

"You love it, mister. Now hush."

He snuck his hand between their bodies to cover hers, helping her set the perfect pace. Slow on the upstroke, faster on the downstroke. Their eyes locked while their hands moved, and she felt drawn in. Connected. Part of him, almost.

Cruz's throat bobbed with a gulp. Did he feel the same thing? For all that they'd already shared, it felt like the most blissfully erotic moment of her life.

Note to self, she thought. *Keep eyes open during sex.*

As soon as she settled into the perfect pace, Cruz reached lower, making her groan.

"Shh," he murmured. "Soon."

It was crazy, how badly her body needed his. He touched her, drawing a line down her folds at the same pace she moved over him. And damn, that was even better. Slow in one direction, a little faster in the other, with a little circling motion that she mimicked at the tip of his cock. She tipped her head and watched for a moment, unconsciously licking her lips.

Which might have been the catalyst for Cruz to suddenly reach for the dresser drawer and grab a condom. He had it on in a flash, then pushed her legs wider with one knee. With one hand, he pulled her arms over her head, pinning them firmly to the mattress.

She pulled in a rattly breath. This was going to be so good.

I swear it will be, his eyes said. His *glowing* eyes, which just went to show how out of her mind she was.

When Cruz dragged his cock along her body in long, deliberate strokes, she gasped. And when he stopped at her entrance, she held her breath.

"You're good, right?" He tilted his head, giving her one final way out.

She gave a curt nod instead of making a pathetic mess of herself by begging, *Please, yes, please,* and wrapped both legs around his waist.

Then she moaned — almost howled — as he slid in with one smooth stroke.

"Yes," she cried a second later, hovering on the razor's edge of pleasure and pain.

He inhaled so deeply, she could hear it over the sound of pouring rain. He withdrew slowly, then slid forward again. Her head flopped back — so much for eye contact. But the burn was overwhelming, and if she didn't block out some sensory input — like the woodsy smell of the thatched roof above, the splash of rain over leaves outside, or the look of total concentration on Cruz's face — she'd lose what little composure she had left.

So she let her head tip back and gasped with each successive thrust. And when Cruz dropped lower to kiss and nip her neck, she angled her head, silently begging for more.

"So perfect. So beautiful," Cruz murmured. Not so much to her as to himself — or maybe to that alter ego he seemed to have muted conversations with from time to time. He found the perfect spot at the curve of her neck and suckled while he drove into her at the same relentless pace.

Jody pulled her legs higher around his waist and clenched hard, making him groan. A drop of rain — or sweat? — landed on her chest.

"So good. . . "

She arched and bucked against him, driving the inner tension higher.

His teeth were bared, his brow furrowed.

"Harder. . . " She arched into him, meeting every thrust, straining for more.

He took both her hands in one of his and lowered the other to her breast, making little black spots dance in her eyes. Two hard strokes later, he dropped his hand to her clit, making her buck.

"Yes... Yes..."

She clenched her inner muscles and hugged his body with her legs. Her breath came in raspy rushes in time to Cruz's thrusts, and his was hot and heavy by her ear. Every muscle in his body flexed as he reared higher, locking eyes with her again.

Look at me, his expression demanded. *Watch as I drive you totally over the edge. Like I promised — I am going to fuck you senseless until we both come undone.*

The longer she gazed into those golden eyes, the more the nuance became clear to her. Cruz wanted her to watch *him* come undone. He wanted to share that with her, to open up that much more of his soul.

"Yes," she whispered, urging him on.

His hands tightened around hers. He pumped harder. Harder. Faster. Muttering under his breath as the steady pace became a sprint. His jaw jutted, and his eyes blazed.

"Oh... Yes..." Jody cried, keeping her eyes open and her legs wrapped tight.

His thick cock stretched her, pistoning into her again and again. He rolled his hips, finding a whole new spot to push against, then rocked harder, slamming into her at an angle guaranteed to drive her over the edge.

"Yes—"

Her *yes* cut off in her throat when Cruz buried himself deep and groaned with his release. Her high hit half a breath later, and she clawed at the air. Everything blurred and exploded in her mind. It was like flying off the edge of the biggest, craziest wave she'd ever ridden and getting swirled around in its foamy wake. Like hanging on by the skin of her teeth, refusing to miss one second of wild pleasure before submitting to the lull after the wave.

Then she went as boneless as a clump of seaweed tossed up on the beach. Cruz lowered himself onto her body, distributing his weight carefully so as not to crush her. She reached around his shoulders and locked him into a hug. Her legs hugged him, too, and he hugged her back. He let his hands drift over her hair and skin as he whispered words she could barely hear. Low and garbled but happy. Undeniably happy.

She grinned. Cruz Khala — tough guy extraordinaire — had a lot more heart than he let on. Maybe even a sensitive soul.

She chuckled and spoke softly. "So, tigers don't purr, huh?"

He stiffened a little as if on guard against what she might say next.

"What about tough guy bodyguards?" she went on. "Are they allowed to purr? Because I'm pretty sure that's what I'm hearing."

He exhaled and let his muscles go loose again. "I think that's Keiki."

She laughed, and he did, too. "Right. Keiki. Sure." The calico was nowhere in sight, but she'd let Cruz have his excuse.

She was a mess, as was the bed, and she was afraid Cruz would roll away and end this quiet bliss. But instead of rolling, he slid sideways, dropped the condom beside the bed, and came face-to-face with her. He blinked once, twice, then started nuzzling her with his cheeks and chin. The world's most thorough nuzzle that rubbed his scent into her skin.

Jody rubbed back like a bird in a timeless mating ritual. Or maybe even like two mighty felines who nuzzled and growled their devotion to each other before settling back and lording over their shared domain.

She was sticky. Wet. Her hair, a matted mess. But she'd never felt this good.

Cruz broke off slowly and held her snugly against his chest.

"Hey," she whispered, kissing his skin.

"Hey," he replied softly.

She closed her eyes and imagined waking up this way every morning.

He tightened his hug. Was he imagining the same thing?

She sighed and wiggled closer, determined to enjoy the present. The soft play of his hands over her shoulders, the puff of his breath on her hair. The background music of an island awash in cleansing rain.

Minutes passed. She could have rested there a full hour. Days, even.

"I love it here," she cooed. "So peaceful."

"It was until you arrived," he joked.

She popped up to look at him. "Until you brought me here, you mean. I think this was all part of your master plan."

He laughed outright. "I wish I were smart enough to have that as my master plan. I'm improvising, honey."

She kissed him, and the snappy remark on the tip of her tongue vanished from her mind.

"Whoa," she said a few minutes later. "You really are purring."

Cruz laughed. "That's Keiki. Really. Look."

A soft thump sounded as Keiki jumped into view and trotted over to Cruz, who scratched her under the chin. Keiki plucked at the sheets with her tiny claws and purred louder.

"Aren't you a cutie?" Jody said, coming up on one elbow. She waited a second then delivered the punch line. "And the kitten's not half bad either."

Cruz swatted her with a pillow, then chased her across the mattress and pinned her under his body again. "Who are you calling cute, lady?"

He tried to look menacing, but it didn't work. Especially not when Keiki jumped on his shoulder and looked down at her, too.

"You," she giggled, flailing with no hope of getting free. Not that she wanted to budge. "And you're cute, too," she assured Keiki.

The kitten purred, kneading Cruz's muscled shoulder like a rug.

Cruz shrugged Keiki aside and flopped down beside Jody, spooning her to his chest — really holding her like he didn't want to let go. Keiki, meanwhile, pranced over and peered at the two of them from up close.

"You're the queen of this place, aren't you?" She chuckled, scratching the kitten under the chin.

"That, she is."

Jody laughed. "I think I've figured you and Silas out. Especially you and your thing for cats."

Cruz went still. Very still.

"Yep," she breezed on. "Some crazy old widow died and left the estate to her cats, and you and Silas are the caretakers. So the cats are actually the ones in charge." She laughed. "What do you think of my theory?"

Cruz let out a long exhale and kissed the top of her head. "I think your theory is as crazy as you are. Now, be quiet and listen." He gestured toward the pouring rain outside.

She closed her eyes and tuned in — not so much to the relentless drumming of rain but to the beat of his heart. Keiki curled into the space by her stomach, purring and plucking at the sheets as Jody petted her head.

"Pretty perfect," she sighed.

Cruz ran his fingers down her arm, getting her all heated up again. It truly felt perfect, especially now that she was a free woman again. She had the rest of the afternoon and all night to do whatever she wanted. Whatever she and Cruz wanted to do, that was.

"Pretty perfect," Cruz agreed, tickling the side of her breast.

Chapter Fourteen

Cruz woke slowly, reluctantly, shooing away a fly that tickled his temple. His eyes opened a crack then fluttered shut again. He and Jody had made love for most of the night, and now, the world was at peace. *His* world was at peace, anyway. The rain had stopped, and the only sound in the forest was that of dripping leaves. In another hour or two, the morning sun's rays would pierce the sky, but he still had plenty of time to snooze.

Jody's chest rose and fell in the snug curve of his arms, lulling him back to sleep. The only thing she was wearing were those bangles of hers, and God, her skin was so soft. He brushed a strand of her hair from her cheek and sniffed. The forest was rich with that special after-rain scent — the scent of something old and rotten slipping away and something new thriving in its place. But right in front of his nose was the best fragrance ever — the scent of Jody with a little bit of him mixed in. The scent of recent sex and the deep sense of contentment that followed.

It was perfect. Even his inner tiger was quiet, lazily curling his tail.

Yes, everything was perfect — except for that damn fly, pestering him. He scratched his head and squeezed his eyes shut, yet the tickle persisted.

Cruz. A faint voice sounded in his mind. *Cruz...*

He groaned quietly. That wasn't a fly. It was Silas, calling into his head. Man — couldn't a guy sleep in for the first time in years? That's what civilians did, right?

He caught himself at the thought. This had to be the first time he'd felt like a civilian in... in, well, ever. The first time he wanted to let his guard down and relax. The first time...

He took a deep breath and wrapped his hand around Jody's. The first time for a lot of things, like relishing the flutter in his heart and the warm glow in his soul.

Not now, he grumbled back at Silas.

Now, the dragon shifter insisted, using his ranking officer's voice. *It's about McGraugh.*

Cruz wrinkled his nose. His informant, McGraugh, was dead. That news was days old, and it had cut him to the bone. But this was not a time to mourn. It was a time to revel in the bright side of life.

Do we have to talk about it right now? He sighed.

For once, he didn't want to wallow in misery. He wanted to sleep in and give Jody's *believing* theory a try. *Life is beautiful. Love is beautiful. You just have to believe.*

He shifted his chin over her shoulder and tucked his legs under her body, keeping her nice and close.

Silas's voice was a grim monotone in his mind. *It's not that McGraugh died, but how.*

Cruz lifted his head from the pillow. What the hell did that mean?

Come and talk, already, Silas barked.

Cruz made a face. So much for a nice, quiet morning. Slowly, reluctantly, he backed away from Jody, covering her with the sheet as he went. He sat on the edge of the bed for a full minute, looking at her.

"Mmm," Jody mumbled, refusing to release his hand.

He kissed her on the shoulder and took in her sleepy smile, the satisfied curl of her body.

Perfect, his tiger hummed.

Cruz! Silas barked.

"I'll be right back," he whispered to Jody, forcing himself to move.

He got halfway across the rope bridge to ground level before pausing. Normally, he'd pad across the estate in tiger form — the quickest, easiest means in the dark. But with Jody there, he should wait until he was out of sight.

But I want her to see me, his tiger protested. *I want her to know me.*

His imagination ran away with a dozen impossible visions. Like Jody leaning over him and hugging his tiger body, cooing at how soft his fur was. Or Jody grinning wildly while she petted him under the chin. Or how nice it would be to swim in tight circles in his rock pool, making space for Jody to paddle beside him.

She'd make a great tiger, his inner beast hummed.

He snorted. *Sometimes I think she'd make an even better mermaid.*

Whatever. His tiger shrugged. *As long as she's mine.*

Shouldn't he hate her — or hate himself for falling for her? But he couldn't. He just couldn't. Not with every instinct telling him she was the one.

He looked at Jody one second longer, then stepped into the darkness and shifted. A quick, effortless shift that indicated how ready his tiger was for some time on four feet.

Just one more second near her, the beast begged.

And damn it, without thinking, he set off on a loop of his place, placing his paws carefully so as not to make a sound. He brushed his striped sides along the central trunk of the tree, marking the turf as his. Then he leaped up on a thick branch and climbed higher, reveling in the power of the muscles rippling under his skin. He ascended higher still, watching his sleeping lover the whole time. When he reached the topmost platform of his tree house, he lay down quietly and looked down at her.

My mate. My destined mate, his tiger hummed.

He lowered his muzzle to his two front paws and watched her. God, he could do that for hours. Just watch Jody sleeping peacefully with a smile playing across her lips. A smile he'd put there.

He rubbed his chin against his paws, tilting his head left and right. He was slipping into dangerous territory, because it was all too easy to picture nuzzling Jody — Jody, in tiger form as if they were mated and she had become a shifter, too. He could teach her all about being a tiger. That would be nice.

Really nice. And Jody could teach him all the things she knew about, like laughing and smiling and embracing life.

His chest rose in a deep sigh, and he couldn't tell whether the ache welling up inside was hope or the first warning signs of impending heartbreak.

Cruz! Silas hollered into his mind.

It might as well have been the ghosts of his family admonishing him. *How can you betray us by falling for a human?*

He snapped his head up and growled. It was Silas, not a ghost, but that was bad enough.

Coming, damn it. Coming.

The magic of the moment was gone, but he kept his eyes on Jody's sleeping form as he leaped from branch to branch, stealthily making his way to the ground. After one final look back, he set off in earnest.

Footsteps sounded behind him, and he whirled with his heart in his throat. For a second, his overeager imagination made that sound Jody, following him. Accepting him. Trusting him...

But the footsteps were too light to be Jody's, and when he looked down, he spotted Keiki. The kitten had taken off once things heated up in bed, but obviously, she hadn't gone far.

Keiki scampered up and pranced alongside like a warrior maiden insisting on joining the army's march. Most house cats freaked out at the sight of his tiger, but this little kitten seemed to think she was as big as him.

Carefully, so as not to bowl Keiki over, Cruz butted heads in greeting the way his dad used to do with him, then walked on at a slower pace — partly so the kitten could keep up and partly because he was in no rush to hear whatever bad news Silas was sure to share.

You can come if you behave, he chuffed at Keiki.

Funny, his dad used to say that, too, whenever Cruz had tagged along, so many years ago. Funny, too, that the thought made him smile instead of bringing back all the pain.

Keiki mimicked his low, long strides. Her shoulder blades slid smoothly with each light step, and Cruz couldn't help chuckling a little inside. Hunter liked to say that Keiki had the nose of a bear, but Cruz swore she had the soul of a tiger — just in a tiny, calico package. She even flicked her tail in time to his.

Whatever bounce Keiki helped put back in Cruz's step disappeared as he approached the meeting house. Silas stood at the edge of the building, arms folded over his chest, glaring at Cruz every step of the way.

"What took you so long?"

Cruz replied with a low grumble of warning. Silas might rank highest among the shifters of Koa Point, but every self-respecting tiger had the right to show his moods.

It's five in the morning, he snarled.

"Eight o'clock on the mainland," Silas shot back. "Ella just called."

Ella, a desert fox shifter, had been the only woman in their Special Forces unit. Nowadays, she lived in Arizona and worked for the Twin Moon wolf pack, contracting out as an investigator on the side.

Spy is more like it, he remembered Ella chuckling.

He wondered who Ella was spying on now, and for whom.

It better be important, Cruz grumbled with another look at the clock.

"It is." Silas reached for a steaming mug of coffee. "Are you going to keep prowling around like that or are you going to come in and talk?"

Cruz preferred prowling, but Silas looked awfully serious. And now that he'd come all this way, he might as well find out what was going on. Slowly, painfully, his tiger gave way to his human form. He reared up on two legs and ground his teeth a few times as his tiger fangs receded and his shoulder blades flattened into position on his back.

Keiki gave a plaintive meow and pranced around, trying to shift, too. Then she gave up and butted her head against Cruz's leg. He scooped her up and ducked under the roof of the meeting house, setting the kitten down long enough to pull on one of the spare pairs of pants they kept in a corner so as not to lounge around naked after shifting. Silas, ever the proper one, had made that rule ages ago, and a good thing, too, now that there were women living at Koa Point.

Silas pushed a pot of coffee, cup, saucer, and cream toward him. Everything the dragon shifter did, he did with style. Cruz poured cream into the saucer and let Keiki lap away while he brought the mug of black coffee to his lips. So much for sleeping in.

Silas's eyes narrowed on him, and his nose twitched. "You slept with Jody, didn't you?"

Cruz kept sipping, refusing to make eye contact. He didn't interfere with Silas's private life, and he damn well expected Silas to do the same.

"Damn it. What were you thinking?"

Cruz stirred his coffee slowly, watching it swirl around. Sleeping with Jody hadn't involved thinking so much as doing. Reacting to the incredible pull she had on him.

"You can mess around with anyone you want but—"

He growled. "Not messing around."

Silas's eyes went wide at the admission. "Listen to yourself. You know you can't be a reliable bodyguard if you're emotionally involved."

"I'm not emotionally involved," he snarled.

Silas arched an eyebrow, reading his mind. "No?"

Cruz clenched his fists. Okay, so he might be getting involved.

"What did Ella say?" he asked, steering Silas back to the point.

Silas scowled deeply. "She called to report that McGraugh wasn't just murdered. He was killed by a vampire."

Cruz's blood ran cold. "Vampire?"

Even Keiki looked up, sensing his demeanor change. Vampires were as sick as any sick bastard could be. And with their supernatural strength and speed, they were incredibly hard to kill.

"She's sure?" Cruz demanded.

Silas nodded. "She's sure. It was covered up as a slashing, but Ella found the puncture marks."

Cruz's mind spun, trying to put it all together as Silas did the same aloud.

"First, McGraugh provided misleading information that had you believing Jody was a target..."

Cruz gripped the edge of the counter, remembering how close he'd come to pulling the trigger.

"Then McGraugh denied wrongdoing and swore to us he'd get to the bottom of it..."

Cruz put up his hand. "Are you saying a vampire killed McGraugh before he could uncover the source of the false information?"

Silas stirred his coffee slowly, and the rich scent filled the air. "I suspect the vampire was the one providing false information."

"Why would McGraugh trust a vampire?"

Shifters and vampires usually kept apart — miles apart. Vampires stuck to cities; most shifters preferred quieter places, and on the rare occasions when the two clashed... Well, the body count tended to be high.

Silas's frown deepened. "The question is why anyone would want to target Jody in the first place."

Cruz pushed away from the counter and paced, muttering the whole time. He'd find whoever that was and rip them limb from limb. He'd track them to the end of the earth and make sure those bastards got what they deserved. He'd—

"See what I mean?"

Cruz's head snapped up at Silas's remark. "See what?"

"You're emotionally involved."

"And you wouldn't get emotional when vampires are involved?" The second the words were out of Cruz's mouth, he made a face. Silas never got emotional...except when Moira was involved. Which made his mind spin in an entirely new direction. "Moira."

"What about her?" Silas's voice was dangerously low.

"She's behind the whole Elements line, right?"

Silas's chin dipped in a reluctant *yes.*

"Would she stoop to hiring a vampire?"

Silas paced to the edge of the building and looked out into the night. A hint of electric energy still hung in the air, and the palm trees swayed uncertainly.

"Obviously, I'm not a good judge of what Moira is capable of." Silas's shoulders slumped.

Keiki tilted her head at Cruz, asking if she should pad over to comfort the dragon shifter.

"Not sure if that will help, buddy," he murmured, scratching her between the ears.

Another gloomy minute ticked by, and Cruz found himself yearning for Jody's soft voice and sunny smile. A few minutes without her and he was as grouchy as ever instead of blissfully blank-minded the way he'd been in bed.

Life is beautiful. Love is beautiful. You just have to believe, Jody had said.

Once upon a time, he'd found that impossible to believe. But with Jody in his life, believing seemed easier than carrying around his own personal storm cloud all the time.

"I'm just glad Jody is finished," he muttered out loud. No more Richard, no more need for her to endure a job she hated. She could send the money to her family, get back to surfing, and—

Then it struck him. What would she do now that the modeling job was done?

His tiger snarled and lashed its tail. *Can't let her leave. Can't let her go.*

Silas whirled. "What do you mean, she's done?"

Cruz leaned back, crossing his arms. "She finished her contract with that last photo shoot. She's done with Elements."

Silas stalked closer. "How can she be done? What about the Spirit Stone?"

Cruz pushed forward, bristling. "That was just a hunch, and the manager couldn't get the jewel he wanted in time. So I'm guessing our Spirit Stone theory was wrong."

Silas stared at him. "Wait a second. No sapphire?"

Cruz scratched his brow, remembering Richard yell out to Jody as the storm broke.

Wait, Jody. We can get that gem, after all...

That doesn't mean it's a Spirit Stone, his tiger pointed out. *No need to mention that to Silas.*

But he couldn't lie to Silas. The man was like a brother to him.

We could do a bonus session. I'll pay you extra, Richard had said.

"Damn Spirit Stones are more trouble than they're worth," Cruz grumbled.

"If they get into the wrong hands, they'll be more than trouble. They could be a disaster for us all."

Cruz hung his head. If the gem Richard mentioned was a Spirit Stone, it meant Drax, the most powerful dragon lord of all, would be hot on its tail, too.

Drax. Moira. Vampires. How had Jody gotten sucked into all this? He thumped a fist onto the countertop, making poor Keiki jump. He hurried to comfort her then muttered under his breath.

"The product manager did say something about one more session if Jody agreed."

"One more session — with a jewel?" Silas stalked closer, his eyes glowing red.

Cruz barely refrained from shoving him back. "A jewel we can't be sure is a Spirit Stone. And only if Jody agrees."

"She has to agree. You know the power of the Spirit Stones."

Cruz frowned. He'd witnessed the power of one firsthand. The Earthstone had made the ground shake and set an entire cliff toppling into the sea — and with it, an enemy who would have used the stone's powers for his own foul means. The Lifestone had sensed the evil in the heart of a woman who dared steal it and had killed her outright. The same stone — a ruby — hadn't harmed Nina, its rightful owner, but damn. Cruz didn't want to imagine the power the Waterstone might wield. Could it set off a tsunami or start a tropical storm?

"Jody doesn't have to do anything," he snarled. "It's too risky to involve her."

Silas glared. "We can't risk letting the jewel go before we verify that it is — or isn't — a Spirit Stone. If Moira gets her hands on it — or worse, Drax..." He trailed off, shaking his head. "We need Jody to do the extra session."

"Are you nuts? I am not letting her get more mixed up in this than she already was. Not with the possibility of vampires or Spirit Stones — or worse, Drax. Listen to yourself, Silas. It's too dangerous."

"We could all go. You, me, and Kai. We'll protect her."

A low snarl rumbled from Cruz's chest as his tiger protested. *I protect her. No one else!*

But that was selfish and arrogant, and he knew it. If he could round up a platoon of elite soldiers to protect Jody, he would. And yes, he, Silas, Kai, and the other shifters at Koa Point were the cream of the crop when it came to a fighting elite. But better still would be to avoid putting Jody in danger at all.

"Who says she wouldn't need protecting from the Waterstone, Silas? You know how unpredictable the Spirit Stones can be."

"Jody knows water. She's perfect."

That was bullshit, and Cruz knew it. There was no predicting how a Spirit Stone might use — or abuse — its bearer.

"No way. She's not doing it."

"We need Jody."

"You need me to what?" a voice drifted from the edge of the building, making them both whirl around.

Cruz's heart jumped in glee at the sight of Jody, but his gut sank. How could he possibly put her at risk?

Jody stuck a hand on her hip and pinned Silas with her unwavering blue eyes. "You need me to what?"

Chapter Fifteen

Jody looked from one man to the other. Twenty minutes ago, she'd been sleeping like a baby. But gradually, a gnawing sense of dread set in along with bizarre dreams full of vampires and twisted, grotesque monsters she couldn't name. It was almost as if her father's crazy aunt Tilda had snuck into her mind and rattled off spooky stories — spooky enough to make Jody wake up in a cold sweat.

So she'd pulled on some clothes and set off in search of Cruz, hoping to work away those silly, unfounded fears. And there he was with Silas, standing over mugs of coffee so strong, she could smell it half a mile away — and looking like a fight was about to break out. What was wrong?

For a second, she'd even wondered if they had shared those crazy dreams. But big, tough soldier types focused on real threats, not dreams. So what could it be? Silas's eyes were glowing red embers. And as for Cruz — the soft, dreamy look she remembered was gone, replaced by something deadly and cold.

No way. She's not doing it, she'd overheard Cruz saying moments ago.

We need her, Silas had said.

Curiosity killed the cat, but she couldn't resist asking again. "Come on, already. You need me to what?"

Cruz opened his mouth, but Silas spoke first. "We need you to do that extra modeling session."

She stuck her hand up. "Whoa. Wait." The guy might be big and scary — really scary, with eyes that intense — but she didn't take orders from anyone. "I'm done modeling. I finished my contract."

"Cruz said you had an offer to model one more time."

The withering look Cruz shot at Silas would have knocked most men back a few steps, but Silas didn't blink.

"Listen, it's important," Silas said with just enough plea in his tone to make her believe him.

Cruz, meanwhile, beseeched her with his eyes. *Don't listen to him. You don't have to do anything.*

She crossed her arms. "Why is it so important?"

Even Cruz looked at Silas expectantly, as if he had no idea what might come out of his boss's mouth.

And just like that, the fire went out of Silas's eyes. He gazed off into the distance, looking wearier than ever. The man wasn't accustomed to being put on the spot, and he sure wasn't used to asking for help. That much was clear.

Jody tilted her head at him. Maybe it really was important. So she waited. And waited...

It was only when her hand brushed Cruz's shoulder that she realized she'd been inching toward him, yearning for contact. Whatever it was that had Silas so worked up worried Cruz, too. And in Cruz, *worry* translated to *angry*, which really wasn't good. Not when she'd finally gotten him to loosen up and smile.

When she touched his shoulder, he grasped her hand. The tight lines on his brow loosened slightly, and the twitch at the corner of his eye eased, too. Jody smiled and let everything but him fade away. The chirp of insects outside, the muted rumble of surf in the distance, and even Silas's forceful presence. Everything blurred to the background except Cruz and the warmth radiating from his hand to hers. His tight grip said everything he'd never say out loud. *I'm glad you're here. I loved our night together. I never wanted it to end.*

She never wanted it to end either. Before long, she and Cruz were going to have a long talk about what was happening between them and where they wanted it to go. But now was obviously not the time.

"I hate it when real life butts in when I'm having fun," she whispered.

A thin smile formed on Cruz's lips. "Yeah. Me, too. But maybe you just have to believe a little."

She grinned broadly and nearly leaned in for a kiss. But, oops — Silas was there, so she pulled away and settled for brushing her thumb over Cruz's cheek. His eyes closed as he leaned into her hand. And for a moment, he was at peace.

God, she loved being able to do that to him.

Then Silas cleared his throat, and Cruz scowled again. Jody stuck her hands on her hips and forced her attention back to the other man. The sooner she solved his problem — whatever it was — the sooner she and Cruz could go back to—

Erotic, breathless images flooded her mind, and Cruz's eyes flashed.

Jody caught her breath and hurried to reel the dirty thoughts back in.

"Minx," Cruz muttered under his breath, making her smile again.

"Have a seat," Silas said, pulling her attention across the room.

She pursed her lips. *Have a seat* was never an auspicious start to a conversation.

"Coffee?" Silas offered.

She stared at him. Apparently, Cruz wasn't the only one who tended to dance around big issues.

"Sure." She tapped impatiently on the counter as Silas moved around the kitchen.

"Milk?"

She made an exasperated sound. "Wow, you're just as bad as Cruz."

Silas's jaw dropped, and Cruz's brow furrowed again.

She poured her own coffee and waved at Silas. "Just get to the point already."

Silas blinked at her for a full minute before shooting Cruz one of those guy-to-guy looks. The kind buddies used to say, *Are you sure it's worth putting up with this chick?*

Cruz pulled his stool over to Jody's and looped an arm around the back, and she hid a grin. Yeah, she and Cruz definitely had to have a talk soon.

"You need me to do one more modeling session because..." she prompted Silas.

He paced around the room, darker than ever. The effect was slightly softened, though, by the sight of Keiki prancing along behind him, doing her best to imitate his grave steps.

It took Silas a full minute to answer, and he started with, "Miss Monroe."

She shook her head. "Jody."

Cruz brushed a hand over her back, bolstering her resolve as she faced down that simmering volcano of a man.

"Jody." Silas nodded stiffly. "You mentioned a jewel earlier. What do you know about it?"

Jody put down the cup she'd had halfway to her lips. That was not what she expected. Why was Silas interested in a jewel? And why did Cruz tense up at the mention of it?

She shrugged, trying to defuse the tension. "I don't know much. George, the photographer's assistant, mentioned that the Elements bosses wanted to get more attention from the press early on — by making the photo shoots an event in themselves, I think. They'd love to stir up attention and get social media to gossip. There's a lot of pressure from the top, and the product managers of each location — including Richard — are all trying to top each other and get the campaign back on track. George said there's bonus money at stake, and the payoff could be huge if the campaign is as successful as they want it to be. The models and places were chosen by someone higher-up—"

Cruz and Silas exchanged angry glances, and Jody wondered if they knew something she didn't. Still, she went on.

"—which means the managers don't have influence over that. So they're each trying to outdo each other with poses and props to match the themes — earth, air, fire, water. Rumor has it, the 'earth' model has been posing with a boa constrictor. Richard wants to top that, so he's been trying to lease a sapphire — but it didn't work out."

"Until now," Silas murmured.

She stirred her coffee, frowning at the brown and white swirls. "I wasn't really paying attention, but, yes. Richard said something about that. But, listen. I'm done modeling. I can't wait to get back to my own life. To surfing. The next competition is only two weeks away—"

She stopped abruptly and looked at Cruz. Parts of her job, she loved. Other parts, not so much. Long flights. Smiling on cue for the cameras. It was amazing to be able to surf the gnarliest breaks in the world, but now that she'd been on the tour for a while, the thrill was giving way to the reality of loneliness and the constant pressure to win prize money to cover her expenses. The plan had always been to enjoy the pro tour for two or three years then move on to what she really wanted to do — make custom surfboards, like her dad. And damn, she was more tempted than ever to fast-forward to that part of the plan. She could do that here on Maui. Maybe even apprentice for Teddy Akoa, the legendary board builder. She could spend more time with Cruz and find out if what they shared really was the real thing. She could—

She slammed on the brakes there, though her imagination skidded and screeched in protest.

"Surely you could fit in one more session," Silas said.

She tilted her head at him. "Tell me why. Why is a jewel so important?"

"We don't even know if it's the jewel we think it might be," Cruz cut in.

Silas conceded the point with a brief nod. "But if it is..."

The grim silence that followed pushed all the fresh air out of the room. Jody squirmed in her seat.

"It's not the jewel itself so much as..." Silas trailed off, fishing for words. "As what it represents. As where it comes from..."

He was dancing around the heart of the issue, and Jody knew it. Cruz grew more and more tense beside her, and looks flew between the two men like knives.

Silas put both hands on the counter and turned to her, more earnest than ever. "I don't wish to keep the truth from you, Miss Monroe. But the more you know, the more you enter a world you may not wish to be part of."

Goose bumps prickled over her arms. Did Silas mean a world of crime? She didn't want any part of that. But she found it hard to believe these two men were part of a shady underworld. Of course, there was something different about them. Something even an elite military background didn't explain, like that prowly, animal feel to both of them. Cruz and Silas were both so haunted. So mysterious. So private.

"The truth could endanger you, Miss Monroe. I wouldn't keep it from you for any other reason."

Silas looked so pained and sincere, she had to believe him.

"There's a possibility that the jewel — if it's the one we fear — could find its way into the wrong hands," Silas pressed on.

She studied his face closely. Did he mean *fear* literally? Neither Silas nor Cruz struck her as the type to fear anything.

"Which is why we want to get close enough to make sure it's not the one," Silas finished. His tone gave extra gravity to the last words — not just *the one* but *The One.*

Jody couldn't begin to make sense of it all, but she could tell he meant every word.

"It's not worth putting Jody in danger," Cruz growled. "We still don't know who tried to kill her and why."

She gulped some coffee. A blissful night in Cruz's arms had pushed that minor detail right out of her mind.

"We'll be there to protect her. You, me, and Kai. All we need is one look at the jewel," Silas insisted. "That's all we need. All you need to do is one more session."

Jody made a face. Just when she thought she never had to model again... Of course, these men had done a lot for her. They'd given her safe harbor and protected her when they could have walked away. Shouldn't she help them in return?

Her stomach turned at the thought of working with Richard. But then again, it wasn't as if she was doing it for free. Richard had offered extra payment, right?

"No. It's too dangerous." Cruz banged his left fist on the table. His right arm, meanwhile, pulled her tighter against his side.

Jody pursed her lips. How much danger could she be in with Cruz as her bodyguard? And if she could help him with something important...

"I agree that we don't want Jody in danger. But we call the shots. We can make it location-dependent. We can—"

"I call the shots," she said, sharply enough to cut Silas off. He might be the owner, head caretaker, or whatever of this estate, but she was her own boss. "I call the shots."

Cruz bristled at her side as he glared at Silas. "She calls the shots."

Jody couldn't help glowing a little. The man knew when to take charge and when to let her speak for herself. And again, she wished she could talk to her mom just once. *Is this what you felt like with Dad? Is this what love is?*

Silas stuck his hands up. "You call the shots. We'll take care of security."

"I still don't like it," Cruz grumbled, meeting her eyes. "Not one bit."

She didn't like it either, but hell. There were a lot of things in life she didn't like. But she knew what she had to do.

Slowly, deliberately, she put her hand out, and Silas handed her his phone. She looked at it for a good minute.

"It's too early to call," Cruz murmured, giving her an easy out.

She looked at the sky, where the first hints of dawn were starting to show. All but the boldest stars were growing faint, and a fringe of pink tinted the horizon. The clock on the wall said quarter to six.

"I'm guessing Richard won't mind." She flashed a naughty smile. "And if he does, well... His problem, not mine."

Silas didn't look amused, but Cruz grinned.

She dialed Richard's number from memory and held the phone to her ear.

Cruz's face asked, *Are you sure?*

No, she wasn't sure. Not entirely. But she'd figure it out as she went along.

She almost gave up after the seventh ring, but then Richard bellowed over the line.

"Who the fuck is calling at this—"

"Good morning, Richard," she said in her sweetest voice.

And just like that, his voice turned to molasses and honey. "Jody? So good to hear from you, baby."

She rolled her eyes. "Not your baby, Richard."

"Right. Sure. Whatever. Have you thought about my offer?"

Not until five minutes ago, but heck. Spontaneous decisions did seem to bring the best things in life. "I'd like to know exactly what you're offering and what you had in mind."

She gave herself a little nod. This time, she'd know exactly what she was getting herself into.

Cruz leaned closer, listening in as Richard chattered away.

"It's going to be great, baby. Best concept ever. We finally got our hands on that sapphire. Your eyes will match it perfectly."

She made a face. Richard had a way of focusing on objects before people. Or maybe people were just objects to him.

"Tell me more about this sapphire," she prompted, leveling a gaze at Silas.

"What's to tell? A jewel's a jewel."

Cruz shook his head in a way that said, *Maybe not.*

Part of her wanted to shake the whole story out of Cruz and Silas. On the other hand, she wasn't sure she wanted to know.

"It's costing thousands to rent, so the sooner we get the shots we need, the better. As in, today. All I need is one hour, baby. We've got the perfect location, too."

Cruz scooped the air with his hands, prompting her.

"Where?" she asked.

"A waterfall not too far away. It will be great."

She looked at Silas, who tilted his head.

Which waterfall? Cruz mouthed.

"Which waterfall? Where?" she echoed into the phone.

"Who can pronounce these crazy Hawaiian names? Some place in West Maui. George scouted it last week. Hanapaladala-something or other."

"Hanalalai," Cruz whispered.

"You have to fly in," Richard added. "The problem is getting a chopper. They're all booked out for days."

Cruz perked up his ears and looked at Silas. Jody tilted her head in the direction of the helicopter pad, and when the men nodded to her, she replied. "I can organize a helicopter."

"You can?" Richard yelped.

She grinned. It was nice to have friends who lived on luxurious seaside estates outfitted with every high-end toy. If Richard wanted her to pose on the hood of a sports car, she could get him one of those, too.

Which made her remember exactly what she was talking about and how much she hated being reduced to being nothing more than a hunk of flesh.

Silas rubbed his fingers together, reminding her what she stood to gain.

"If I agree to this, how much will I earn?" she asked.

"Fifty thousand," Richard said.

Jody sucked in a long breath. Fifty thousand went above and beyond what she'd imagined. Fifty thousand would be the icing on the cake. The tax on her dad's shop might increase again. Her sister might need more than one or two rounds of treatment. Even if she didn't, the money could help pay part of her younger sister's college tuition.

Little alarms sounded in the back of her mind. Was she getting greedy? Her dad had warned her from the start that money had a way of sucking a person in. *A little makes you want more and more until you're one of those people who pays more attention to bank accounts than the real joys in life.*

Then again, it would only be an hour of modeling. The highest paid hour of her life.

"Fifty thousand, huh?" she asked, buying time.

Silas didn't look too impressed. Cruz shook his head and jerked his thumb up.

She gaped. Was he serious?

Dead serious, his eyes said, and he drew on the table, using a finger as a pen.

She stared at the number he'd drawn. Then she took a deep breath and made the gamble of her life.

"Sixty thousand."

The second she said it, she held the phone away from her ear.

"Are you nuts?" Richard hollered. "Are you crazy? You think you're the only chick with a decent set of tits?"

She winced as Richard raged and complained. When he stopped for a breath, she cut in, feeling bolder.

"Sixty thousand. I want it in writing, Richard. And the full amount for the sessions we already finished has to be transferred to my account today."

Cruz gave her a thumbs-up, and even Silas clapped his hands in a silent *bravo*.

Richard kept up his protest, but she didn't relent. Five minutes later, she hung up with a smile and checked the clock on the wall. By early afternoon, she would have the highest bank balance of her life, and she could look forward to a sixty-thousand-dollar bonus, too. Who said she didn't have a business mind?

She grinned, but her elation didn't last long. Not with Cruz looking so fraught with doubt.

Silas hurried off, murmuring something about Kai and the helicopter, leaving the two of them alone.

Cruz took her hands in his and kissed them, looking grimmer than grim.

"Promise me you'll explain all this to me someday," she whispered, tipping her head against his. "Or at least, as much as you can."

Cruz's hands tightened around hers, and he deliberated a long time before answering. "I swear. I promise I will."

Chapter Sixteen

"Everyone all set?" Kai called, looking around the helicopter cabin.

Cruz clutched his seat belt and forced himself to keep his eyes open.

"Perfect!" Jody said from the window seat next to him, chipper and excited as ever.

"All set," Guy, the photographer, said from Cruz's left.

Richard, of course, had claimed the front seat for the best views. He gave Kai an officious thumbs-up as the rotors accelerated. Neither George nor the makeup lady were there for lack of space, what with all the equipment Guy had.

Cruz clenched his teeth. Takeoff was the worst part. Well, takeoff and flying. Or maybe takeoff, flying, and landing, because felines and feline shifters were not meant to be locked in metal boxes that hurtled through the sky.

"I really like her," Jody said over the headset as she waved to Tessa, who stood waving at them from the lawn at Koa Point.

Cruz glanced at Kai and pictured how nice it would be to have a mate to wake up with, to wave goodbye to, and best of all, to come home to. A little fantasy of Jody moving in with him at Koa Point zipped through his mind. She could live in the tree house with him and make friends with the men and women of Koa Point. She'd have access to some of the best surf in the world and—

She could be my mate, his tiger added enthusiastically. *We could live happily ever after, like Kai and Tessa. Like Boone and Nina. Like Hunter and Dawn. We could—*

Cruz bit his lip. It took a lot to dismiss his hate of the human race, especially once the heat of a sensual night dissipated. But the feeling hadn't worn off. He wanted Jody more than ever. But, shit. Believing in the good parts of life — and having faith that destiny had more than just tricks up her sleeve — was as hard as ever. Did he have it in him?

"I really like her, too." Kai grinned, waving cheerily to his mate.

Cruz liked Tessa, too, but he didn't like the situation one bit. Silas was supposed to have accompanied them, but at the last second, he'd been delayed by a phone call. A damn important call, as Silas's grim expression had made clear. Cruz didn't like that turn of events at all. Neither did Silas, whose face went stony as he stalked away with the phone.

At least Cruz had Kai for backup, but still. He hated the chopper with a passion.

Kai moved the joystick, and the helicopter lurched sideways. One of the photographer's many boxes and bags banged into Cruz's knee.

"Wow! Great view," Jody called.

A single bead of sweat rolled down Cruz's brow. That some people actually paid good money to fly thousands of feet above the ground never ceased to amaze him. To be suspended by nothing more than a couple of scraps of metal and a crazy trust in some obscure laws of physics that couldn't possibly be right. To roar through the air—

Cut it out, already, his tiger barked. *You're making it worse.*

He closed his eyes and focused his attention on the warmth of Jody's hand over his.

"Look at those waterfalls." Jody tapped on the window as they soared toward the emerald mountains of West Maui.

"Look at those clouds," Richard grumbled. "I thought Hawaii was supposed to be sunny."

"The mountains usually cloud up in the afternoon, and the system that moved in yesterday isn't clearing out soon," Kai replied. "Looks like it will be on and off all day. Could be a turbulent ride."

Cruz gave an internal moan. Give him a pit of snakes. Inhospitable deserts dotted with lurking enemies. Haunted houses full of the undead. Any of those things, he could handle. But flying...

The helicopter bumped and rattled along for what seemed an eternity as Jody oohed and aahed over every gushing cascade and ridged volcanic slope. "It's beautiful!"

It was beautiful — from the ground, where a tiger was meant to be. Cruz longed to show Jody all his favorite places. Just her, no one else. He'd pad along in front of her, swishing his tail, and she'd—

He caught himself there. She'd what? Scream and run away when she saw tiger stripes emerging from his skin?

Jody doesn't scream, his inner beast huffed. *She's not scared of anything.*

True as that might be, he doubted she'd flash that brilliant smile once he showed his fangs.

I'll keep them covered, his tiger insisted. *I promise.*

Somehow, the stupid beast wasn't getting the crux of their problem.

"We get some of our most scenic flights after rain," Kai said. "All the waterfalls are flowing, and flowing fast. But you'll have to watch yourselves out there."

The helicopter dipped and turned, and another box bumped Cruz's shin. He reached out with all his senses, trying to distract himself with thoughts of a possible Spirit Stone. The sapphire had to be somewhere among the ridiculous amount of equipment Richard and Guy had brought. But where?

Do you sense anything? he asked Kai silently.

Not a thing. Kai shook his head, swinging his earphones from side to side. *Not a single vibe like the other Spirit Stones give off.*

Which boded well, Cruz figured, that the sapphire Richard had leased wasn't a Spirit Stone.

Of course, we didn't feel the Earthstone while it slumbered either, Kai went on.

Cruz frowned. That was the thing with Spirit Stones. They were impossible to tell from any ordinary gem until something happened to stir their hidden powers. And that *something* was rarely good.

"Oh my gosh! Is that the Iao Needle?" Jody asked.

Kai nodded at the striking rock formation tucked deep in a lush valley. "Kuka'emoku is what locals call it."

Richard snorted. "It looks phallic."

Cruz growled from the back seat. Native Hawaiians revered the Iao Valley as a spiritual place, and it was best not to mess with those beliefs. Especially not when you were thousands of feet up in the air in a flying coffin.

The second we get a chance, we talk to Jody, his tiger insisted in one of those *I might die, so let me make my final resolutions* moments.

Cruz nodded grimly. Somehow, he'd find a way to reconcile the ghosts of his past with the woman destiny intended for him. Somehow, he'd explain what he was and what true love really meant.

But what would Jody say? And would the spirits of his family haunt him forever if he took a human as his mate?

The helicopter dipped suddenly, making his stomach lurch.

"Sorry," Kai murmured as he guided the chopper through a long, winding valley.

"You're a good pilot," Guy said. "I know. I've seen a few. You have an instinct for flight, huh?"

Kai grinned and kept his reply for Cruz's ears only. *A dragon better have good flying instincts.*

Cruz nodded with his eyes shut, counting the seconds until they touched down in a hidden valley deep in the West Maui mountains. He popped his seat belt before the door was open, and the second he got outside, he crouched and touched the moist, fertile earth, exhaling hard.

"This is incredible," Jody said, turning in a slow circle once the helicopter's rotors stopped.

Birds sang and chirped from all around. Water roared somewhere nearby — the powerful crash of a waterfall mixed with the chuckle of a stream. Fingers of mist groped over the shoulders of the surrounding mountains, and rich beams of sunlight pierced the valley.

"Incredible," Cruz echoed, gulping huge lungfuls of blissfully clear, fresh air. Then he straightened quickly and started hauling equipment away from the chopper. The sooner they got this started, the sooner they'd be done, and the sooner he could get Jody home. Within seconds, sweat soaked his back as the humidity made itself felt.

"There's a good location over there." Kai pointed from the slab of volcanic rock he'd landed on — the only spot not choked by vegetation. The bowl formed by the lee of a ridged mountain pulsed with waterfalls, each plunging hundreds of feet from the cliff above. "And there's another set of falls down there with a pool at the base. You'll have to do some trekking to get to it, though."

Cruz circled and sniffed, inspecting every inch of surrounding jungle. At least there was that — the danger to Jody seemed low. There was no way anyone could have followed them into this remote valley, as the only way in was on foot or by helicopter.

He shot a glance at Kai, who was helping unload equipment. *Still nothing?*

Kai shook his head. *Nothing I can pick up on.*

At exactly that moment, Richard reached into his jacket pocket, pulled out a black case, and motioned for Jody to step over. He drew a brilliant blue sapphire out and reached around Jody's neck to put it on.

Cruz ought to have focused on the gem, but all he could see was Richard's too-intimate gesture. The bastard was dressing Jody the way a husband might help his wife before a night out.

She's mine, his tiger roared inside.

He took a step toward Richard, who immediately went white. Within a heartbeat, the man had dropped the jewel around Jody's neck and backed away.

Cruz stood steaming for another full minute before finally tuning in to Jody's breathless words.

"Wow. This is beautiful. So blue..." She held it up, letting the sun reflect through each facet of the gem.

The light glinted off Jody's golden hair, and her beauty struck him all over again. She was like the sun and the sky, full of hope and love and life.

You just have to believe... Her words ghosted through his head.

"Not sure," Kai muttered.

Cruz glared.

Kai tilted his head toward the jewel. *I don't feel a thing. If that's a Spirit Stone, it's not just slumbering, it's downright hibernating.*

Cruz blinked. Oh. Right. He really ought to study the gem instead of obsessing about Jody, true love, and destiny.

He looked at the sapphire, feeling the air for a ripple of some supernatural force at work. The jewel was a remarkable sky blue worked into a fine teardrop shape and hung off a simple silver chain. But there was no undercurrent of power, no pulse of energy. Thank goodness for that.

"You lose it, you owe me thousands," Richard barked.

Jody gulped and pressed the sapphire against her chest.

"Listen, if it starts raining, we need to abort quickly," Kai said. "No telling when a flash flood could rip through."

Cruz wondered if anyone even listened. Well, Jody did — as her glance at the surrounding bowl of mountains affirmed. But Guy just walked around, sighting for angles and checking the light. Richard, meanwhile, snapped his fingers at Jody. "Get dressed."

Jody sighed and whispered to Cruz. "Let the final photo session begin."

Getting dressed translated to getting *undressed,* and it was all Cruz could do to hold back open snarls of discontent as Jody shed layer after layer. She only stopped when she was down to a tiny string bikini and a white T-shirt that made the blue of the jewel stand out. Resolve flashed in her eyes, and her lips moved with a mantra he couldn't quite make out. Was it *I'm doing this for my family,* or *I swear I'm never doing this again?*

Cruz's gut roiled. He had let Silas pressure Jody into this. He had let Jody talk herself into doing something she hated. Was it really worth it?

"Let's go." Guy motioned, setting off for the lower falls.

Kai stayed with the helicopter. Jody bounded through the jungle as easily as she cruised over waves. Richard cursed every step of the way. Cruz followed closely, keeping his senses on high alert. The peaty scent of the valley filled his nose, and his ears flicked with every rustle in the thick underbrush, but nothing seemed amiss.

"Wow. This is amazing," Jody gushed when they stepped into the clearing at the foot of a lower, broader waterfall with a clear pool at its base.

"Let's get started before the weather breaks," Guy said, turning to Jody. "Hair back."

She caught Cruz's gaze as she finger-combed her hair, and he licked his lips. God, if she did that minx thing again, he'd be a goner.

"Good. More lip gloss," Guy ordered, tossing her a stick.

Cruz averted his eyes, because watching Jody pucker her lips would definitely get him off track.

"Better. Now lose the bikini top," Richard said.

"What?" Jody squeaked.

Cruz whirled, ready to pummel the guy.

"You can keep the shirt on," Richard said. "And the sapphire. Just no bikini top underneath."

Jody looked from Richard to the waterfall and down at her chest. The second she got under the waterfall, the white T-shirt would be soaked and...

"No way." Jody crossed her arms over her chest.

"We're paying you sixty thousand dollars," Richard snapped. "Do you want it or not?"

Cruz stalked forward, but Jody intercepted him with one hand on his chest. "I call the shots, right?"

He glared at Richard over her shoulder and forced himself to nod. "You call the shots. But you don't have to do this, Jody."

She dipped her chin twice. "I don't have to, but I want to. It's worth it."

He searched her eyes before she hustled him off to one side for some privacy. "How could this be worth it?"

"I picture my sister and her husband cuddling their baby. I see my dad splashing in the water with his grandchild. I picture his surf shop, staying right where it belongs until my dad is ready to retire." She nodded firmly. "It's worth it."

Cruz's heart thumped as he wrapped his hand around hers. God, he loved this woman. And damn, he really had to find a way to tell her that.

Soon, his tiger growled. *Soon.*

"Just one thing," Jody added.

"Anything."

Anything, his tiger agreed.

She pursed her lips. "Don't take this the wrong way, okay?"

His heart sank. What was she getting ready to say?

"I'd rather you didn't watch this time," she said.

Her words nicked his heart like a chisel over stone, chipping off one chunk at a time. They'd spent an incredible night together. He'd touched, kissed, and licked her everywhere. Yet suddenly, she didn't want him to see her half naked under a waterfall?

"This isn't me," she whispered, holding his hand — the one he wanted to yank away. "Not the real me."

He stared. The pictures Guy snapped here were bound for magazine and billboards all over the world, but Jody didn't want him to see?

His face must have shown the hurt, because she smoothed a hand over his chest and added, "I don't mean it in a bad way. I just don't... don't..."

You just don't want me anywhere near you, he nearly said.

Give her a break, his tiger tried. *She's human. They do strange things sometimes.*

Yeah, he shot back. *Humans are unpredictable. Irrational. Even dangerous sometimes.* Dangerous to fools like himself who didn't protect their hearts. He shook his head slowly, feeling sick to his stomach. *I thought she was different.*

She is different. She's special, his tiger insisted.

But suddenly, he wasn't sure what to believe any more.

She's right. This isn't really Jody. The real her is who we saw at home, his tiger said.

Cruz knew that made sense, but all he felt was the rejection. Richard and Guy could watch her, but he couldn't?

"You call the shots," he mumbled, backing away slowly.

Jody looked stricken, but Richard and Guy hurried her off before she could say a word, and that was that.

Cruz turned his back and stared at his shoes as his tiger raged inside.

Don't make a big deal of it. Just try to understand.

Kind of ironic, having his tiger lecture his human side for a change.

"Step under the waterfall, honey. Beautiful. Now lean toward me..."

Cruz closed his eyes, wishing he couldn't hear Guy instruct Jody. Wishing he couldn't hear the camera click away.

You need to blow off the steam, his tiger said. *Move a little bit.*

Cruz felt like running into the woods and snarling until his ire echoed across the mountains, but he couldn't do that. Not when he was committed to protecting Jody.

Of course, there was no reason why he shouldn't check the surrounding area, so he took off into the jungle until the sound of the waterfall and rustling leaves drowned out Guy's voice. Every step he took tempted him to shift and run, and before long, he gave in to the urge, leaving his clothes bundled on a rock. He let his tiger take over his body, wincing throughout the shift. When his two sides were in accord, changing shapes was a smooth, effortless transition he barely felt. But when his two sides conflicted, shifting was a creaky, painful process that made seconds feel like torturous hours. His shoulders ached as they dropped into their feline position. His skin burned as tiger stripes broke out over his body, and his jaw stretched.

All your fault, his tiger grumbled, giving himself a hearty shake when the transition was finally complete. Then he took off, sticking to the undergrowth. He dipped his nose to the ground then pointed it up to sniff the air. He didn't really expect to find a whiff of danger, but—

The valley filled with the sound of an engine, and he rushed to a rocky outcrop.

What the hell? Kai? he called, watching the helicopter take off and soar away.

Bad timing, but there's a mayday call, Kai replied in a tense tone. *A couple of teenagers headed out on windsurfers and haven't come back. Emergency services is calling for everyone in the area to help locate them before the weather deteriorates.*

Cruz looked up. Mist was wafting over the mountaintops, but the real issue was the dark, angry clouds that were inching into sight. *How long do you think the weather will hold?*

The valley is still clear, but shit, you should see the clouds rolling in from the northeast, Kai said from his vantage point high above.

Cruz jumped back off the rock and pawed the earth as he called to Kai once more. *Get back as quick as you can. We need to get Jody out of here.*

Roger, Kai said as he sped out of view.

Cruz muttered to himself and circled back toward the waterfall. He jumped over a mossy tree trunk, heading back to the place he'd left his clothes. Then the wind shifted, teasing him with a faint new scent.

He froze, immobile but for the twitch of his whiskers and the sharp flick of his tail. The earthy scent of lobelia permeated the valley, along with native ferns and even a whiff of the rare Nau plant. But somewhere back behind them all...

He jerked his head around, following the faint smell of mammal. Of shifter. Of...of...a fellow feline?

The hair along his back prickled and stood as he rushed up the valley, chasing the unfamiliar scent. He couldn't even bring himself to stalk it properly. Instead, he rushed headlong to confront the intruder who had no business that deep in the mountains — or that close to Jody. The ground blurred into a patchy green-brown rug under his feet. Vines whipped his sides as he hurtled along.

Ahead, branches snapped, the telltale sound of panicked flight. Leaves swayed, shedding water as the intruder raced away, and the pungent scent of fear speared into the air. Cruz sprinted in hot pursuit, catching glimpses of tawny fur and a tufted tail. He ran, fast and furious, driving the beast upslope. Then, with a final burst of speed, he launched himself at the intruder. They both exploded into snarls as they tumbled downslope, flailing at each other with deadly claws and fangs.

Cruz roared and threw his weight to one side, dragging his enemy to the ground until he had it pinned, belly up. He stared at the dark nose and furry neck.

A lion. What was a goddamn lion shifter doing on Maui?

He clacked his teeth a hair away from the beast's throat, sending a clear message. *Move and you die.*

The lion, young and inexperienced — that much was immediately evident — panted wildly and held his paws still, submitting immediately.

Who the hell are you? Cruz barked. Most shifters could communicate mind-to-mind, and though it was harder to hear an unknown shifter's thoughts, similar species could often make themselves understood.

He'd better well make himself understood, Cruz's inner tiger snarled.

Don't hurt me, the lion cried in terror. *Don't kill me.*

The ruff around his neck hadn't thickened into a proper mane, he was that young. Young and stupid, Cruz thought. And definitely from off-island. Cruz didn't know of a single lion shifter on Maui.

What the hell are you doing here?

Just, uh... uh...

Yeah, the kid was up to no good, all right. Cruz leaned closer and snarled in a deeper tone while perking his ears. He doubted this cub of a lion had wandered all this way by himself. Were there other shifters out there?

Who are you with? he demanded. *What are you up to?*

Nothing. The lion yelped. When Cruz snarled again, he capitulated. *All I'm supposed to do is watch from up here. I swear I'm not even going to get close. I'm just supposed to watch and learn—*

The lion snapped his mouth shut, aware he'd said too much.

Cruz showed every inch of his teeth. *Learn? From whom?*

The lion hesitated until Cruz waved the claws of his left paw in front of its face.

My uncle. I'm just supposed to watch. I swear I wasn't going to do anything else.

Cruz's mind spun. Was there a pride of lion shifters moving in to Maui? Were they working for Moira or trying to sabotage the photo shoot? Did his family ever cross paths with a pride of lions who might want to cause trouble for him now?

None of it made sense, no matter how he tried piecing it all together.

A helicopter buzzed back into the valley, and Cruz exhaled. If Kai was back, he could help get to the bottom of this.

Cruz lifted his head and sniffed deeply. And just then — in that split second of inattention — the young lion shifter bolted into the underbrush.

Cruz snarled but didn't bother setting off in pursuit. With Kai back, one fleeing lion wasn't much of a threat. The question was what other shifters might be out there, lying in wait.

No matter how he sniffed, though, he couldn't pick out anything but the scent of the rapidly retreating lion.

He padded back downslope, flicking his ears at the buzz of the helicopter. The pitch sounded higher than before. Was Kai in a rush? He bounded up to a boulder for a clear look as the chopper touched down.

Whoa. Wait, his tiger snarled inside.

Kai's helicopter was brown with red and yellow stripes, but the chopper swooping in now was a big blue A-Star. Cruz growled under his breath as five bulky men stepped out. Big, meaty, mercenary types, except the leader, who was taller and leaner. Lion shifters?

When he sniffed again, his blood ran cold. Among the other scents came one singular smell. Not so much a scent as an interruption of scents that ought to have been there.

What kind of creature didn't smell like anything? What beast chased scents away rather than carrying its own?

Then it hit him, and he cursed. Vampire. That lack of scent was the hallmark of a vampire.

Cruz didn't watch a second longer, because he'd chased the young lion a long way upslope, and the newcomers were much closer to Jody than he was.

Shit, he cursed, tearing down the slope with his heart in his throat. *Jody. Jody...*

Chapter Seventeen

"Lift your chin higher. Turn a little more," Guy said. He was crouched by Jody's knees, aiming the camera upward to catch the water cascading over her body.

She did her best to channel her inner minx, but she just couldn't force herself to do it. Standing under the waterfall ought to have been cool and refreshing, but she felt dirty and used, especially with Richard leering from the background like that.

"What's with you today?" Richard complained. "Where's the magic we had in the last shoot?"

She hid a scowl. The magic was Cruz, but she'd sent him away. Worse, she'd upset him. Didn't he understand why she didn't want him to watch? She'd bared her truest, most private self to him the day before, and she wanted him to treasure that, not pollute the memory with this caricature of herself. And damn it, she was helping him by doing this, too. Wasn't he grateful for that?

But Cruz had barely looked at the sapphire after a first glance, so maybe it wasn't the jewel he and Silas were interested in.

Doubt clouded her mind. What if Cruz didn't care? What if he was only interested in a jewel — a different jewel — and not truly interested in her? What if he had been using her all along?

Without thinking, she brought her thumbnail to her mouth to gnaw on, then yanked it away before Richard could comment. Had she been too trusting, too eager? Had she been too entranced by the dark, brooding warrior so shrouded in mystery?

"Center the necklace and lean forward," Guy said.

When she bent at the waist, the sapphire swung away from her chest. She caught and steadied it, then glanced down. Despite the cool temperature of the water, the gem felt warmer than it had at first. Was that from her body heat?

She scowled. Her body heat that wasn't all that high, not with Cruz gone.

"Try lifting it up," Guy said. "Let's see if we can get it to catch the light."

She held the gem higher. Clouds were sneaking over the sky as he spoke, but sunlight still pierced the valley — for the moment, at least.

"Right there. Great. I love how it splits the light," Guy said.

Jody studied it. Wow. The jewel really did reflect the light.

"Get under the waterfall. Put your head back like you're in the shower."

Letting go of the sapphire, she did as she was told. A warm spot on her chest told her where the gem lay, though her attention jerked away when a helicopter zoomed overhead. Not Kai's brown striped machine — a different one. Moments later, several men appeared on the rise she'd hiked down from.

"Who's that?" she asked, breaking out of the pose.

Richard snubbed his cigarette against a rock and tossed it into the pool at her feet. "Must be the guys from the Elements corporate office I invited." He rubbed his hands together. "When they see these pictures and bring them back to the boss, we'll be the primary ad team, for sure."

You what? she wanted to yelp, but she held back — barely. The last thing she wanted was more people to watch her prance around half naked. Of course, the photos would end up being published, but having people see her pose in person seemed even more an invasion of her privacy.

"Concentrate," Richard grunted.

Jody did her best, but the water skipping over her body came in thin, irregular bursts, and having the men watch from above made her skin crawl. Where was Cruz?

"I wish we had a little more water," Guy said.

Jody knew just what he meant. The waterfall split into six separate streams, and each was more of a trickle than a shower. She imagined the rock pool at Cruz's place. That had been just the right amount.

A second later, she squealed as what felt like a bucket emptied over her head. Guy jumped back and turned to protect his camera from the splash. Jody blinked, looking up at the waterfall.

"Ha. Watch what you think, sweetheart," Guy joked. "Now quick, while it's running. Look this way and hold the sapphire against your heart."

She expected the jewel to feel cold and edgy, but it was surprisingly comfortable — almost as if it wanted her to hold it close.

"Perfect! Hold it right there so I can get the light reflecting off it."

She couldn't help peeking down. That wasn't just the light. The sapphire was glowing.

"Come on, honey. Let's have some of that magic from the other day."

She didn't have an ounce of magic in her, not with Cruz gone. But, wow — maybe the sapphire did, because the light streaming off it intensified. The facets didn't just reflect daylight — they seemed to project their own luminescence.

"Good. Now, shut your eyes..."

She closed her eyes and found herself adrift in images of water of all kinds. Rushing river water. Roiling surf at the edge of the sea. Pitter-patter rainwater. Babbling brooks. All those scenes merged together like one of those relaxation videos city dwellers used to conjure peace.

Footsteps splashed nearby, and at first, she thought that was part of the menu of water conditions bubbling through her head. But then Richard called out in greeting.

"Gentlemen, gentlemen. Glad you could make it."

Jody snapped her eyes open, and her hands flew to her chest. She'd grown accustomed to Guy and Richard — more or less. But five newcomers had appeared — big guys with long, leonine hair — and to have them look on...

"Oh, don't let us hold you up," the tallest one said, looking right at Jody.

Guy coaxed her on. "Come on, honey, one more set. Chin up..."

Jody shivered. The clouds marched steadily on, and the temperature dropped. She cast her eyes around for Cruz, feeling naked and vulnerable. Clutching the sapphire made her feel more grounded, though. More powerful, somehow. Slowly, she straightened her shoulders.

I can do this. I can do this...

"Good. Now angle that way..."

She did her best, but it was hard with those men there, undressing her with their eyes.

"Nice. Keep that up. Bring it right up to your eyes," Guy said.

She blinked as she cupped the jewel with both hands. Light danced and flickered within the facets, taking on a life of its own.

Guy muttered to himself, as he always did. Richard chattered away at one of the big guys flanking the tallest, leanest man. And then — in spite of all the distraction and the noise of the waterfall — she heard the tall man's sharp intake of breath. His eyes shifted to the sapphire, and his lips moved.

A shiver went down her shine, and she clutched the jewel tighter.

"I love the way the light reflects in that stone," Richard said.

Thunder rumbled over the mountaintops, making everyone peer up.

"Damn it. We'll have to hurry to get these last shots," Guy said, fumbling with his lens.

The tall, lean man stepped forward, hopping from one rock to another with incredible speed and grace. One second, he was far away, and the next, he was far too close. Every step he took forward made Jody retreat, pressing her back to the waterfall.

"Miss Monroe?" he asked.

His eyes were black and eerily dull. The whites of his eyes were a jaundiced yellow. His hair was shiny and slicked back, his voice deep and commanding.

"Hang on there, Vasco," Richard said. "Let Guy finish shooting."

She could see anger flare in the newcomer's eyes. Vasco. Who was he?

"I say when you're done shooting," Vasco said in a scary monotone. His eyes locked on hers, a predator fully focused on its prey.

Richard shook his head. "We're on a tight schedule."

Richard, she wanted to whisper. *Be quiet. Don't push him.*

Vasco had a simmering undercurrent of strength, much like Cruz. But unlike Cruz, he exuded a scary feeling of ruthlessness. Of evil, almost. She tore her gaze away from him to search the hillsides. God, where was Cruz?

"Moira LeGrange may be the big boss," Richard blustered, "but I'm the product manager of this shoot, and I say—"

Vasco twisted the hand Richard placed on his shoulder and shoved so hard, the manager fell backward into knee-high water. He came up sputtering, but the other men grabbed his arms, pinning him in place.

Guy, oblivious, played with the zoom. The camera was so close to his eyes, he hadn't noticed the shove. "All right, now I need you to—"

Jody's heart pounded as she backed a few inches along the face of the waterfall. The tall, lean man was clearly capable of terrible deeds. The urge to run coursed through her bones.

"You are Jody Monroe, daughter of Ross Monroe?"

"Wait a minute," Guy yelped as Vasco stepped into the frame.

Jody was so terrified, she couldn't speak. Horrible images raced through her mind. Had this thug done something to her father or sisters?

"Now, you listen to me," Richard said.

Vasco didn't even look back. He simply raised one hand and snapped his fingers. The men holding the manager put him in a headlock and twisted.

One second, Richard was wide-eyed and panicked. The next, he was dead.

"Richard," she screamed when they snapped his neck like a twig and dropped his body without showing the slightest emotional response.

"Jesus," Guy yelped, spinning around.

Vasco didn't pay the least attention as Guy fled, only to be caught by the other men.

Jody searched wildly for something to defend herself with. A stick. A rock. But she could barely move, let alone think.

"You are Jody Monroe, correct?" Vasco repeated in a frighteningly controlled voice.

"What do you want with me?" she cried, clutching the sapphire. Water splashed over her shoulders as she sidestepped through the thin curtain of falling water.

Vasco broke into a grin. "A sip. Just one little sip," he whispered, looking at her neck. "A taste of your blood."

His canines were much too pointy. His fingernails, too. Jody froze, horrified.

There are all kinds of evil spirits out in the world, her great-aunt used to say. *Ghosts. Demons. Vampires...*

She wanted to scream that there must be some mistake. That there was some other Jody Monroe in the world who'd somehow attracted the interest of this monster.

"Let me go," Guy protested from behind. A second later, he grunted as one of the other men punched him in the stomach.

Cruz! Jody screamed silently. *Help! Cruz!*

Vasco's grin grew. "All right, maybe I want more than one sip. But don't worry, I won't drain you dry. Someone as unique as you..."

Unique? She wasn't unique. She was just her.

His eyes dropped to the necklace she wore, and he clucked in appreciation. "Such a nice jewel you have there. Moira will be so pleased with this unexpected gift."

Her fingers closed around the sapphire instinctively, and a surge of power pulsed through her arm.

It's not the jewel itself so much as what it represents, Silas had said. *But the more you know, the more you enter a world you may not wish to be part of.*

Jody had a sneaking suspicion she'd just stumbled into that world, whatever it consisted of. Murderers? Worse, vampires? Was there really such a thing?

Vasco lunged for her so quickly, the movement blurred. Jody barely managed to jump backward, slipping out of his grasp. One of Vasco's long, pointed fingernails scratched her forearm as she moved, and she yelped, covering the wound.

"Ah." Vasco grinned. "A little appetizer. Just what I've been dreaming about."

He held up his finger and slowly licked the drop of blood the way a child might lick a lollipop. He closed his eyes, savoring the taste as she backed away, disgusted.

"Jesus, who are you people?" Guy yelled.

Vasco's yellow-tinted eyes snapped open as his lips moved, testing the flavor. "Wait a minute..."

When he jumped forward and grabbed for her, Jody froze, catching sight of his pointed canines.

Vasco slashed down her forearm, leaving a three-inch gash. Only then did she pull away, watching him lick her blood a second time. His tongue darted out, tasting. Testing. Then his face darkened.

"Human? A mere human?"

Jody wanted to scream. What else would she be?

Dark, remorseless eyes stared at her. "Are you or are you not Jody Monroe, daughter of Ross Monroe?"

Her mind spun. Whatever interest this lunatic had in her blood, it was misplaced if he was looking for a relative of Ross Monroe — the best father ever, but not her biological father. Not that she dared mention that. What if this monster tracked down her father next? Or maybe her younger sister, who really did carry their father's blood?

Jody tried to run, but all she could coordinate was a splashy shuffle over a large, flat rock.

Then a voice boomed from above, and a shadow loomed. She ducked, yelped, and then cried out in relief.

"Cruz!"

He vaulted from the top of the waterfall, landing in a crouch in one eerily silent move. And, man, she'd never been happier to see someone. Even — whoa — a naked someone. What was that all about?

"Back off," Cruz snarled at Vasco.

As Cruz straightened, he flung an arm backward, protecting her. She reached out to touch his back, desperate for that sense of sanity. The moment they made contact, a burst of energy pulsed through her, and she gasped, blinking. Fear had slowed down her mind and limbs, but suddenly, she felt invigorated and fully alert. As if she'd just plugged in to a new power source — Cruz. The heat coming from the sapphire seemed to double, too.

There's a possibility that the jewel — if it's the one we fear — could find its way into the wrong hands, Silas had said.

She held it tightly. Vasco was definitely the wrong hands. But, shit. What could she do to protect it?

"Are you okay?" Cruz growled without taking his eyes off Vasco.

Jody wiped the cut on her arm, letting the waterfall cleanse the blood away. "Yeah," she said, hiding the shake in her voice. Because, crap. Even with Cruz there, how was she going to elude five men?

"Take the jewel if you want. Just leave us alone!" Guy cried.

Vasco didn't blink an eye. He just looked Cruz up and down.

"Now, who do we have here? The hotheaded Mr. Khala, I presume?"

Cruz snarled. "Don't presume anything about me, asshole."

Jody kept her hand on his back, trying to keep him calm. Wondering how Vasco knew Cruz. Wondering what the hell was going on.

Then the gears in her mind clicked into place, and she pointed at Vasco. "You were there that night at the party. You tried to kill me."

Rage bubbled up inside her, and suddenly, Cruz was the one clutching her hand, trying to calm *her* down.

Vasco tut-tutted. "I don't try, my dear. I succeed. The shooter was an associate of mine." He glared at one of his men. "An associate who might have been punished for ineptitude if his actions hadn't revealed who you really are."

She stared. What the hell did that mean?

Vasco's eyes narrowed, and his lips formed a thin line. "Unless, of course, you are not as special as I was led to believe. Or is it that your bloodlines are so diluted, the flavor isn't there any more?"

His words didn't make any sense, but they turned her stomach all the same.

"Listen, I don't know what's going on here, but—" Guy started to protest. His yelp was followed by a bone-chilling snap and a dull splash.

"Oops." A big man chuckled as he dropped Guy's body. Like Richard, Guy floated facedown in the pool, lifeless.

Jody gasped. "You... You..."

Cruz turned slightly, shielding her. His eyes met hers, blazing with outrage and giving her courage at the same time.

Vasco sighed at the killer. "Now, how are you going to cover that up?"

Jody couldn't believe his casual tone.

"No problem," the man who'd killed Guy said. "We just make it look like humans did it."

Jody did a double take. There it was again. *Humans.* What did that make these men?

Cruz's body went stiff, and a low, dangerous growl escaped his lips.

Another man snorted to the first and gestured to Jody. "No one will ever buy that she killed them."

Jody's jaw hung open. They wanted to frame her?

"It doesn't take much," the first man said. "Plant a little evidence, spin a little tale..."

Cruz's face turned a scary shade of red. "Planting evidence? Where else have you done that? India, maybe?"

Vasco took a slight bow. "A true aficionado travels the world to sample its best flavors, my dear tiger."

Jody stared. His dear *what?*

"You did it. You killed my family." Cruz's hands curled into fists, and his voice dropped to a murderous growl.

Jody grasped at the threads in her mind. Cruz's family had been killed in some horrible event he refused to speak of. By Vasco and his men?

"You killed them, and you covered it up." A vein in Cruz's neck pulsed wildly as he stepped toward Vasco.

Jody grasped at his shoulders, trying to restrain him.

"And you, I see, bought the whole story." Vasco grinned.

Jody cried out. "Why would you kill anyone? What kind of monster are you?"

Vasco's smile grew, the points of his teeth showing again. "I'm not a monster. I'm a connoisseur, if you must know. A collector of rare tastes."

She blanched. He was talking about blood as casually as some people discussed wine.

Vasco's eyes took on a faraway look. "Once you taste shifter blood, you never want to go back."

Jody's ears got stuck on one word. Shifter?

Cruz hissed. "You bastard."

But Vasco wasn't done. "Tiger blood. Wolf blood. Even mermaid blood, or so I'd been led to believe." His eyes drifted to Jody.

"You're crazy," she cried, looking around for some means of escape. The man was delusional. A first-class lunatic she had to get the hell away from.

Thunder rumbled in a long, angry drum roll, and dark clouds swept overhead. The temperature dropped another ten degrees, though the sapphire remained warm against her chest. Jody looked up, checking if there was any way to climb up the waterfall. But the flow was too steady, the rocks too slippery.

The water in the rock pool swirled urgently around her feet, and an image formed in her mind. An image of turbulent water, pulling her enemies away.

No telling when a flash flood could rip through, Kai had said.

She shook her head, trying to keep her wits about her instead of grasping at straws.

Cruz squeezed her hand, signaling something. His left shoulder dipped, and he tugged her forward. What exactly was he planning to do?

An engine buzzed in the sky, and for a moment, Jody hoped it was Kai in his helicopter. But it was only a small plane on the way back to its home base in the impending storm.

"Jody," Cruz whispered under the engine noise, pulling her close. "The second I say run, you run. You got that? Run and don't look back."

She'd witnessed Cruz in a dozen dark moods, but she'd never seen him as grim. His yellow-green eyes glowed, and a muscle in his jaw twitched.

His gaze dropped to the gem around her neck. "Use that."

Her lips moved, but no sound came out. What use was a jewel in a situation like this?

"Don't look back," he repeated in the split second that Vasco and the others were distracted by the plane. "And trust me. No matter what happens, please trust me."

Jody's heart pounded and not just from the anticipation of whatever might happen next. Cruz wasn't just telling her. He was *begging.*

Please trust me.

"Of course, I trust you," she whispered.

Cruz didn't look so sure, making her wonder what exactly he had in mind. But there wasn't a moment to ask, because Vasco turned his attention back to her.

"I'm not crazy," he murmured, stepping closer. "Just hungry." He motioned his men closer and looked Jody right in the eye. "Hungry for new tastes, which is where Miss Monroe comes in. But you, Mr. Khala, will do nicely, too."

Chapter Eighteen

Jody couldn't keep herself from screaming at Vasco. "You're a monster." A lunatic, too, but she left that part out.

He shrugged. "We're all monsters, are we not? Humans wage war. They maim and steal. Shifters change allegiances with the seasons."

"Some do," Cruz muttered, shooting murderous looks at the others. "Others know the difference between right and wrong."

Jody stared. What were they talking about?

Vasco went on, unfazed. "Even my kind. We stalk. Select. We suck our prey dry. Oh yes," he said, seeing the horror on her face. "Vampires. You thought we were bedtime stories?" He laughed, showing his teeth. "Well, let me show you the truth."

Clouds swept down the mountains, and another roll of thunder shook the air.

"Jody," Cruz hissed. "Don't listen to him. We're not all like him."

Her eyes went wide. We? What did Cruz mean by *we*?

"Hubner, Smith." Vasco snapped his fingers at his men. "Show her."

One of them grinned and took off his jacket. The other grimaced, not as happy to comply. But they both took off their shirts, revealing broad, steely chests. Then they dipped their chins, curled their backs, and—

"Oh my God," Jody whispered, backing away.

It wasn't possible. It wasn't happening. Those men weren't turning into wild beasts in front of her eyes.

Except they were. Tawny fur sprouted from their backs as they fell forward on all fours. Teeth extended from muzzles that doubled in length, and their noses darkened to black. No matter how many times Jody shook her head, she couldn't force reality back into her mind.

"No..."

Cruz stepped forward, shielding her with his body. "Shifters, Jody. Some are evil. Some are good."

Vasco cackled. "Evil is in the eye of the beholder, my friend. Why don't you show her your true colors? Or should I say, your stripes?"

Cruz held her hand so tightly, it hurt. His voice was a gruff whisper. "Don't listen to him, Jody. When I say go, run and don't look back."

Vasco laughed out loud. "Oh, I think she should stay and watch, don't you? Or don't you want to discover what your bodyguard really is? Oh, wait. Not just your bodyguard. Your lover. Am I right?"

Jody was too busy eyeing the beasts prowling at the edge of the rock pool to retort that her love life was none of his business. Somehow, the lions' smooth, stealthy movements reminded her of Keiki. No, wait. Not Keiki. Cruz. Why would they remind her of Cruz?

She glanced at him, trying to will away the doubt crowding her mind.

Cruz balled his fists and turned his gaze to her. The green specks in his eyes grew darker, more menacing. "Don't listen to him, Jody."

Vasco laughed. "He wants to keep you in the dark, Miss Monroe. Do you know why?"

Jody wanted to jam her hands over her ears.

"All he wants is the jewel, you know. Do you know about his past? He's a killer. A sniper."

"Jody," Cruz said. "Please trust me. No matter what, trust me."

She didn't have time to answer. She *couldn't* answer because Cruz dropped to his knees in front of her and let out a low groan.

"Cruz," was all she managed as she reached for his shoulders.

"Here, kitty, kitty." Vasco laughed.

She wanted to punch the man, but she couldn't leave Cruz. Something was wrong with him. A seizure of some kind? His torso shook, and his hands clutched at the rock.

"Trust me," he grunted in a strangled voice.

"Cruz," she cried, touching his back. Then she froze, because his skin was softer than it ought to have been. Furrier. He pushed his legs back, stretching out in a long line, and then—

Jody fell back and landed on her ass, frozen at the sight of a man blurring into a beast just inches away.

"Cruz?"

But Cruz was gone, and in his place was a tiger. An honest-to-God, orange-and-black-striped Bengal tiger. She stared, wondering when she'd wake from this awful nightmare, watching as the beast's yellow-green eyes swirled and focused on her.

Trust me, they said.

She stared. "Cruz?"

His nose twitched, and sorrow consumed his eyes. Then rage took its place as he whirled to face Vasco.

"Ah, such misplaced courage." Vasco flapped a hand. "Such futility. Either way, I will kill you, Mr. Khala. I will kill her too, and I shall take the stone. Moira will be so pleased. And I'm sure she will pay me whatever price I ask. Funny, isn't it, how fate makes things work out?"

Jody forced herself to stand, though her knees shook. The tiger paced in front of her, snarling at Vasco, the three remaining men, and — holy shit — two lions. The soft fur of the tiger's sides brushed her shins as he stalked two steps right then left, swishing his tail the whole time.

"You find killing funny?" She spat the words at Vasco.

"I find business funny." He smiled. "This all started as a small job. One little shooting at a society event — just the thing to stir up a little publicity for dear Moira's new enterprise."

Jody's lips twisted into a snarl of her own. "What kind of person sets up a shooting as a publicity stunt?"

"You don't know Moira." Vasco chuckled.

The tiger snarled. Or, more precisely, Cruz snarled. Jody stared at him, trying to get that through her head.

The bushes parted, and yet another lion stepped into view. A slightly smaller, younger one, from the look of it.

"Ah, my dear nephew," Vasco sighed. "Don't mind him."

Jody looked around, counting foes as Vasco went on.

"The beautiful part of the plan was the idea of pinning it all on Mr. Khala with some carefully placed misinformation. Everyone would have bought it, too. You know, the unhinged war vet who couldn't handle transitioning back."

Cruz snarled, and Jody voiced the words coded into his tone. "What do you know about transitioning back?"

Vasco ignored her completely and rambled on. "Of course, the blunder my associate made just opened the door for opportunity. For me, not for Moira. I have the chance to sample a new flavor, and the stone is icing on the cake." His eyes dropped to the sapphire then slid to Cruz with a look of utter disdain. "Perhaps it was an opportunity for Mr. Khala, as well."

Jody balled her hands into fists. "You're crazy."

"Am I?" Vasco raised an eyebrow. "All he had to do was pretend to rescue you and take you back to that lovely estate. The perfect place to woo and seduce you."

Cruz let out a ferocious snarl that made the lions step back.

Jody's jaw hung open. What was Vasco suggesting?

The vampire pointed at the sapphire. "After that, he used you to obtain a Spirit Stone. Ah, Mr. Khala. You're smarter than I imagined."

Jody backed up as far as she could without falling into deeper water. She was marooned on a slab of rock with a tiger, wondering if Vasco's accusations were true.

Cruz raised one paw and slashed at the air, gnashing his teeth the whole time. His tail whipped back and forth, and his shoulders hunched, one step away from an all-out attack.

"All bark and no bite." Vasco made a dismissive motion.

Jody frowned. She didn't know what to believe, but one thing was clear. The only reason Cruz hadn't torn the man's throat out yet was because she was so close. He kept nudging her back with his haunches, keeping her shielded from the others. His eyes met hers one more time, pained and sincere.

Don't listen to him. Trust me. Please trust me.

Jody held her breath then dipped her chin in a weak nod. She might be going crazy, but she'd go with her heart on this one, for sure.

He flicked his tail once, warning her to be ready to run.

Jody's teeth were chattering too much for her to nod, but sure — running sounded like a great option right now. Away from Vasco, away from men who turned into beasts. She nodded again and bent her knees, ready to move.

Cruz whirled to face Vasco, and all hell broke loose with a mighty roar that echoed off the surrounding mountains.

Jody watched just long enough to understand about the *don't look back* part. Saliva dripped from the tiger's jaws. Massive claws slashed four long lines across Vasco's chest, drawing parallel lines of blood. The vampire pushed back with incredible strength, showing inch-long fangs.

Jody whirled and hurried away. *Run. Run. Run!*

She couldn't begin to digest everything she'd seen and heard. With footsteps splashing behind her, though — the sounds of men in close pursuit — she didn't have to do much thinking.

Just run, damn it, she ordered herself. *Run!*

She splashed through knee-deep water, using every lesson she'd learned as a kid who'd grown up on the beach. Lifting your knees high worked better than dragging your feet, but the men behind her didn't seem to know that. She looked for a branch to use as a club, but there was nothing except Guy's lifeless body, floating a few yards downstream. Her heart rose in her throat as she ran toward him. Guy wasn't her favorite person, but it gutted her to see him killed. Richard, too. Both of them murdered in cold blood.

You'll be murdered in cold blood, too, a dark voice said in the back of her mind. *Hurry!*

Cruz. What about Cruz? she wanted to protest.

"I want her alive!" Vasco yelled.

A tiger's snarl boomed, reminding her Cruz could take care of himself. Or so she hoped. She glanced back, but it was impossible to tell who had the upper hand as the tiger and Vasco fought in the shadow of the waterfall. Water flew everywhere, and grunts punctuated slashes and growls. Thunder rolled and raindrops began to fall, splattering on her face. God, how could this get worse?

"Finally, we get to hunt. A real hunt." One of the men stalking her grinned. "We haven't been able to do that in a while."

The other man chuckled, moving to the opposite bank of the stream.

Jody had no choice but to run. The sapphire bumped and bounced against her chest, and a slew of images raced through her mind. Visions of water in every possible form: waterfalls catching rainbows. Drenching storms. Pitter-pattering rain. Dewdrops. Swirling, rushing rivers... A whole menu of options, almost.

Options for what? she wanted to scream.

She nearly raced past Guy's body, but at the last second, she reached out and yanked the camera from his shoulder.

I'm sorry, Guy. So sorry. She wanted to stop and cry. *But I need this.*

She ran another three steps, listening to the panting behind her grow louder. Closer. At the last possible second, she spun.

"Leave me alone!" she yelled, swinging the camera.

"Hey," the man shouted.

The camera smashed into the left side of his face with a heavy thud, and the lens shattered. The man grunted and stumbled sideways. Jody yanked the broken camera back before sprinting onward. There were more men after her. Or rather, one man and what sounded like one lion. They splashed along the shoreline, and the man yelled at his accomplice.

"You go that way. I'll go this way."

Like a lion could understand that? Apparently, yes, because the lion did as he was told.

"Damn it," the man she'd struck grunted as he slipped from rock to rock, back in hot pursuit.

The rain intensified, splattering against the water in countless tiny darts. Bruised, swirling clouds slipped overhead, dimming the valley.

If it starts raining, we need to abort quickly, Kai had said. *No telling when a flash flood could rip through.*

Jody winced at a burning sensation on her chest. Was that the sapphire? She pulled it away from her skin and glanced down.

Use that, Cruz had said.

Use me, the eerie blue glow seemed to echo.

How? She wanted to scream. *How?*

The glow flared, and the water around her legs rose an inch, swirling and rushing. Not high enough to push her off-balance, but enough to send wild images through her mind. She saw gushing water tearing through a lush landscape. Enough to create a swirling flood that swept everything away.

She stared at the sapphire. No wonder Silas had mentioned fearing the gem. The thing seemed to have a mind of its own.

Power. The sapphire seemed to say as it glowed brighter. *I do have power. Not just a pretty glow.*

Which was crazy, but... If men could sprout vampire fangs and turn into wild animals, who was to say a jewel couldn't hold special powers, too?

God, Silas hadn't been exaggerating, had he? *The more you know, the more you enter a world you may not wish to be part of.*

No kidding, she wanted to snort.

Another feline snarl split the air, and she jerked around, coming face-to-face with a lion.

She dropped the sapphire back to her chest in time to swing the camera with both hands, bashing the lion in the nose. The beast yowled and stepped back, then stalked forward with a low growl. Jody inched backward, trying not to panic. And damn — the irony! So many people warned her about the danger of sharks while surfing, and here she was, facing a grown lion in the closest life-or-death moment she'd ever experienced. The lion moved awkwardly, though, picking up its paws and edging around the shallows with distaste.

"Don't be such a pussy," one of the men called. "Get her, already."

She thought of the rock pool near Cruz's tree house. From what she knew, tigers liked water. Lions — not so much? Still, she doubted that would hold him for long.

I can hold him, the prickly heat of the sapphire seemed to hint.

Jody looked around, afraid to turn her back. If she lost her footing, they'd pounce and rip her throat out — or worse, save her for Vasco.

We stalk. We select. We suck our prey dry.

Her skin crawled as the stone pulsed in her hand.

Jody. Use it.

She couldn't tell whether she was remembering Cruz's words or hearing them all over again in her mind. But it didn't matter. The more she tried to think things through, the more the process slowed her down.

Sometimes it's better not to think, her dad said in those first surfing lessons he'd given her, so long ago. *Just do. Listen to your heart and trust what you can do.*

Jody took a deep breath, then exhaled slowly. *Listen... Trust...*

A second later, she took off, splashing over to a boulder high in the middle of the stream. She clambered up on it, ignoring the enemies in pursuit. From the top, she squinted through the rain, watching Cruz and Vasco grapple.

Don't think. Just do.

She pulled the necklace off and held the sapphire out. The sun had long been chased away by rain clouds, but the last rays of light caught in the facets of the gem. She tilted it this way and that, magnifying the light.

"Shit," one of the men who'd been chasing her muttered. "Fucking Spirit Stone. You don't mess with that."

Jody held the jewel higher and glared. "Back off."

She had no clue what she was doing, but still. The sapphire felt more and more like a weapon, and she'd use whatever help she could get.

The lion grumbled, and the man snickered. "Sure. Try me."

Anger rose in her, turning her thoughts into a swirling, tempestuous mess. And instead of controlling that mess, she let it run wild.

Yes, the sapphire seemed to say, glowing brighter and brighter. *Yes...*

Jody closed her eyes, concentrating on the raindrops dripping down her skin. Blocking out the sounds of the men around her — including the one who muttered, "Just get her, already."

Flash floods. White water rapids. Crashing waves. She'd been sucked under a few in her time, so she could picture it perfectly. The way water crashed against rocks, then split and reformed around obstacles, plowing on relentlessly. One eddy would spin one way, while the neighboring eddy went the other. She could feel the yank of the leg rope on her ankle, tethering her to her surfboard. The force of the waves, pulling her and the board in opposite directions before releasing both. Sometimes, the power of water frightened her. Most times, it mesmerized her. She'd spent years learning to harness the power of water. Surely, she could harness it now.

"Go on, get her," someone said.

"Damn current..." another grumbled.

She opened her eyes and looked toward Cruz. No matter how many times he slashed, bit, or kicked Vasco, the vampire retaliated. A lion backed Vasco up, jumping in for dirty strikes whenever Cruz was at a disadvantage, then scurrying back to safety again. An uneven, unfair fight — and all for her sake.

Her hand trembled around the sapphire. This had to end. She had to end it.

She gritted her teeth against the burning sensation in her hand, picturing rushing currents. Flash floods. Crashing waves.

"Shit, it's getting faster," one of the men said, chest-high in the water near her boulder.

Light poured out from between Jody's fingers, struggling to break free. She kept her eyes on the water rising around the rock slab Cruz fought on and around. The men had no idea how fast the water was about to get. And frankly, she didn't either. All she knew was that the sapphire was burning hotter than ever, its force building. The sky crackled with energy beyond that of the thunderclouds.

Let me free, the sapphire seemed to tell her. *Now. Let me release my power.*

So, so tempting — but, hell. She'd never been the angry, vengeful type. It was hard to summon that kind of hate — unless, of course, she thought of Vasco and his horrifying quest for "flavors." She might not have the blood he sought, but if he went after her younger sister...

Her stomach roiled, and anger washed over her. Vasco had to be stopped.

The moment she lifted a finger, uncovering more of the gem, a rumble sounded in the mountains.

"I'm out of here," one of the men muttered, running back toward dry ground.

Jody lifted another finger, releasing another brilliant ray of blue light.

Please, please, don't hurt Cruz, she prayed, wondering how exactly to control a flood once she set one in motion.

The sapphire didn't provide an answer, no matter how hard she listened or wished. The lion jumped to a nearby rock and looked toward her, judging the distance for a leap.

Now, the sapphire ordered. *Now!*

Jody widened her stance and opened her fingers, letting the sapphire lie exposed in her palm. A burst of energy shook her, but she focused on the images in her mind. Rushing water. Swirling eddies. Water dividing and reuniting, slamming anything in its path.

The gurgle of the stream became a hiss, then a roar. Separate strands of the waterfall thickened and joined, turning into a single torrent of water that gushed off the rock face and crashed into the pool below.

"Cruz..." she whispered, even though he was too far to hear. "Stay right there. Stand like that."

But Cruz was anything but still. He jumped through the air, slashing at his foes. One second, he was facing upstream, and the next, he stood side-on to the river. The rocky slab disappeared under rushing water, closing over his feet.

"No..." she muttered, afraid of what she'd unleashed.

"Fuck," a man yelled, looking up.

Jody held her breath as a wall of water swept around a curve of the river and over the falls. A two-story wall of water, rushing at her.

"Cruz!" she cried. The tiger had pounced upon Vasco, who lay on his back, trying to wrestle the beast off. But the tiger opened his jaws wide and—

Jody looked away as blood gushed.

"Oh God. Cruz..." she whispered. The flood was about to hit.

There was no way he could have heard her, but his head whipped around.

"Don't move," she breathed, every muscle in her body tensing.

He did move, though — long enough to shove Vasco's body off the rock ledge. Then he crouched low, looking up at the wall of water. His tiger claws flexed at solid rock in a desperate attempt to hold on.

"Don't budge," Jody whispered — as much to herself as to him. The only movement she allowed herself was tilting the sapphire the slightest bit.

Split, damn it, she ordered the water. *Split. Go around him.*

She nearly screamed when the wall of water engulfed Cruz's position, but she forced herself to focus. As the water roared toward her, she imagined a mighty mountain in front of Cruz. One big and solid enough to withstand the greatest flood. Big enough to split the water and force it to seek a new course.

"Run!" a man yelled.

The lion fled, too. Both too late, because a second later, the flood hit and swept them away. They flailed and shouted as the water stole them away. Then they were gone, sucked under for good.

Jody leaned forward as if she were bracing against a barn door and not the sliver of thin air dividing her from the rushing flood. But the sliver held, and the water rushed by on either side, leaving her untouched. It splashed and grasped greedily at her hair and her feet. But she fought off the onslaught and kept the sapphire high, imagining a path for the water to follow down and out of the valley.

Vasco, she wanted to chant. *Take Vasco and the others. Do with them what you want. But leave Cruz.*

I take whom and what I want, the hissing water said.

Jody held her ground. *Take the evil. Leave the good. Leave Cruz.*

Leave me, she wanted to add, but she didn't dare.

The roar built to a crescendo so loud, she was sure she'd be swept away, too. But the sapphire gradually dimmed along with her fading focus. Exhausted, she lowered her hand. The water level lowered, too, going from a gush to a jog and finally a babble as the rocks in the riverbed reappeared. Jody fell to her hands and knees, unable to look. What if Cruz was gone? What if the flood had spared her but claimed him?

Rain tapped on her shoulders. Wind teased her hair. Both those forces were dying down, too. Everything grew quieter — everything but her nerves. Her heart thumped erratically as she clutched the jewel. What had she done?

A minute ticked by, then another. The surrounding forest went from too-silent to humming with hidden life. The water bubbling around the boulder flowed evenly — until something disturbed it. Something big and four-footed, Jody realized after a breathless minute. The pitch of the splashes indicated shallow water, which wasn't a good sign. The moat that had arisen to protect her was flowing away.

She cracked one eye open and looked at the sapphire. The fire had gone out of it, and she was tempted to dismiss everything as a hallucination. Until a soft growl sounded beside her, that was.

She froze and tensed all over again, closing her eyes. The growl sounded again, closer still, and her arms shook. She shouldn't be such a weenie, but somehow, she just couldn't work up the nerve to look.

Everything went quiet, even the growl, until the only hint of company she heard was the deep, ragged breath of an animal that had been through some great trial.

An animal. Shit. An animal.

Moments later, two soft thumps sounded against the boulder. Jody took a deep breath, opened her eyes, and—

Startlingly clear greenish-yellow eyes gazed into hers from six inches away. The eyes of the tiger, standing on his hind legs. His front paws touched the boulder not far from her toes.

He huffed once and twitched his nose. *Please,* those eyes said. *Please trust me...*

Never had such a powerful creature looked so lost or lonely. Never had a moment of triumph been so muted and sad, as if he'd lost a battle, not won.

"Cruz," she whispered.

One by one, her muscles loosened — every one but her tongue, because she still couldn't utter a word. Slowly, she inched a hand forward until she touched his chin. The tiger closed his eyes and sighed. Really sighed, as if that was his greatest victory — being accepted by her.

She scratched his surprisingly soft fur until he hummed with pleasure.

"You said tigers don't purr," she murmured in a shaky voice. Her hands trembled in his fur, but she went on scratching all the same.

The tiger blinked at her. Once. Twice. Then he leaned forward, asking for more.

"You like that?"

I love that, the dreamy look on his face said. At least, Jody was pretty sure that was a dreamy look. She wasn't exactly an expert on tigers.

"And...um... If I come down from this boulder — you promise not to bite, right?"

He blinked like he'd never heard such a preposterous thing.

Jody grinned in spite of her fear. That was Cruz, all right. She shuffled around and slid off the boulder, hopping to the ground two feet from the tiger's side. Cruz came down on four paws and held his ground, giving her no choice but to approach.

"Is that really you?" she asked, crouching down. The eyes were all Cruz. But the black dots around his whiskers, the orange centerline, the paintbrush stripes... Well, those would take some getting used to.

He blinked. *Yes. This is me.*

Jody decided it was another one of those *Do, don't think* moments and fell into a hug. A huge human-to-tiger hug that worked surprisingly well. Cruz held perfectly still, but she could hear his heart hammering inside. A little like hers, she guessed.

"Cruz..." She hugged him tighter as they both lay on the ground. Then she cried — and laughed a little, too — out of sheer nerves. She leaned more and more of her weight on Cruz, letting go of more and more fear, until at some point she opened her eyes again and found herself eye-to-eye with a man. *Her* man. Cruz.

His dark hair was a mess, his eyes as deep and mysterious as ever. But his arms were firm over her shoulders, and his brow was furrowed in a pattern that matched the stripes that had disappeared.

"You okay?" he whispered, brushing a finger across her cheek.

The sun pierced the sky on the tail edge of the storm, shooting rays through the thick, low clouds.

Jody swallowed away the lump in her throat. "I feel fine, but I might be going crazy. Can you live with that?"

His gaze, she noticed, jumped briefly to the sapphire, and part of her feared Vasco was right. But there was no greed in Cruz's eyes. More like relief and a healthy dose of respect. A heartbeat later, his eyes locked on hers, and a smile ghosted across his lips.

"I can live with you if you can live with..." He searched for words before trying out two. "This. Me."

She glanced around. The rain had ceased, and the outline of the sun was starting to show behind the cloud cover.

"You, I can deal with. But the others..."

He touched her shoulders before she could start trembling again. "They're gone. The flood took them. We're safe."

She nibbled her lip. "So I'm not going crazy?"

"Only crazy enough to trust me."

She laughed and dropped to his chest. Maybe the truth didn't have to be terrifying. Maybe she could deal with this if she followed her heart.

"So, a tiger, huh?"

"Tiger shifter."

She thought it over. "Silas and Kai, too? Or are they lions?"

Cruz made a face. "Not lions. They're—"

An engine roared to life not too far away, and both of them looked up as a helicopter took flight. The helicopter Vasco and the others had arrived in. Which meant...

Cruz rolled to his feet and pulled her up. "Quick. One of them got away. We need to get out of the open."

Jody's heart pounded in her chest. Now what?

The helicopter made a slow turn then rushed straight at them.

"We need to—" Cruz started, then pulled up short as a dark shadow swept overhead.

Jody ducked. "Whoa. What the—?"

"Get down." Cruz pushed her to the ground and covered her body with his.

Jody looked up, watching the helicopter rush into a tight U-turn. Its engine strained as it hurtled toward the mountain-tops, suddenly the hunted instead of the hunter.

"Go, Silas," Cruz breathed, letting her up.

Jody wasn't sure she wanted to get up. Not when she saw what the helicopter was fleeing from. An impossibly huge creature with leathery wings and—

The dragon rushed after the helicopter, belching fire until both disappeared over the ridge.

"That's Silas?" she squeaked.

Cruz nodded.

"Silas is a... a..." She couldn't quite get the word out.

"Dragon," Cruz said, helping out.

Jody took a deep breath and looked down at the sapphire. "And this is..."

"A Spirit Stone."

"A Spirit Stone," she echoed in a careful monotone. "Boy, do you have a lot of explaining to do."

Cruz gave a solemn nod, and she threw her arms around him.

"But not right now," she begged, holding him tight. "Right now, all I need is you."

Chapter Nineteen

Two days later...

Cruz woke slowly, gradually. Totally unhurried and totally relaxed. It was two days after the fight in the mountains, and Jody was in his arms. Two days after he'd discovered how wrong he'd been about humans, and two days after he'd confirmed how deep his love for Jody ran.

Like I didn't know that from the start, his tiger grumbled.

He hugged Jody tighter. She was okay. He was okay. Everything was all right. Right enough that he could let his eyes ease open instead of snapping to attention the way he usually did. There wasn't a nightmare in his mind nor a ghost rattling its chains in his head. On the contrary, the peace went deep enough to tell him his family would be glad for him, too.

Morning light filtered softly through the woods where every songbird in Maui seemed to be chirping and tweeting at the top of its lungs. Singing about the beauty of life and love because they believed. He smiled and let his eyes droop shut again, because that's what civilians did. They snoozed, something he'd gotten surprisingly good at in the past two days. Jody called it catnapping, laughing at her own pun each time.

Catnap. Get it? She'd grin.

"I get it," he whispered, kissing her bare shoulder.

"Hmmm?" she mumbled, still half asleep.

"Nothing." He breathed deeply, scrubbing his chin against her skin.

So, okay, his version of sleeping in was still a few hours shorter than most people's, but that was okay. He could lie spooned around Jody for hours.

His tiger chuffed, ridiculously proud of himself. *I can do more than lie around with my mate for hours.*

Cruz grinned. He and Jody had spent the better part of the last few days in and around the bed, and not too much of that time had been spent asleep. Why sleep when he could make love to his mate?

Make love? his tiger laughed. *Is that what you did to her when you lifted her against the wall? Or when you laid her down beside the waterfall at the rock pool?*

Cruz shushed the beast, even if he had to admit that he and Jody had sometimes veered over into *desperate fucking* territory. She had her wild side, too, and her appetite was right up there with his. Other times, though, they'd made slow, sweet love, staring into each other's eyes the whole time. And each time brought him closer to the woman he loved. Each time made him feel more complete.

My mate, his tiger hummed.

Without thinking, he slid his hand from her belly to her breast.

"Mmm," Jody murmured, nestling closer.

He'd done his best to explain to Jody about shifters over the past two days, and though his words came out clunky at times, it went a lot more smoothly than he imagined. Jody had made him shift back and forth a few times. She'd gulped and held very still the first time, but soon after, she'd petted him all over.

You look good in stripes, she'd joked when he came out of one shift, naked. *But I like this look, too.*

And off they'd gone into another round of frenzied sex just because they could.

The easiest part was telling her about destined mates. Jody had nodded right away, like she'd known all along.

"You knew you were my mate?" he'd asked, stunned.

"Sure." She'd shrugged. "Just like my mom and dad. They just knew. Well, it took me a little while to realize that, but I think I felt it, deep in my heart. You don't have to be a shifter to sense that."

Humans were funny creatures, he decided. Unpredictable, irrational — sometimes, in the best possible way.

"Mmm," Jody murmured, putting her hand over his. The only thing she wore was the bracelets that touched his skin, warm from her heat. "Time to wake up?"

He tucked a strand of hair behind her ear and kissed her shoulder again. "Only if you want."

Jody chuckled sleepily and pressed her hand against his, guiding his palm over her breast. "I definitely want to wake up. But I could use some help."

Oh, he'd help her, all right. He circled the soft flesh as his tiger hummed with approval.

"What did you say?" she mumbled.

Cruz cleared his throat. They hadn't exchanged mating bites yet — a subject he hadn't directly broached — but he swore she was already close to reading his mind.

Here's a little test, his tiger said, thinking all kinds of dirty thoughts. Like taking her from the back on all fours while delivering the mating bite.

Cruz took a sharp breath because, damn. A hard-on that sudden hurt.

"I like the sound of that," Jody mumbled, grinding back against him.

She was still half asleep, so he did his best not to run away with the thought. He did nip her neck, though, eliciting another hum of delight.

"Best way to wake up," she sighed.

He snuck his leg between hers and slid his hand from her breast to her belly and back up. "I think the rest of you needs waking up, too."

She arched, reaching over her head to touch his hair. "You know what I think?"

"What do you think?" he murmured, reaching between her legs.

"I think we're a perfect match." The last word turned into a coo as he furrowed his fingers through her folds.

Her legs flopped open, and she pushed back against him, proving her point. She was always eager for his touch, and she loved to toe the line between submitting to his dominant tiger and asserting her own desires. She reached around and groped for his cock, stroking in time with his moves.

"Cruz..." she murmured, starting to rock.

"Minx," he said, gritting his teeth. He'd assumed they'd start the day all slow and sweet, but she was rapidly pushing him over toward hard and hot.

She moaned as he slipped a finger inside her and started circling. "Not my fault you have magic shifter hands."

Cruz pressed his mouth against her shoulder to suppress his own moan. She was so slick, so tight. His cock was going to explode, especially with her perfect ass pumping against him like that.

He scraped his teeth over her neck, then suckled the spot while his finger continued to circle around and around. It was going to be so hard to resist the mating bite.

His tiger groaned inside. *How can I wait?*

Jody cooed, wiggled, and moaned — then croaked an unsteady, "Wait."

Cruz froze while his heart pounded away.

"I promised myself..." she started then stopped, taking deep breaths. She gripped his forearm hard, hugging it to her chest. "Damn it, I promised myself I wouldn't get all carried away again." She rolled in his arms, coming face-to-face, and pointed an accusing finger at him. "You, tiger, are too irresistible for your own good."

He exhaled a little. Whew. Maybe there was no need to get all alarmed. He crooked an eyebrow at her, trying to ignore his burning erection.

"Um... I'm sorry?"

Not sorry, his tiger growled. *Not one bit.*

She shook her head and held a hand up, asking him to wait. As her chest rose and fell, the tips of her nipples tickled his chest. God, she was going to kill him. Ujjayi breathing again?

"Okay," she mumbled, pulling away slightly. "When is this meeting again?"

He propped himself up on his elbow. Was she worried about meeting the other shifters of Koa Point? As of last night, everyone had returned to Maui — Boone and Nina, Hunter and Dawn — so Silas had called a meeting of all hands.

"It's at ten o'clock. Plenty of time."

Jody gulped a little. "Ten, huh? And everyone will be there? Dragons... bears... wolves..."

He held her tighter. "Everyone will be there. Don't worry. You'll do great."

Her eyes drifted to the necklace hooked over a bedpost. "I guess we'll talk about *that* then."

He nodded, waiting for her to finish, because she'd trailed off and held her lip between her teeth.

"So, maybe..." she started again, haltingly. "Maybe you and I ought to talk first."

His chest rose involuntarily, because this was it. The talk they'd been putting off all along. And a good thing, too, because it was becoming harder and harder to hold his inner tiger back. The instinct to claim her with a mating bite was so strong—

He cleared his throat and ordered his tiger — and his dick — to calm down.

"Yeah, I guess we should," he murmured, letting her start. Left to his own devices, he'd blurt everything out in one breath. *I love you. I need you. Please, please let me mark you with the mating bite and never, ever leave my side. Okay with you?*

All that rushed through his mind. But on the outside, he held perfectly still.

Jody pursed her lips and cupped his face in her hands. "I love you, Cruz. I love you, and I want to be with you."

His tiger danced around. *She loves me! Wants me!*

"But..." she added, making his heart stop.

Shit. She was going to tell him she couldn't stay. That she was a free spirit and had to keep moving. Or maybe she'd say she had to stay in California to help her dad with his shop. Or that she'd had second thoughts about the whole shifter thing.

"...there are a few things I need to see through before we take the next step," she whispered.

His blood barely seemed to move through his veins. Was she talking about taking a break? Humans might do that, but destined mates didn't. Destined mates didn't leave each other's sides after finding true love. They devoted themselves to each other for the rest of their lives.

"Like what?" he managed.

"I need to visit my family. After everything that's happened..." She closed her eyes and held him tightly. "And I really want to finish the tour. Just this season. You know, to finish what I started and all that. Do you think you can handle that?"

He took a deep breath and tried to summon the strength to say, *You bet I can handle it,* even if he wasn't sure he could.

"Of course, I may need a bodyguard," she said, smoothing her hands over his shoulders.

His blood rushed, chasing away the chill in his soul. "You mean..."

She hugged him tight. "You think I could leave you?" She shook her head firmly. "No way. But I was hoping you might not mind hitting the road for a little while before we settle down here. I mean — if all that's okay with you."

Of course, it was okay with him. "More than okay," he said, holding her against his chest.

Her next words were muffled but happy. "I just have three more months on the pro tour. Three months to try to crack the top ten. Even if I don't, I'll know that I tried, like my dad always says. It was getting harder and harder to motivate myself to do, but if you were there..."

Hell, yes. He'd be there. She'd have to chain him to the gate of the estate to keep him from following.

"Anywhere you go, I go."

She touched his nose with one finger and pretended to be stern. "But no snarling at every bare-chested surfer dude who crosses my path. I'm not interested in anyone but you."

"Can't promise that," he growled.

She laughed then grew more serious again. "It's funny — all I could think of these last weeks was earning money to help my family. And now that it's in my account—"

Cruz smiled, remembering the look on her face when she'd checked her statements. She hadn't received the extra payment for the final photo shoot — after all, the photographer and camera had disappeared in the flood — but the first payment was big enough to make her whoop and start planning how to break the news to her family. Her father's shop would be saved, and hopefully, her sister's greatest wish would come true.

Funny, how it no longer seemed criminal to bring a child into the world.

My sister will get to be a mom, and my dad will get to be a grandfather, Jody had said, looking into the distance with shining, hopeful eyes.

And we'd get to be uncles, his tiger had added quietly, ridiculously pleased with the notion.

"—now that the money is in my account, I can finally think about what happens after I quit the tour. I was thinking I might be able to score an apprenticeship with Teddy Akoa. You know, shaping custom boards." She looked around. "But I'm not sure I can ever live in a regular house again."

He took her hands in his. "You never have to live in a regular house again. You can live here."

"You sure that's okay? I mean, the owner of the estate. . . "

Cruz made a face. He kept forgetting that the place wasn't actually his.

"Who owns it, anyway? Can you tell me now?" she asked.

"No. I mean, I'd tell you if I knew, but I don't."

"Seriously?"

"Seriously. I don't know."

She thought it over for a minute. "My money's on Silas."

Cruz shook his head. "Every time I think it's him, something happens to make me decide it isn't. And what with that query out there. . . "

"What query?"

"There's a rumor going around that someone approached the zoning committee about developing this property and the one next door. Silas says he doesn't know anything about it, but I'm not so sure."

Jody nuzzled her nose against his, helping settle down the worry in his gut. "I guess no one really knows what the future holds. And that's the beautiful thing."

He kissed her, keeping his lips pressed to hers for a long, long time. That was his mate. Always seeing the bright side of things.

"And you know what else is beautiful?" she giggled, sliding her hands down his back.

His tiger perked his ears.

"What?"

"Ten o'clock is a long way away. Plenty of time."

He grinned, sneaking his hands toward her breasts.

"There is one more thing," she said, gently holding him back.

Anything, his tiger said, lashing his tail intently. *Anything you want, we do.*

"You told me about, well..." Her cheeks grew pink.

He cocked his head. What was that about?

When she mumbled the rest, he leaned closer to hear. "What?"

She made an exasperated sound and play-slapped his chest. "The mating bite."

He touched her cheek, hoping he hadn't scared her off when he'd explained it the previous day. "Not until you're ready. We wait as long as you want."

She slid her hand from his chest to his neck, making every nerve tingle. "What if I don't want to wait?"

His heart went from a steady beat to a heavy thump. Was she serious?

"You have to be sure, Jody."

His tiger yowled. *Don't talk her out of it, idiot!*

He didn't want to talk her out of it. But he couldn't live with her having any regrets. "You're so new to all of this..."

She smiled a crooked grin. "It'll be an adventure."

He took her hands in his. "Seriously, Jody..."

"I am serious. And you ought to know by now that when I'm in, I'm all in. Got that from my dad, I guess."

He smoothed her hair back into place. Someday, he was going to shake her dad's hand. And someday, he hoped to hell he'd get the chance to be as good a father as Ross Monroe. But right now...

"You're sure?" His voice was all scratchy and rough.

"I'm sure."

"The change initiated by the mating bite will take some time, but eventually, you'll be a shifter, too."

She looked deep into his eyes, looking wary but resolute. "Will you help me?"

He nodded so hard, it hurt his neck. "You bet I will.

Her eyes dropped to his neck, and her fingers played over his skin. Was she imagining it right now?

One way to find out, his tiger murmured.

He leaned in slowly, peppering kisses from her ear to her neck, inhaling the scent of her desire. The air was thick with the sweet aroma, even stronger than that of the surrounding woods and tropical flowers.

"Mmm," she murmured, lying back as he tiptoed his fingers over her chest.

He kissed her jaw, her collarbone, her neck, getting drunk on her scent.

She cooed, arching as he touched her breast.

She's ready. She's sure, his tiger assured him.

He caught a nipple and rolled it between his lips. The pure taste messed with his mind until he couldn't see straight. When he slid his hand between her legs, touching her again, his groan was nearly as loud as hers.

"More..." Her hips rose, forcing his hand deeper. Her legs split and hugged his, begging for more.

Mate, his tiger hummed. *My beautiful mate.*

He circled her entrance then slid a finger in, still kneading her breast with his left hand. Nipping and suckling more insistently. Slowly losing control.

"Yes... Yes..." She put her hand over his and pushed him deeper. Faster.

His rock-hard cock pulsed against her hip, and when she grasped it, his vision flared. She tapped on the tip, torturing him.

"Jody," he rasped, at the end of his self-restraint.

Her eyes locked on his, wide and blue as the sky, and she reared up to kiss him hard. Then she rolled onto her belly and popped up on her elbows the way she popped up on her surfboard, ready to tame the wildest wave.

"This way. Please. This way..."

Before she'd so much as wiggled her rear, he kneeled behind her, knowing just what she meant. He dragged her hips against his, exercising just enough restraint to drag his cock through her slick folds. Once. Twice...

"Please..." She pushed back, making it clear he wasn't the only one about to explode with need.

When he took firm hold of her hips and slid home, Jody threw her head back and cried out. When he withdrew, she moaned and dropped her chin.

"Need you..."

He needed her, too. Desperately. But he wasn't all animal, and he wasn't going to hammer away until she was absolutely ready. She was still tight inside, deliciously tight, and each steady thrust was a slide through the best kind of pleasure-pain.

"Soon," he panted, pausing just long enough to push her hair to one side. His eyes narrowed, focusing on her bare neck.

Mate, his tiger chanted. *Make her mine.*

"Yes..." she panted as he started thrusting into her again. Edging deeper and deeper. Everything blurred away — the dappled sunlight around the tree house, the scent of the woods, the call of songbirds — until his world funneled down to Jody and nothing else. Pure tunnel vision, pure ecstasy as he rocked back and forth.

"Yes..." Jody cried, bracing her arms. Her back glistened with a mixture of his sweat and hers, making his tiger growl.

Yes. Mark our mate with our scent.

He plunged harder and harder until his balls were so tight—

"Please," she cried, turning her head to offer her neck.

He ran his tongue over his teeth, letting the canines extend. His heart hammered in his ears as he sniffed along her neck, letting instinct guide him.

There, his tiger howled. *Right there!*

He inhaled and thrust deeper still, then exhaled, relishing the burn in his cock. And on the next inhale—

Jody made a choking sound as his teeth sank into her neck. For one brief instant, he panicked that he'd done it wrong. But a heartbeat later, her thoughts exploded into his mind. A flood of ecstasy, a high that bridged over to him and rushed through her body. He saw rolling tropical waves and brilliant sunsets. He heard laughter and squinted at the sunlight shining in her soul. His nostrils went wide as all her favorite scents surrounded him, and he gripped her hips tighter as her ecstasy rose higher and higher.

Hold tight, his tiger grunted.

He kept his lips firmly sealed as his hips pumped furiously.

"Yes..." Jody groaned in one long syllable as she clenched down hard. Every muscle in her body flexed, claiming him as hers.

Cruz slammed into her one more time before his cock jolted and emptied inside her. He saw rainbows dancing over waves. Sunshine sparkling off the ocean. A sky so blue and clear, it made his heart swell.

Mark her forever, his tiger chanted wildly.

They'd already given up on condoms, and the skin-to-skin rush drove his tiger wild. But he didn't let up on the bite until her head sank into the pillow.

Slowly, carefully, he retracted his teeth, keeping his tongue over the bite marks. The skin sealed under his touch, and some instinct from deep in his soul told him it was all right to let go. He fluttered kisses over her neck as a thick, satisfied weariness filled his muscles, letting him relax at last.

Jody shuddered, milking him throughout her high, then slowly dropped to her stomach. He sank down over her, pinning her down with just enough pressure to make her murmur once more.

"So good..." she said, melting into the sheets.

"So good," he echoed, holding her tight.

He closed his eyes, breathing in her scent. The heat radiating from her body, the satisfied sighs. Each reminding him that life was beautiful. Love was beautiful. He just had to believe.

And damn, did he believe. He'd believe every day for the rest of his life.

They lay against each other, counting heartbeats, feeling at peace. Eventually, Jody rolled to face him with sparkling, satisfied eyes. Then she grinned and tried a little roar.

He laughed. "Not bad."

"Not bad?" Her brow knitted. "You better watch out. I'll be out-tigering you any day now. I just need a little practice."

He didn't doubt it. Not one bit. "You can practice on me all you want."

She chuckled, putting a finger under his chin. "Wait. Are you getting a sense of humor?"

He shrugged. "Not my fault. You seem to have infected me."

They grinned at each other like a couple of teens who'd just scored for the first time, but then they gradually grew serious. The good kind of serious, like a couple of adults who were done messing around. Looking into the future and liking what they saw.

He smoothed her hair back into place. It was mussed and wild — probably like his. He sniffed the air and grinned, finding their scents wrapped so tightly together, he could barely tell what part was hers and what part was his. When they met with the other shifters of Koa Point, there'd be no mistaking how he and Jody had spent their morning.

Good, his tiger said firmly. *Let everybody know she's mine.*

He thought back to the day Kai and Tessa had come to a similar powwow after the dragon duel in which they'd secured the Lifestone. Boone and Nina had come hand in hand to their first formal meeting, smelling distinctly of sex and joy. Hunter and Dawn had covered each other with their scents after three days ensconced in his cottage, and who could blame them after so many years of holding back?

Well, now it was his turn — a day he'd never thought would come — and he damn well was going to show off his mate. He was in for some ribbing, for sure, especially about the human part. He still couldn't quite believe that Vasco had made it look as though the local villagers were to blame for the deaths of his family or that he had bought into the lie for so long. Now he realized that humans were just like shifters — there were good and bad of each. He'd be vigilant for the latter, but he'd also do his best not to drive himself crazy with anger or hate.

Life is for living, his tiger agreed. *Loving. Laughing.*

Jody slid closer, brushing her finger across his lips. He closed his eyes as the touch turned into a long, deep kiss. A kiss he never wanted to end. She rolled closer, letting their chests touch, getting him all heated up again.

"Good thing that meeting isn't till ten," she murmured, pulling back slightly. She tipped her head to the right. "Because there's a rock pool with your name on it not too far away."

He kissed her deeper, stirring her up the way she stirred him. "You been thinking dirty thoughts again?"

She nodded through the kiss. "You'll have to wash me well. Really, really well. But first..."

He arched his eyebrow. "First?"

She grinned from ear to ear. "First, we get to be dirty all over again."

Chapter Twenty

Jody twisted her bracelets around and around as she followed Cruz over the bridge that divided his private world from the rest of the estate. Ten o'clock had seemed so far off, but once again, time had gotten away from her. They'd ended up rushing to get dressed.

"Are you sure I look okay?" She tugged on Cruz's hand, making him stop.

His eyes wandered up and down her body, giving her all kinds of bad ideas, and she gave him a little shove. "Forget I asked. I'm not sure you're thinking straight."

"Of course, I'm not thinking straight. Can I help it if you're gorgeous?"

Truthfully, she felt gorgeous, though it was only because of him. She even felt radiant — literally. The bite marks on her neck had already healed over, but her body still tingled from the high. The first chance she got, she was going to have Cruz repeat that bite just to make sure it hadn't been a wild fantasy.

"You already know Kai and Tessa," he assured her.

At least there was that. Tessa was super nice, and so was Kai, who'd been incredibly worried that awful day up in the mountains. The second he'd helped locate the lost sailors, he'd rushed back to the waterfall. Too late to assist in the shifter fight, but just in time to bring her and Cruz back to Koa Point.

What a day, huh? Kai had sighed when they'd touched down.

The understatement of the year, which was one reason Jody had spent so long holed up with Cruz. But she couldn't hide away at the tree house forever. And if everyone was as nice as Cruz said...

They were, as it turned out, and Tessa even strong-armed Silas into putting off the meeting until everyone had eaten.

"I'm sure that can wait an hour, Silas. We all need to settle in a little first. Plus, Dawn gave me a great new recipe I want to try out."

Dawn grinned. "Pancakes, Hawaiian style."

Even Cruz licked his lips at that, and before long, everyone was gathered around the kitchen, shooting the breeze. Dawn and Hunter had just returned from what sounded like a lovely honeymoon in Alaska, and they barely had eyes for anything but each other. Nina, a sweet brunette, and her mate, Boone, were just back from the East Coast, and everyone was friendly and talkative. Well, Hunter, the bear shifter, wasn't so talkative, but he tipped his head and listened to every word. They asked Jody about surfing and told funny Cruz stories he pretended to resent. It was like a big family gathering, and Jody's heart warmed. The men were all tough military types, but they obviously had their softer sides, too. The women were intelligent, outgoing, and plenty assertive if the men got out of line.

"Watch it, wolf," Tessa scolded, smacking Boone's hand away from the pineapples she'd diced.

"Hey, someone has to do quality control," he protested.

Jody looked closely but couldn't find the slightest hint of wolf in Boone. More like cheery lifeguard or happy-go-lucky ski bum. It was only when his tousled hair fell over his eyes that she caught a hint of canine. And when he looked at his mate, Nina, his eyes lit up so bright, it was easy to picture him wagging a tail.

Jody exhaled and looked around. Okay, so maybe shifters weren't all scary, after all. Not this bunch, at least.

Then she remembered the scene in the mountain valley and corrected herself. She was lucky to have survived the experience unscathed. And, damn. Her new friends could be downright scary when they chose to be.

"Hey, did you see this?" Boone asked Kai, holding up a newspaper.

Helicopter Crashes in West Maui Mountains, a headline said. *Lightning Strike Sets Aircraft Ablaze.*

"Lightning, my ass," Kai laughed, looking at Silas.

Jody tried not to dwell on the article at the top of the paper — *Seven Lost in Flash Flood.* She was genuinely sad for Richard and Guy, though she couldn't summon any sympathy for Vasco and his men.

Property damage minimal, the article continued. At least there was that — no innocent citizens of Maui had been impacted by the shifter fight.

"Can I help with something?" Jody asked Tessa to get her mind off the unpleasant memories.

Even with four skillets going at the same time, Tessa had everything under control. Still, she let Jody tend one while engaging in small talk that settled Jody's nerves again. Nina insisted on doing all the serving, claiming it was in her blood, and in the end, all Jody really did was eat.

"Oh my gosh, these are so good," Dawn gushed, biting into a mouthful of coconut-pineapple pancakes.

"Everything Tessa makes is good," Kai agreed.

"We really have to start doing pancake Sundays," Nina sighed. "I mean, now that everyone is back home and things are settling down."

Jody pursed her lips. *We* was a big word. Could she really fit in at Koa Point? Was it really home?

Nina's friendly smile reassured her, and Cruz backed that up with a throaty rumble that warned everyone they'd better accept Jody — or else. Not that they needed the reminder; as he'd promised, everyone was as welcoming as could be.

It was only when the stacks of pancakes grew lower and everyone leaned back, patting their bellies in satisfaction, that they got around to discussing the unavoidable.

"So, you're part mermaid, huh?" Nina asked as she cleared the table with Boone.

Jody shook her head. "Not really. My dad is, apparently, but I'm sure he doesn't know." Which meant her younger sister was part mermaid, too. Did that mean her life was in danger?

Cruz smoothed a hand over her leg, reminding her the vampires were gone. But what if another came along?

Slowly, she let out a long breath. Sooner or later, she'd figure out how to break the news to her sister and find a way to keep her safe. But first, she'd get to share good news, which made her smile all over again. Her sisters and dad would be so excited. Proud, even. The way she liked to think her mom would have felt.

"No one in my family ever mentioned anything about mermaids. Well, except my crazy old aunt..." She trailed off, looking at her bracelets. Maybe old Tilda wasn't as nutty as everyone said. She would definitely have to pay the old woman a visit soon.

Tessa looked sympathetic. "I went most of my life not knowing I had some dragon blood."

Dawn mused over her coffee mug. "Can you imagine my surprise when I changed into an owl instead of a bear on my third shift?" Her eyes sparkled at Hunter.

"You make a great owl — and a great bear." His soulful brown eyes shone at his mate.

Jody sighed and glanced at Cruz. And wow, his eyes were sparkling just as intently at her. She let out a long, slow breath. How did she ever get so lucky?

Nina laughed. "I was always just plain old human."

Boone took her hand and kissed it. "Nothing plain about you."

An ocean breeze wafted through the open space, carrying the sound of breakers from the reef. Jody might have guessed the *koa* of Koa Point meant *heavenly place of love and tranquility* if hadn't been for what Cruz had once said.

Koa is a class of warrior, named for the hardest type of wood.

Well, that fit, too, she decided, looking at the men and women gathered around the table. Their love was tender yet fierce at the same time.

Tessa fingered the pendant around her neck. "Maybe your bracelets are a mermaid thing. You said they were a family heirloom, right? Maybe they give you some mermaid qualities, too."

Jody looked down and fingered the design.

"Nah," Cruz cut in. "Jody has all the qualities she needs all on her own."

Her cheeks went warm, and she couldn't resist cupping his cheek. Who knew a grouchy tiger could be so sweet?

"So what was with the lions?" Hunter asked, frowning for the first time.

"Vasco was a rare mix," Silas explained. "Half vampire, half lion. The lion part seemed recessive, the vampire dominant. Hence his taste for blood and the thugs he surrounded himself with."

"Lions," Cruz muttered in distaste.

"And they were after Jody because...?" Dawn asked, showing her police officer side.

Jody traced a finger over the tablecloth, trying not to tense up all over again.

Silas stirred his coffee. "From what we've gathered, Vasco wasn't originally after Jody. One of his men was hired to shoot at Jody—"

"To kill Jody," Cruz grumbled, leaning into her side.

"—in an attempt to create publicity for the advertising campaign." Silas shook his head wearily. "A good thing Toby has been cleared of all charges."

"Toby?" Dawn exclaimed. "The valet? He wouldn't hurt a fly."

"I hope no one roughed him up," Hunter said.

Dawn scowled. "The Maui police don't rough people up."

Kai grinned. "Don't worry. I made it all up to him. I let him drive the Rolls-Royce yesterday."

Silas jerked his head up. "You let Toby drive *what*?"

Kai shrugged. "Come on, Silas. Give the poor kid a break. He was thrilled. And careful," he hurried to add, looking between Hunter and Silas. "Very careful."

"Wait. Someone wanted to kill Jody as a publicity stunt? Who would do such a thing?" Nina asked, aghast.

Silas looked at the floor. Kai looked at Cruz, and Cruz looked at Silas.

"Moira," Cruz said at last.

"Moira?" Tessa yelped, then covered her mouth.

Silas went still as a stone, as did everyone in the room. Jody, too, because Cruz had told her about Moira — the woman who'd broken Silas's heart.

Jody crinkled her nose. She hated Moira as much as everyone, but all she felt for Silas was sorrow. It did explain a lot, though. His solitary lifestyle. The yearning in his eyes. She wouldn't have thought a dragon would show flashes of vulnerability, but she'd glimpsed that side of him a few times.

"The gunman Vasco originally sent was a vampire, too," Cruz growled, rescuing Silas from the awkward silence that ensued. "That would explain why I couldn't pick up a scent at the resort."

"But the attempt on Jody's life failed, which is when Vasco came in," Silas added wearily. "Apparently, he did some research and discovered there was mermaid blood in Jody's father's side of the family."

"My stepfather, technically," she explained to the others. "So it's not in my blood. Poor Vasco was so disappointed." Her voice dripped with sarcasm.

"There hasn't been a mermaid sighting in decades, not even among shifters," Silas said. "All the more reason for a vampire to want to—"

Cruz growled before Silas got to the *suck Jody's blood* part. "The guy was sick, even for a vampire." His eyes burned with hate.

Jody squeezed Cruz's hand. He wasn't just thinking of her; he was thinking of his family members murdered by Vasco for their rich tiger blood.

"He won't be collecting any more flavors," she reminded him. "You took care of that."

"You, too," Cruz whispered.

"You both did," Kai added.

A quiet minute ticked by, and everyone grew somber. Each couple snuggled a little closer as if remembering their own trials. Cruz had filled Jody in on a few of their stories, so she knew she wasn't the only one to have survived a nightmare. A nightmare with a happy end, she reminded herself, happy to have Cruz's reassuring bulk at her side.

"Both of us did it, along with this." She pulled the sapphire necklace from under her shirt and set it on the white tablecloth.

"The Waterstone," Tessa said in a hushed voice. "Wow."

"Your hunch was right," Cruz said to Silas. "A Spirit Stone."

Silas's pained expression said he wished he hadn't been right.

"It scares me a little," Jody whispered, looking at it. Even now, the stone shot all kinds of watery images into her mind. Tranquil ones, like placid, misty lakes and quietly meandering rivers, but still. Who knew when the stone might demand that she summon a tidal wave?

"All the stones are scary in a way," Nina agreed.

"All?" Jody looked at the others. Cruz had mentioned other Spirit Stones, but she'd had so much to absorb in such a short time, she hadn't asked for details.

One by one, the other women pulled off necklaces or drew jewels from pockets. Dawn set out a glittering amethyst. Nina laid out a brilliant red ruby, her face soft with memories. Tessa added a glowing emerald to the collection and kept her hand on a lookalike pendant she wore around her neck.

"The Spirit Stones," Silas said in the silence that ensued. "A long-lost dragon hoard with magical powers. The Lifestone. The Earthstone. The Firestone." He pointed to each in turn. "And now, the Waterstone. In the right hands, their powers can be controlled — or at least directed toward worthy ends."

Jody frowned at the sapphire. "I'm not so sure I did much controlling."

Silas shook his head. "Few could direct a flood of that force, but you did."

Tessa shot Jody a proud wink, while Dawn and Nina nodded, bolstering her mood. A lump grew in her throat as she saw the men join in, too, dipping their chins with respect for what she'd done. Her, the not-even-a-mermaid.

She looked at Cruz, who smiled, making her heart beat faster. Prouder. The Waterstone glowed, shooting a faint beam of blue light in her direction.

"In the right hands, the power of the Spirit Stones is not to be feared so much as respected," Silas said. "But in the wrong hands..."

No one said a word. No one even shooed Keiki off the table. The kitten pranced from person to person, blissfully ignorant as each person petted her, lost in their own thoughts.

"So that's that. It's over," Jody said, looking around. "Everything's okay now, right?"

The silence in the room was resounding, and everyone looked pained.

"What?" she asked, looking from face to face. What was wrong?

No one seemed eager to be the bearer of bad news until Tessa spoke up. "There's one more Spirit Stone."

Silas tapped his fingers on the tabletop. "The Windstone."

Jody tightened her grip on Cruz's hand. Why did that not sound good?

"The Spirit Stones call to each other," Cruz said in a low, raspy voice. "When one awakes, it calls to the others."

"They call to shifters, too. Powerful shifters," Kai added.

Jody clenched her fist before her fingers trembled. "Such as?"

Kai shrugged, but the gesture didn't mask his concern. "All kinds of shifters. But dragons above all."

Jody glanced at Silas. She'd never forget the size of his dragon's shadow or the thunderous roar he'd emitted along with crackling flames. In human form, he seemed so controlled, so sophisticated. As a dragon, he had been terrifying.

"Good dragons?" she ventured. After all, Kai, Tessa, and Silas were all dragon shifters, and they were nice. That boded well for the species, right?

Tessa shook her head. "Bad dragons are after the Spirit Stones, too."

"Drax," Kai spat out the name.

Jody leaned back in her seat. Whoever Drax was, she never wanted to tangle with him.

"And now Moira," Kai muttered. "Sorry, Silas. It has to be said. Whatever she was in the past... She's changed."

Silas fingered the tablecloth, rubbing one spot as if to erase a smudge. If Keiki hadn't come over and pawed at it, too, he might have scratched a hole right through the fabric.

"Here, Keiki," he whispered, leaning over for a ball of yarn. He threw it across the floor, watching the ball unravel.

Jody watched, too. Something about the long red strand reminded her of a dragon's tail, and not in a good way. Then Keiki pounced, conquering it.

Kai spoke loud and clear as if hoping those other dragons, wherever they were, could hear. "If nothing else, they haven't been cocky enough to march in here and take us on in a direct fight. Our power has grown, Silas. They respect that."

It was a pep talk, Jody realized, though it didn't seem to bolster Silas much.

"Maybe," he murmured, still intent on the tablecloth.

"Definitely," Tessa said, backing Kai up. "We have four stones. Drax has none. The Windstone is slumbering, and you know what?"

Her defiant tone made everyone look up.

"We have a lot to celebrate," Tessa continued. "Another stone brought to safety. A new friend and ally." She raised her glass at Jody then smiled mischievously at Cruz. "And best of all, we can celebrate the fact that Cruz hasn't been pacing holes into the ground or complaining about humans for an entire hour."

Everyone laughed, and Boone added, "Amen."

Cruz looked ready to protest, but Kai slapped him on the back, teasing him. "So whatever happened to humans being... what was it, again?"

"Unpredictable," Tessa filled in immediately.

Cruz aimed a finger at Jody. "She is unpredictable."

"Hey!" she protested.

"What about irrational?" Boone joked.

The dawn of a smile played over Cruz's lips, but Jody saw him fight it away. "She is irrational."

She snorted. "Says the man who lives in a tree house."

"What about dangerous? I seem to remember something about that." Kai laughed.

"Have you seen her surf? She is dangerous."

"Am not," Jody laughed, looping an arm across his shoulders.

Cruz caught her free hand and looked at her with sparkling eyes. "You're all of those things — and more. That's why I love you."

Tessa sighed. Kai grinned from ear to ear, and Nina sniffled. Well, Jody thought that's who it was, but she wasn't sure, not with her vision focused on Cruz. The outside world was fading away again, leaving everything a blur except her and him.

She nodded to herself. It was easy to get caught up in scary thoughts. But the truth was that life was beautiful. Love was beautiful.

"I believe," she whispered to no one in particular.

Cruz seemed to know exactly what she meant because he murmured, too. "I believe." Then he snapped back to attention and looked around with chagrin. A moment later, he was on his feet and pulling her with him.

"You believe what?" Boone asked.

"I believe my mate and I have... What was it? Pressing business," Cruz announced, heading for the trail to his place.

Jody's neck tingled, and her cheeks flushed as a dozen steamy scenarios flashed through her mind.

"Thanks for the pancakes," she called over her shoulder, barely remembering to be polite to her new, um — friends? Neighbors? Family? Yes, family sounded good. Then she dashed off with her man. "They were delicious."

"I'll show you delicious," Cruz growled, breaking into a trot.

She giggled as they turned the corner, and by the time they made it to the footbridge, she'd undone the top button of her blouse, thinking ahead. She thought back, too, over everything that had happened since that crazy night at the golf club. Cruz had gone from potential enemy to ally, bodyguard, and lover.

Mate, a voice grumbled in her mind. A feline voice, throaty yet feminine at the same time.

Wow. It was really happening. Someday, she'd be able to shift like Cruz did. But right now... She was all human, full of human desires.

She stopped Cruz with a firm tug, wrapped him in a surprise hug, and covered his lips with hers. Suddenly, she was insatiable with more than just human desires.

"Tiger desires," Cruz mumbled, reading her mind. He ran one hand up the inside of her shirt and the other down her rear.

She pressed her body against his, trying to touch him everywhere at once. "Watch out, mister. When I get this tiger thing down pat, I'll be coming at you with my own mating bite." She nipped his neck.

"I'll watch out, then." He chuckled.

"You'd better believe it."

"That, I do." He grew serious and cupped her face in both hands. "I believe, my mate."

Epilogue

Silas looked around the meeting house. Not long after Cruz and Jody made their hasty exit, all the other couples did, too. A little more subtly, perhaps, but all more or less along the same lines of, *If you'll excuse me, I really have to go shag the amazing mate I adore.*

The sea breeze toyed with a napkin on the table, and the clock ticked as he stared off into the distance. An eternity later, it ticked again. Hell — if a minute was that long, how would he ever drag himself through all the years remaining to the end of his life?

He slid a heel across the woven mat floor, watching the shadows of the palms outside. Sunshine flooded the world everywhere but the place he inhabited. There was one exception, though — Keiki. She jumped, scampered, and pounced, chasing the ball of yarn across the floor like a mortal enemy, eviscerating it with tiny claws.

Silas curled his fingers and looked at his nails. In dragon form, they would extend to huge claws. Claws he would love to sink into Drax, the dragon lord who'd stolen everything from him. Everything. A long list unrolled in his mind.

Family treasures.

Personal treasures.

Moira, his inner dragon added, mentally spitting a plume of fire.

His heart ached just thinking about her. He didn't want to believe his ex-fiancée was at the heart of the recent attacks. But then again, he hadn't wanted to believe she would leave him, and leave him she had. For Drax.

Drax, who rubbed salt in his wounds at every turn. Drax, who seemed intent on dominating the shifter world. Drax—

He cut off the thought. Drax didn't deserve to take up so much of Silas's time or his tightly wound emotions. Neither did Moira. They were the losers; he was the winner — the one living at Koa Point with a group of men and women he respected and admired. A joyous group, especially lately, what with love blossoming all around. He was happy for them. Truly. His friends deserved their happiness — even grouchy Cruz, who had found an amazing woman to make him see the sunny side of life. Bit by bit, each of his brothers-in-arms had inched his way over to a quieter, more meaningful life.

Everyone except him.

Keiki purred and butted against his legs until he picked up the yarn and wound it in. She attacked it as he went, throwing her furry body this way and that, honing her fighting skills.

"Skills I hope you never have to use, little one," he whispered, tossing the yarn again.

She scampered after it, rolling head over heels in her own private battle.

He smiled — a little, at least. That kitten had the heart of a dragon. A pity she wasn't a shifter.

The sound of the dishwasher hummed in the background. Thanks to everyone's combined efforts, the place was neat, tidy, and ready for the next communal meal. He really had no reason to hang around now that the meeting was over, but he had no urge to head home. The house he lived in — the owner's place, high on a bluff — was huge and airy. In some ways, the perfect dragon's lair. In others, a prison of his own making. Solitary confinement for a dragon who'd been rejected by the woman he loved.

We didn't love her, his dragon said firmly. *Not truly.*

If that was the case, why did it hurt to breathe when he thought about Moira? Why did all his dreams revolve around what might have been?

We never loved her, his dragon insisted. *We just thought we did.*

He snorted at the beast's pride. Love was all in the head anyway.

Love is in the heart, and hers is made of stone. It always was. His inner dragon stretched his wings and lashed his tail.

Keiki trotted back and jumped into his lap, purring until he petted her the way she liked best. Ever since her two closest buddies, Cruz and Hunter, had partnered up with their respective mates, Keiki had sought out his company more and more. As if it was her mission to bring a little cheer to grouchy, scarred bachelors like himself.

She meowed so loudly, he could swear she was claiming all of Koa Point as her own. Sassy little thing.

He frowned as he petted her soft fur. Koa Point might be Keiki's realm for now, but it might not be for long. The rumors about developing the property weren't just rumors, and he wasn't sure he had the power to ward off the threat.

Keiki swatted playfully at his sleeve as if to belabor the point the others made from time to time. *Who's the owner of the estate? Is it you? Who has the power here?*

In truth, it was a long story, and a complicated one. And once he got to the end — if he ever reached the point where he had to reveal it all — everyone's jaws would drop. But he wasn't ready to share that yet. Not until he knew more about encroaching threats from the outside world. The danger wasn't imminent, and the others might as well enjoy their well-deserved downtime before the proverbial shit hit the fan.

As for him, he'd remain watchful. Vigilant. And above all, unemotional. He'd be the one they could all count on when push came to shove. A good unit relied on its leader, and a leader couldn't afford to become distracted by petty details like love.

"Hey," a voice pulled him from his thoughts. It was Tessa, sweeping back into the meeting house.

He forced the frown from his face. He really didn't want a lecture about how much he needed to relax.

"Hey," he murmured back.

"I forgot this," she said, touching the Lifestone. She laughed. "I know, I know. It's not something I ought to forget.

But sometimes..."

Her cheeks turned pink, and it was easy to guess the words she had swallowed. *Sometimes, you get so lost in the lure of your dragon that everything else fades to background noise.*

The phone rang — definitely not background noise — and Silas shot a glance at it, annoyed. He'd already had a long talk with Ella, their informant, and wrapped up all the loose threads surrounding the Waterstone. Or so he thought. Had Ella found another morsel of information or another startling surprise? Or was it the developer, calling yet again to try to sweet-talk Silas into a deal he would never support?

"Do you want me to get that?" Tessa asked.

No, he didn't. He wanted the outside world to leave him alone for a little while. Just long enough to get his head — and heart — in the right place so he could carry on without showing the strain. Well — he knew Tessa saw through the chinks in his armor, but if he could pretend they didn't exist, she could pretend, too.

He nodded, trying to roll the tension out of his shoulders.

"Koa Point. Hello?" Tessa answered the phone, her usual bright and cheery self. A second later, her smile fell away, and her brow furrowed. "Who may I say is calling?"

Silas made a face. So, it wasn't Ella. More likely the developer or the lawyers he hadn't been able to get off his back.

Tessa's face went chalk white, and she froze before walking stiffly toward him.

"It's for you." Her voice wavered as she held out the phone.

He took it, ready to get whatever unpleasant business over with. "Hello?"

Tessa slowly backed away, giving him his space. The line was silent for a moment or two before coming alive with a voice that sliced straight through his heart.

"Silas."

It was a statement, not a question. The woman on the other end of the line sounded a little breathless. Or was she faking the hint of emotion the way she had faked so much else?

He remained perfectly still. Everything but the throbbing vein at his temple. Finally, he grunted his reply, working hard to keep the pain out of his voice. The betrayal. And worst of all, hope. Hope that would kill him if he didn't watch his step.

"Moira," he murmured, wondering what she'd say next.

Books by Anna Lowe

Aloha Shifters - Jewels of the Heart

Lure of the Dragon (Book 1)

Lure of the Wolf (Book 2)

Lure of the Bear (Book 3)

Lure of the Tiger (Book 4)

Love of the Dragon (Book 5)

Lure of the Fox (Book 6)

Blue Moon Saloon

Perfection (a short story prequel)

Damnation (Book 1)

Temptation (Book 2)

Redemption (Book 3)

Salvation (Book 4)

Deception (Book 5)

Celebration (a holiday treat)

The Wolves of Twin Moon Ranch

Desert Hunt (the Prequel)

Desert Moon (Book 1)

Desert Wolf: Complete Collection (Four short stories)

Desert Blood (Book 2)

Desert Fate (Book 3)

Desert Heart (Book 4)

Desert Yule (a short story)

Desert Rose (Book 5)

Desert Roots (Book 6)

Sasquatch Surprise (a Twin Moon spin-off story)

Shifters in Vegas

Paranormal romance with a zany twist

Gambling on Trouble

Gambling on Her Dragon

Gambling on Her Bear

Serendipity Adventure Romance

Off the Charts

Uncharted

Entangled

Windswept

Adrift

Travel Romance

Veiled Fantasies

Island Fantasies

visit www.annalowebooks.com

About the Author

USA Today and Amazon bestselling author Anna Lowe loves putting the "hero" back into heroine and letting location ignite a passionate romance. She likes a heroine who is independent, intelligent, and imperfect – a woman who is doing just fine on her own. But give the heroine a good man – not to mention a chance to overcome her own inhibitions – and she'll never turn down the chance for adventure, nor shy away from danger.

Anna loves dogs, sports, and travel – and letting those inspire her fiction. On any given weekend, you might find her hiking in the mountains or hunched over her laptop, working on her latest story. Either way, the day will end with a chunk of dark chocolate and a good read.

Visit AnnaLoweBooks.com

Made in the USA
Coppell, TX
29 November 2020